pretend i do

misha bell

♠ mozaika publications ♠

Published by Mozaika Publications, an imprint of Mozaika LLC.
www.mozaikallc.com

Cover by Alex McLaughlin

ISBN: 979-8-89796-002-6
Paperback ISBN: 979-8-89796-004-0

1
sawyer

a.k.a. the girl who really, really hates plain espresso

SHIVERING from the icy wind blowing from the East River, I scan the Starbucks before I dare step inside it.

Whew. No beards on the baristas, nor on any of my fellow caffeine junkies.

Oh, and... wow. One of the patrons is a broody, clean-shaven guy who must be the most stunning specimen I've ever seen. Tall, broad-shouldered, with chiseled everything, he looks like he belongs in Hollywood instead of here on Wall Street. His neatly cut hair is jet black, with just the tiniest, flattering touch of gray at the temples, and unlike me with my puffy jacket, he's not wearing anything over his clearly bespoke suit, which only enhances the—

Crap. His piercing gray eyes catch me staring, so I quickly look away.

Shit. What was I thinking, ogling him? I have to focus on the task at hand: the most important interview of my life happening in twenty minutes. The reason I'm here is to get the caffeine necessary to boost my odds of success.

Gritting my teeth, I pointedly ignore the dark and handsome Suit as I waltz up to the barista and order a matcha latte.

"What size?" she asks.

I sigh. "Venti."

As always, the programmer in me is annoyed at the inconsistent names for the cup sizes. They start with "Short" and "Tall," but the latter isn't anywhere near their biggest size. For those, they arbitrarily decided to switch to an Italian (or maybe Spanish) word for "big" with "Grande" (which is, again, not their biggest size), followed by two Italian numbers representing the actual number of ounces in the drinks. Well, at least in the hot drinks.

It's like they designed their sizing convention while backpacking through Europe drunk and stoned.

"Would you like anything else?" she asks, making me realize I've been staring at her this whole time, like a perverted owl.

"No. Just please don't make it too hot. Thanks." I tap my card and ask for access to their bathroom.

Once inside, I take care of business, then take off my hat and make my hair more presentable for the interview. Since Octothorpe is right next door, I should be able to get there without a hat. For that matter, I don't need my puffy jacket either, so I take it off and adjust my pantsuit.

After exiting the bathroom and walking to the pick-up counter, I stand in such a way that I can sneak glances at the Suit without him seeing me.

"Sawyer!" the barista shouts.

Ah. Great. I run over and take the cup from her hands. Out of the corner of my eye, I see the hottie move toward me, but then he stops.

Good. I don't really have time for him to pick me up —if that's what he was about to do.

I need to head over to the interview.

I dart for the door and step outside into the cold, taking a greedy gulp of my latte... only to spit it out, like I'm auditioning for *The Exorcist*.

The drink tastes so bitter it's like licking a cactus dipped in grapefruit juice. And if that weren't enough, it's also hotter than dragon jizz.

Turning on my heel, I step back in—and hear the barista call my name again.

Huh?

What's even weirder is that the Suit walks up to the counter and takes the drink she's holding.

Wait a second. Is that why he—

Yep. As if to confirm my suspicion, when he tastes his—I mean, my—latte, he cringes.

Fuck me. How is it possible that he looks so good with such an expression on his face?

"This isn't what I ordered," he growls at the barista. "Whatever this is, it tastes like it was made from grass and drowned in a tub of sugar."

"I think there's been a mix-up," I say to both him

and the barista. "My name is Sawyer—and yours might be as well."

His gray eyes widen. "I thought I heard them call my name earlier, but then you went to get the order, so I thought I misheard."

"I'm sorry." I approach him and catch a whiff of a delicious woodsy scent, the kind that has always given me girl wood. Doing my best to hide it, I extend my hand with the cup filled with bitter grossness. "Here. I only took one sip and I'm in good health."

"I can give you new cups," the barista offers. "Or make new drinks."

"I'm in a rush," I reply. "I'm fine taking his." I gesture at Sawyer. "That is, assuming you're not sick or anything."

"I'm in perfect health." He takes his cup from my hands, and his fingers brush mine, making the fine hairs on my arm stand on end from the surge of electric awareness that blasts through me.

My breath catches, and it's all I can do to mutter something along the lines of, "You do look healthy," as he hands me my cup. Our fingers brush once more, and this time, the zing goes directly to my clit.

"Thanks," I say on a gasp.

"No problem," he replies and sips his drink with such gusto you wouldn't believe it was liquid despair.

I take a dainty sip of mine too, trying to ignore the fact that by drinking from a cup after him, my lips are touching where his did, making this a kind of kiss by proxy.

"You really like that concoction?" he asks, studying my expression.

"I do," I reply with a slight eyeroll. "Do you like yours?"

He looks down at his cup. "It's espresso. Everyone likes it."

"Maybe with sugar and cream," I counter. "Not straight like that." Also, if I had that amount all at once, my heart might burst from my chest and bounce off the walls.

"I'm in it for the caffeine," he says. "But the taste isn't bad either."

Sure it's not—if you have no taste buds. "I got this for the caffeine too, and since my drink is green tea based, the caffeine will release slowly into my bloodstream."

He cocks his head. "Why can't you just drink another caffeinated beverage later?"

"Because I'm going to an interview." And really should get going instead of blabbing with him.

"Oh. Good luck then," he says. "And I'm sorry if you overheard me criticize your drink. I usually don't yuck other people's yum."

"No problem. I'm sorry if I implied that yours is more bitter than the child of Ebenezer Scrooge and Miss Havisham."

He scoffs. "My drink is the normal kind of bitter—from coffee. There's a reason they sprinkle it on things like tiramisu. Yours, on the other hand, tastes like dried poison ivy."

This time, my eyeroll is less subtle. "Matcha is in more desserts than coffee. Have you never had green tea ice cream? And in Japan, they use it in a million other sweets—there's even a matcha KitKat."

He smiles, and it feels like winter has instantly turned into sunny summer. "Are you interviewing to be a lawyer?"

"Shit. The interview." I turn toward the door. "I have to run."

"I get it," he says. "I'll walk with you as far as I can."

Nodding, I sprint outside, jacket slung over my arm, only to feel a large, strong hand land on my shoulder.

"You'll freeze to death," Sawyer says. "Put on your jacket."

Who died and made him my keeper? "You're wearing only a suit yourself."

"I work right there." He points at the door that is my destination.

"Oh." I turn to him. "Octothorpe?"

Disappointment flits across his face. "That's where your interview is, isn't it?"

I nod. "Why, are you going to be my boss or something?" I know it's crazy, but I really, really don't want him to turn out to be my boss—or anyone else it would be a bad idea to date. Which is crazy. I need all my focus to be on this job and not—

"Not your boss, no," he says. "I'm guessing you're interviewing to be a developer for our trading platform?"

"Yes. That's the job I want." I take a big gulp of my latte.

"That team works with mine," he says. "Which is why I was asked to interview you later today—if HR and your potential teammates like what they hear."

Crap. "I hope you won't hold the coffee incident against me."

He waves that off. "I'll judge you based on your qualifications only."

We walk up to the revolving doors, and he lets me go first, then rotates them for me.

"She's here for an interview," he informs the security guy once we're both inside.

"I'll still need to see some ID," the security guy replies.

I hand over my driver's license and soon find myself waiting for the elevator with Sawyer in an uncomfortable silence.

"It sure got chilly quick," I say, shifting from foot to foot.

Sawyer's expression turns arctic. "I can't abide small talk."

What? Is that an actual thing, or is he upset with me for some reason? "You seemed fine talking to me earlier."

"I don't have a problem with a real conversation," he says. "Only with trite air movements."

Wow. "Okay. What constitutes small talk?" I need to know what to avoid in the elevator—and during the interview that I'll hopefully have with him.

"Weather—obviously. But also, tired questions like: 'How was your weekend?' or 'What are your plans for vacation?'"

The elevator comes at that moment, and as we step inside, he presses forty-three for me and then forty-four, presumably for himself.

So we won't be working on the same floor? There go my fantasies of running into him by the proverbial water cooler.

"Okay then." I take a big sip of my latte. "I guess we could discuss the answer to life, the universe, and everything?"

He grins. "That's easy. The answer is forty-two."

"Seems like we both like *The Hitchhiker's Guide to the Galaxy*," I reply. "But wait. Is talking about books considered small talk?"

"Books—no. But movies... maybe. Did you know that in the first Harry Potter book, Harry discovered that he's a wizard on page forty-two?"

I chuckle. "Obviously he would."

"And is it a coincidence that the Titanic was going forty-two miles per hour when it hit that iceberg?"

"Wow. That got dark quickly." I catch another whiff of his sexy scent and fight the urge to step closer to him.

"You want even darker? Elvis was forty-two when he passed away... assuming that he did."

"How about something less bleak?"

He shrugs. "Molybdenum's atomic number is forty-two."

"And molybdenum is…"

"An element that just so happens to be the forty-second most common in the universe."

The elevator stops.

"This is me," I say. "I hope I see you again, since that'll mean I did well on the prior interviews."

"Me too," he says.

It takes all my willpower not to do something crazy, like kiss him. Instead, I force my legs to move and carry me out of the elevator. It's not until the elevator doors close—and his woodsy scent is gone—that I'm able to get back to my senses, shake off all the libidinous thoughts, and chug the rest of my latte.

"Hi," says an aggressively attractive receptionist as I approach her desk. "Can I help you?"

I tell her who I am and why I'm here.

"Take a seat," she says.

As soon as I sit down, a sturdy woman lumbers over, her hand outstretched.

"You must be Sawyer Baker?" she booms in a rich baritone reminiscent of Barry White.

I leap to my feet. "You're Mrs. Ramsey, right?" When I accept her handshake, my hand looks like that of a doll in hers.

"Mrs. Ramsey is my Nanna." She pushes her ginormous bejeweled glasses higher up her nose. "Call me Henrietta."

"Of course, Henrietta. It's a pleasure to meet you."

Grinning, she squeezes my hand to the point where

I almost squeal in pain, then blissfully releases it. "Follow me, dear."

As we walk, I scan faces for beards, but thankfully, I see none. Additionally, most of the men here are attractive—though none as hot as my namesake. Oh, and the women are also unusually pretty.

As we progress deeper, I spot a ping pong table, a dozen bean bag chairs, and countless whiteboard walls covered mostly in doodles. The vibe is that of a startup —or kindergarten—and the last thing I'd expect to see on Wall Street.

"Henrietta," says one ridiculously tall guy as we turn the corner. "What are your plans for the weekend, considering this weather?"

Sawyer is lucky he's not here for this double whammy of small talk.

Henrietta bats her eyelashes at the guy so hard her glasses seem to float up. "Jasper, you rascal, I can't fly to the Bahamas with you. I'm a married woman."

What? Jasper doesn't seem surprised by what she says. He actually winks and says her husband is a lucky man.

"That's what I keep telling him." Henrietta stares into Jasper's eyes and licks her lips.

Jasper either didn't notice the lip thing, or has learned to ignore it, because he doesn't even blink an eye. Nodding at me, he says, "New recruit?"

"Oh, where are my manners?" Henrietta gestures at me. "This is Sawyer Baker. She's here for an interview. If all goes well, she'll be on your team." She drags her gaze away from Jasper and looks at me as she adds, "Sawyer, this is Jasper Knight. He joined the company relatively recently, so he might be a good person to ask questions—if you're hired, of course."

Jasper smiles at me. "I was just looking at your resume. Impressive."

"Save it for the interview," Henrietta says. "Come, Sawyer. Dreamatorium awaits."

At least I think she says "Dreamatorium." It could also be "crematorium" or "moratorium."

Nope. Dream is the root of the made-up word—as that's what it says on the door of the meeting room we're entering.

"Take a seat," Henrietta says.

I carefully perch onto one of the Herman Miller chairs surrounding the long mahogany conference table, and she sits opposite me.

"All right," she says. "Tell me a little about yourself."

"Sure." I go into my prepared spiel. "I've recently graduated *summa cum laude* from MIT, where I majored in Computer Science and minored in Finance. For the last two years, I worked as a software developer at MIT's Finance Department and—"

Henrietta emits a loud snore, which—combined with the fact that her eyes are closed—makes me realize she's fallen asleep.

Am I that boring, or is she narcoleptic?

I clear my throat.

Henrietta blinks her eyes open. "Very impressive,"

she says, as if nothing's happened. "Why do you want to work here, at Octothorpe?"

Obviously, I'm not going to tell her the truth: that according to my intensive research, this company is the most surefire way to financial independence. Instead, I tell her how impressed I am with how quickly Octothorpe is becoming indispensable in almost every sphere of life. I also claim that I've always wanted to work for a company on the cutting edge of technology, and that it doesn't get any more cutting edge than Octothorpe.

The latter is very true, actually.

"Yes, yes," Henrietta says. "We've gone over the edge."

Gone over the edge? Doesn't that mean losing control and becoming unstable?

"So, tell me," Henrietta says. "How would you describe the color yellow to a blind person?"

Ah. This. Octothorpe is famous for weird interview questions, so I'm prepared—or as prepared as you can be.

"I'd describe yellow using other senses. I'd tell them to think about how they feel on a warm sunny day, and about the tartness of a lemon, and the scent of daffodils, and—"

"Thank you," Henrietta says. "What are your thoughts on garden gnomes?"

I hate them as much as I hate other bearded monstrosities. But I don't tell her that.

"Garden gnomes have a decorative appeal," I say

diplomatically instead. "And I think their origin is German, so—"

"All right," Henrietta says. "If you could invent a new toothpaste flavor, what would it be?"

"Ginger," I say confidently. "Real ginger, not some artificial flavor. It has anti-inflammatory properties that—"

Someone knocks on the conference room door.

"Ah," Henrietta says. "Your next interviewer is here."

The man who walks into the room looks eerily like a praying mantis—though that's not why I find him unpleasant. That honor belongs to the five o'clock shadow on his face, a slippery slope that can lead to a beard.

"Hi, my love," the guy says to Henrietta. "Is it my turn at her yet?"

My love?

Seeing my confused expression, Henrietta says, "This is my husband, Harlan." Turning to him, she replies, "She's done well thus far. Go for it."

Whew. I didn't realize I was doing well, not when—

"What do you think about in the shower?" Harlan asks as his wife exits the room.

Is that a pervy question?

"Investment strategies," I reply—and it's not a complete lie. I've definitely thought about some on a rare occasion. "Specifically, dollar-cost averaging, which is—"

"What animal do you most identify with?" he

interrupts, and as I try to think of an answer, he texts someone—hopefully not security to escort me out.

"An owl," I say, figuring I can't go wrong with an animal associated with wisdom and intelligence. "They are great hunters, which means they have good analytical skills. They're also super adaptable, so—"

"Would you eat an owl?" he asks, eyebrows waggling.

What the fuck? "Of course not. To start, they are a protected species, not to mention—"

"What if you were starving?" he insists.

"I still wouldn't eat an owl," I reply, and do my best to keep a pleasant, nonconfrontational expression on my face.

I'm sure he doesn't know about—and didn't mean to remind me of—my childhood and the times I was actually on the verge of starvation.

"How can you be so sure?" he says. "Starving people eat other *people*. Owls would hardly be a stretch."

A knock on the door spares me from having to elaborate further.

This time, it's a woman. Her name is Susan, and she turns out to be my potential manager.

"She's doing amazingly well," Harlan says on his way out.

"I figured," Susan says coldly. "Why else would you text me to stop by?"

"Always so serious," he mutters as he stands up.

"I hope he didn't make you uncomfortable," Susan says once he's gone.

"No," I lie. "Why would he?"

She sighs. "It's ironic that our HR power couple are the least appropriate people in the company."

"Oh?" Could this be a trick to get me to bad-mouth the people who have just interviewed me?

"Their questions are a sham," she says. "All they care about is how attractive the candidate is." She gestures outside the room. "Notice any ugly employees?"

"I didn't pay attention." Especially not to one particular, ridiculously handsome employee. Henrietta must have squealed when she interviewed *him*. "Maybe the HR department doesn't actually go by looks. It could be the halo effect at play."

"The halo effect?" She arches an eyebrow.

"It's a cognitive bias where perceiving someone as attractive also makes one assume they are intelligent and competent. Actually, I think this could be useful for developers to know about—if you make a pretty interface, maybe people are more likely to think the software is capable, even if it might not be."

"Interesting." She sighs. "I'm sorry I said anything in the first place. You're probably eager for questions that are actually relevant to this job."

"Those would be nice," I say cautiously.

She nods. "How would you explain the time complexity of your favorite sorting algorithms?"

Ah. It's a good thing that Advanced Algorithms was one of my favorite classes. By the time I get to the time complexity of Heapsort, she smiles and nods approvingly.

"One sec," she says and texts someone.

Did she just call in the next interviewer? That would be a great sign.

"How do you plan to maintain the quality and maintainability of your code?" she asks after she looks up.

I tell her what I did for my last project, and again, she nods approvingly.

After a few more questions from Susan, another guy shows up. Susan tells me that I did well and wishes me luck talking with the rest of the team.

I ace the guy's questions—or so I assume, because he calls in another woman, and she calls in yet another.

Is it weird that part of my excitement about doing well thus far is that I might see Sawyer again?

No. That's crazy.

Crap.

A new interviewer walks in, and I know him already.

Jasper.

"Hi again," he says. "You're doing amazingly well, if they're asking a newbie like me to interview you."

"Thanks," I say.

He asks me a few questions, then says, "Okay. You've got my vote, but the next person you'll speak with will be from another team. Be careful—the guy is a tough audience."

My heartbeat speeds up. "How so?"

"He's extremely antisocial—and I mean more than

is expected in the software development business. I tried to talk to him once, and he snarled at me."

I'm pretty sure he's talking about Sawyer, and that it was small talk that prompted said "snarling."

"Thanks for the tip, Jasper. I'll do my best not to get snarled at."

At that moment, Sawyer enters, and my heart rate speeds up more.

"Speak of the devil. Sawyer Baker, meet Sawyer Worthington." Jasper stands up and wishes me a hushed, "Good luck."

If he means good luck keeping my panties on, then yeah, I'm going to need it.

2
sawyer

TURNING TOWARD ME, what's-his-name who recently joined the trading platform team says, "Hi there, Sawyer! Any of your trading algorithms ready to become Skynet?"

I scoff. "If an AI were to become dangerous, I doubt it would be one of our financial algorithms."

What's-his-name looks confused—probably because he didn't actually want to start a discussion.

On the other hand, the pretty amber eyes of my namesake from the coffee shop light up—and fuck me, she's still as disturbingly beautiful as she was earlier. I was wondering on my way down here if I was just having a random testosterone spike when I met her. I've never been this sexually attracted to anyone before, not even Delilah, and that was a relationship that—

"Anyway," What's-his-name says. "I'd better let you two have that interview." He leaps to his feet and skedaddles.

"Why not?" Sawyer asks when we're alone again.

I take a seat. "Why not what?"

"Why wouldn't a financial algorithm AI decide to wipe out humanity?" She runs her hand through her pixie-cut hazelnut hair.

Damn it. At this moment, I envy AI. They don't get unwanted erections in the middle of an interview. "Without humans, there would be no markets for the AI to analyze," I say, doing my best to keep a poker face. "So by killing us, the AI would lose its purpose for existence."

She purses her lips. "What if that was the only way for the poor overworked AI to finally retire?"

I shift in my seat, but that doesn't help with the hard-on. "I think the AI would go insane from boredom."

"Or it might explore something new and equally complex—like astronomy."

Hmm. "I'm not sure it would find such different interests so interchangeable. Celestial bodies are more predictable than markets."

She cocks her head. "Black holes, dark matter, and dark energy provide plenty of uncertainty."

Did she have to bring up holes? "I wish we could debate this some more, but I only have an hour with you, and there are actual interview questions I'd like to ask you."

"Ah. Sure. Ask away." Something about her prominent cheekbones and full lips makes her smile mischievous, challenging, and completely irresistible.

"How about we start with a puzzle?" Puzzles are a passion of mine, so I can't resist.

"Sure," she says and sounds almost excited.

Could *she* like puzzles?

I steeple my fingers. "Picture four people who need to cross a bridge in a dark cave."

She nods.

"They have only one torch," I continue. "And it's too dangerous to cross the bridge without a light."

"With you so far," she says.

"The rickety bridge can only hold two people at the same time. Their names are Mr. One, Mr. Two, Mr. Seven, and Mr. Ten, and, coincidentally, it takes them 1, 2, 7, and 10 minutes to cross the bridge."

"Ah," she says. "And they have to walk at the slowest person's speed, right?"

"You already know this one?"

She shakes her head. "It just makes sense. There's only one torch."

"Right. So the big question is: what is the shortest time needed for all of them to cross the bridge?"

"Seventeen minutes," she says without hesitation. "Mr. One and Mr. Two go first. Mr. One comes back with the torch. Mr. Seven and Mr. Ten go together. Mr. Two comes back with the torch. Finally, Mr. One and Mr. Two both cross again."

I sigh. "You lied. You have heard it before."

She throws me a glare. "I merely heard something similar that featured a wolf, a goat, and a cabbage. This is a more advanced version of that."

Wow. If she's telling the truth, the speed with which she got that answer is pretty outstanding. And, weirdly, makes me even harder.

"If you want, I can write the algorithm to solve that puzzle." She gestures at the white board.

I nod, which is a mistake. As much as I want to see how her mind works, seeing her standing is not going to help with the unwanted erection.

Damn it. I was right. Her butt looks amazing in that pantsuit, and I'm just glad the table is not see-through.

I force myself to focus on what she's doing—and it's truly impressive. The code she writes is elegant, clever, and sophisticated, just like the woman herself.

I clear my throat when she's done. "That's great. Now I have a few more problems for you to solve."

She actually looks excited at the prospect, so I ask her to code some classics, like reversing a singly-linked list and various traversals of a binary tree.

She handles every problem so well that I follow up with some of my more advanced questions—ones I usually present to highly experienced candidates.

She aces those as well, making me wish we had an opening on my team.

Wait, what?

No.

I'm lucky she's not going to be on my team. If I had to work anywhere near her, my balls would be permanently blue and concentration would go out the window.

Yeah. Bad idea. Thank goodness she's going to be a

floor away, though a different building might be even better. I don't need another reason to prefer my solitude, but she's just given me one: it's so much easier to control my libido while alone.

"Do you want me to solve this without using recursion?" she asks, pointing at the board.

I shake my head. "I've seen all that I need to see. Based on your responses, I'd rate this interview a ninety-five." I pull out my phone and text my team lead to come over here.

When I look up, Sawyer is frowning.

"What?" I ask.

"Was that ninety-five out of a hundred?"

I nod.

"Then how did I lose five points?" she demands.

"You didn't lose anything." Even her disgruntled expression turns me on, which is insane.

"So why ninety-five and not a hundred?"

I arch an eyebrow. "You had a 4.0 GPA, didn't you?" I can tell because I would've asked the same thing back in college.

She frowns. "Don't change the topic."

"Would it help if I told you that you've snatched the highest rating I've ever given? The next highest was eighty-nine."

She shakes her head. "You're changing the topic again."

"Okay, you know what? You've got a hundred. Happy now?"

"No," she says. "I don't want you to humor me. I want to know how I could've done better."

"This wasn't a test," I say. "This was more like reviewing a movie. And even my favorite movie of all time received only a ninety-four rating by me."

"An interview isn't like a movie," she says.

"Can we agree to disagree?"

She sighs. "Fine. What was the movie?"

"*Solaris*," I say.

"The old Soviet one, or the one with George Clooney?"

My team lead knocks on the door, and I'm relieved.

This interview was starting to feel suspiciously like a date.

3
sawyer

a.k.a. the girl who's just become a millionaire?

WHEN MY NAMESAKE LEAVES, I breathe a sigh of relief. If we spend any more time together, I cannot be held responsible for my actions—and said actions could be slutty.

The next woman who interviews me tells me she's the team lead working with Sawyer, and I do my best not to show how jealous I am. Thanks to Harlan from HR, she's as gorgeous as all the other women here, and she's around Sawyer all day, every day.

After she leaves, I face my biggest challenge yet.

The next guy has a soul patch—at least I think that's what the horrific blob of hair below his lip is called.

I take in a calming breath.

This thing isn't a beard. It's barely even a mustache.

My fight-or-flight response still activates.

Fuck.

Maybe I could pretend it's something much less gross? Like a very, very hairy mole? Or a fuzzy caterpillar that has decided to chillax under his lip for some reason? Or a—

"Are you familiar with Big O notation?" the interviewer asks.

Purely on autopilot, I launch into an explanation, then give a few examples of said notation to compare the efficiency of some famous algorithms.

What I don't add is that the biggest O of all is probably something that only Sawyer could give me, especially if—

"Great," the caterpillar-mole owner says. "Have you used Unix or similar systems before?"

I nod.

"What does the fsck command do?" he asks, pronouncing it as "f-suck."

I tell him, and he follows up with questions about hot-swapping, penetration testing, and a stack dump—which makes me wonder if the topics were carefully selected to be inappropriately humorous. Well, thanks to the horror under his lip, I don't even smile as I reply. Who knew facial hair could help you act professional?

"I think I'm the last person," he says. "Wait here. Someone from HR should come back any minute."

Whew. Finally. I'm glad that guy isn't on my potential team. If he were, I'd probably need to surprise-shave him or something, and that might be misconstrued as assault.

Henrietta comes back in, a big smile on her face. "I have good news," she booms.

"Yes?" I don't dare let myself hope.

"Based on everyone's feedback, we'd like to extend you an offer," she says, and then names an annual salary that is way above the number I expected.

My eyes nearly jump out of their sockets. "This is so sudden."

Typically, companies give you the job offer somewhere between a week to a month after the last interview.

"Here at Octothorpe, when we see a good fit, we move fast," Henrietta says, as if reading my mind. "Even your namesake—our biggest misanthrope—sang your praises."

He did? My stomach feels fluttery at the thought. I'm also tempted to inform Henrietta that not liking small talk doesn't make a man a misanthrope, but I don't want to risk her pulling back the offer.

"Thank you so much," I say. "I need to think—"

"Let me tell you about the stock options," she says conspiratorially. "I bet that will expedite your decision."

Right. They're famous for this.

She tells me how the options work, and even though I expected this spiel—and chose this company because of said options—it still sounds too good to be true. In a nutshell, I will be a millionaire on my first day, and a billionaire if I stick around long enough. All of this is on paper, of course. The catch is that you have to stay at Octothorpe for five years before the initial options vest, and for the rest of your career to get to billions.

At least at the company's current stock price. If it appreciates as quickly as it has in the past... well, I don't even dare to think about it.

"So," Henrietta says. "Are you ready to give me the answer I want?"

I bite my lip. "Thank you again. The stock options are extremely—"

"How about if I bump your base fifteen percent?" Henrietta says. "Will that help you decide now?"

Wow. "Yes," I say firmly.

I mean, I was working up to saying yes before the bump.

"Good," she says. "Can you start tomorrow?"

"I GOT THE JOB!" I SAY EXCITEDLY INTO THE PHONE AS I walk home from the bus stop.

Layla caterwauls like a horny cat. "I can't believe it! Does that mean you're a millionaire?"

"Kind of. I just have to work hard and not get myself fired."

"This is insane," she says. "Tell me all about it."

I launch into a detailed retelling of the interviews, but when I get to Sawyer and explain my initial encounter with him, she caterwauls again.

"How could you not start with that?" she demands. "A hot guy with the same name as you is—"

"A distraction," I say firmly.

"Is he though? Or is he exactly what your cobwebby vagina needs?"

I sigh. Layla is my adoptive sister and best friend whom I love as though she were my identical twin, but when it comes to the subject of men, she often makes me want to strangle her.

"Shouldn't you worry about your own vagina? I bet it has overgrown vines, rusty hinges, faded paint, and a seven-inch layer of dust."

"Thanks for that very visual blow below the belt," Layla says.

"You started it."

"Fine. Moving on. Explain to me how it is that Octothorpe makes everyone who works there uber rich?"

"Ah. Right. They give employees stock options, meaning we can buy the company stock at specific, locked-in prices. And their stock keeps getting exponentially more expensive, so those prices quickly increase in value. As if that weren't enough, they give yearly bonuses in octocoins—a cryptocurrency that Octothorpe invented and one that has also been skyrocketing in price."

"But those prices won't go up forever, right?" she asks.

"They may go up for a while," I reply. "Octothorpe is ahead of all competition when it comes to technologies like AI and—"

She yawns, loudly. "I only wanted to hear about how you're going to get rich, not a million more details about the company that you've been prattling on about for ages. If I learn anything else about all the Octopussy products, I'm going to pull my pubic hair out. In front of you."

"Thanks for that image," I say with a grin. "I'm home and starving. Let's talk later."

I walk into my tiny studio and fix myself a sandwich—which strains my cooking skills to their limit.

Once I'm full, I crack open my most prized possession: an album that contains my stamp collection.

On page one, the Elvis stamp seems to smirk at me.

"Hey, King," I say to the stamp.

As usual, I can imagine Stamp Elvis speaking back:

Hey, mama. Good job on your interviews today. I've always said that ambition is a dream with a V8 engine. Thank you, thank you very much.

I look at the Marilyn Monroe stamp. "Tell me, honestly, did you and Elvis ever go on a date?"

I could have if I wanted to, but no. As I always said: a wise girl knows her limits, a smart girl knows that she has none.

As I flip through the pages and have more imaginary conversations with my stamps, I feel myself relax—which is great, because I need to get good sleep before my first day at the new job.

Only, when I finally get into bed, my treacherous subconscious serves me up an X-rated dream that features Sawyer—and I get very little sleep.

4
sawyer

a.k.a. the guy who could really use a distraction
from his distraction

I SIT up in bed and want to plop back down. I had the kind of night where you wake up less refreshed than you were going in. I blame that interview with Sawyer. After I left her in that meeting room, my whole day was out the window. I was like a zombie at the meeting that followed, and I didn't get much other work accomplished.

Hey, at least today is my work-from-home day.

I swing my feet off the bed, and Hermit rubs himself against them before meowing loudly.

I smile. Like me, the cat likes solitude—but he's practical about it. When he's hungry or wants pets, he'll seek out company, which just happens to be me.

"One sec." I exit the bedroom and head over to the other side of my penthouse—which I have dubbed my Fortress of Solitude. When I arrive in the kitchen, I crack open a can of tuna for Hermit and set it down on the counter, the way he likes.

Was that a grateful meow?

Unlikely.

I head back to the bedroom and do my morning routine—the work-from-home edition—and then settle with a bowl of cereal behind my laptop.

Fuck me.

She got the job.

I suspected she would, but I didn't want to dwell on it too much.

Suddenly, I wish I did go to work in person.

No. That's insane. I'm actually lucky I'm here, away from insane ideas… like asking her to lunch.

I like eating lunch, along with all other meals, by myself. That way, I can work, read, or watch TV at the same time.

Yeah.

As a distraction, I assign myself a bug fix that I usually would've given to someone on my team and then get lost in the code.

I'M SUBMITTING THE NEW CODE WHEN MY PHONE RINGS.

Hmm. It's my father.

"Everything okay?" I ask as soon as I pick up.

"Of course," Dad says overly enthusiastically. "Why? Can't I just call my son when I feel like it?"

"Of course you can." It just so happens that he doesn't do it that often, and when he does, there's usually some sort of an agenda, like to invite me to some celebration or congratulate me on having aged another year.

"So, anyway, how are things with you?" Dad asks.

"All the same," I reply as I fight a weird urge to tell him about meeting Sawyer. "How about you?"

When it comes to people I care about, I can tolerate a little bit of small talk—and even initiate it.

"All the same," Dad says. "I've been spending most of my time on the golf course."

Right. His favorite activity is solo practice.

"I got a new stamp," I say to fill the silence.

Dad scoffs. "How many millions was it this time?"

I sigh. "It's worth every penny. Trust me."

My collection is my pride and joy. When I get a new stamp, I feel like a treasure hunter uncovering a chest filled with gold.

Dad sighs. "Is it another error?"

"Yep. It was misprinted in the eighteen hundreds when they somehow used blue ink on it instead of the intended red."

He snorts. "If I got a defective stamp at the post office, I'd feel like they owed *me* money."

"It's all about rarity," I explain. "I'm pretty sure this stamp is the only one like it in the world. Think about how you feel when you sink a challenging putt."

"Hmm. All right. I guess there are crazy collectors like you all over, and the price will go up with time."

"True, though it's a moot point because I'm never selling my stamps."

"Anyway," Dad says. "Have you heard from your mother recently?"

That's an odd question. My parents realized one day that they prefer to live alone, so they very amicably separated and are friends to this day… Or so I thought, until this question.

"What happened? Are you not speaking with her?"

Dad clears his throat. "I heard she's dating someone —and that's not something I want to talk to her about."

What? "She loves the freedom of living alone," I say, stunned. "Why would she date?"

"Wait. Do you think they're living together?" Dad demands.

"You just told me they *might* be dating. I have no idea what's really happening. Last I spoke to her, she didn't mention anything."

"Ah, I see. Oh, well. It was nice talking to you, kid, but I'd better go."

He hangs up, and I stare at my phone in confusion. That question about Mom was clearly why he called in the first place. But even if what he told me about her dating life is true, why does he care? He likes to be alone. He's happier that way. So is my mom.

Could she really be dating?

Hermit walks into the room and jumps on my lap. As I pet him, some of the cat's famously deadly curiosity must transfer over to me because I swipe across my phone's screen to call my mom.

"Hi," she says cheerfully when she picks up. "How are you?"

Ugh, the small talk. But this is Mom, so… "I'm good. How about you?"

She launches into a story about her knitting circle and speaks for about twenty minutes—without a single mention of dating. Finally, she turns her attention to me.

"So… you meet any nice girls lately?" she asks slyly, as she so often does.

"No," I say, as usual. Though this time, the true answer is maybe. "What about you?"

"I haven't met any nice girls either," she says. "Besides, you told me not to set you up anymore, so…"

"Right." Should I flat out ask if she's dating anyone? Nope. Can't. If it's important, she'll mention it.

"How's your cat?" Mom asks.

I scratch said cat behind the ear. "He's good. How's your dog?"

"He became a father recently," she says. "Which I guess is the closest I'll get to being a grandmother."

Not this again. "Hey, Mom, I just got an urgent work email. I'd better go." Else she'll somehow guilt me into becoming a sperm donor or something equally crazy.

"Of course. Love you."

"Love you too," I say, feeling a little guilty as I hang up.

To my relief, it turns out I didn't lie.

I do have an important email in my inbox, so I immerse myself in that.

. . .

WHEN I'M DONE WITH WORK, I EAT DINNER AND RELAX by solving the most recent puzzle that I bought from the specialty shop.

The puzzle is tricky: a key stuck into a small door. Turning the key doesn't do anything, even when I try turning it clockwise and counterclockwise. Then it hits me: what if I turn the door instead of the key?

Yes! The puzzle unlocks, and everything seems right in the universe for the next few minutes… until I think of my namesake, for no reason at all.

Fuck me. I need another puzzle.

I take a Rubik's cube, mix it up, and solve it in forty seconds.

Ugh. How horrible. My usual time is around thirty seconds. I guess this is a good lesson about distractions —which my namesake is.

Even my stamp collection doesn't take my mind off her entirely, and I end up dreaming of her all night.

5
sawyer

a.k.a. the girl who can't wait to get out of Staten
Island

I ARRIVE EARLY on my first day of work, so I swing by Starbucks to get a matcha latte—obviously to get some caffeine, and not because I am hoping to run into my namesake.

I don't, for the record. Run into him, that is.

And I'm not disappointed at all.

When I enter my new company's lobby, the security guard calls Henrietta before waving me through to the elevators. I ride up to the forty-third floor, where she greets me with a toothy smile on her face.

"Welcome to Octothorpe," she says. "Let me show you to your cubicle."

She leads me over the floor, and a few of the people who interviewed me yesterday say hello.

Just as we pass Jasper Knight sitting in his cubicle, Henrietta gestures at an empty desk nearby. "That's you."

Like the others' cubicles, mine looks like a gamer's

wet dream, from the special Herman Miller chair to the super-high-definition curved screen.

"How do I log in?" I ask her, gesturing at the screen.

"Someone from IT will come by and set you up," she says. "For now, leave your stuff here, and I'll take you to make an ID."

The ID-making takes a half hour, and once I have one, Henrietta drags me into a meeting room to "explain HR policies."

"This is all available on the intranet," she says when we sit down. "But I like to go over the things that would mean instant job termination—and therefore forfeit of your stock options—in person."

"Yeah, sure," I say. "Thank you."

Whatever the rules are, I'll be the last person to break them.

"No harassment and no discrimination," she says. "I figure this one is obvious, but worth mentioning."

I nod.

She mentions more scenarios that are even less likely to be a problem for me, like selling Octothorpe secrets to the competition or chronic lateness and absenteeism.

"Finally—and this has burned a lot of people—we have a strict non-fraternization policy," she says. At my frown, she explains, "That's HR speak for workplace romance."

"Right." I knew that. I just didn't like what I heard, for some reason.

"The details are on the page I mentioned," she

says. "But to sum up: don't date a coworker, don't have an affair with a coworker, don't even kiss a coworker."

I cock my head. "But… your husband works here." Does HR not follow their own rules?

She smiles. "Octothorpe doesn't disallow for spouses to work together—so long as they don't practice favoritism."

"Got it." If I had any doubts that thinking about Sawyer was a bad idea, they are gone now.

There can never be anything between us.

Not while our very lucrative jobs are on the line.

RETURNING TO MY DESK, I NOTICE A VERY UNUSUAL GUY is waiting for me. His pale skin has a bluish tint, which might be why he reminds me of Brainy Smurf. In my defense, he's even wearing a hat similar to that of a Smurf—a pointy one that you might also see on garden gnomes.

Wait a second. Is he why Henrietta asked my opinion on garden gnomes? Does she have a fetish or something? It would explain why she approved hiring him despite—

"Hi," the guy says. "I'm Ishmael Tickle, from IT." He grins. "Call me Ishmael."

"Hey," I say, and thank heavens that—unlike the unholy monsters that are garden gnomes—this guy's face is clean shaven.

"I'm here to give you access to your workstation."

Ishmael waves a weird tape-recorder-like device in front of my face.

"Ah," I say and look at him expectantly.

He presses a button on his device. "Say the following phrase: 'Octothorpe, Sawyer Baker, reporting for the daily grind.'"

Feeling like a goof, I say the phrase.

"Good." He presses a few buttons on his device, then says, "Now say the same thing to your workstation."

Feeling even goofier, I repeat the phrase.

"Starting up," says a chipmunk-sounding voice from the speakers, and then my screen unlocks and I see the desktop.

"Wow. An AI. Is it exclusive to our company?" I ask, relishing the word "our."

"No. We've sold it to a bunch of companies. Still, ours *is* the latest version, and the most sophisticated."

"Cool," I say. "What else can it do?"

He tells me, and I'm very impressed—especially by the fact that this AI can actually tell the coffee machine to make me a drink, or so Ishmael says.

"The coffee machine also has the same AI," he continues. "So you can ask it to make whatever you want, directly."

I narrow my eyes at him. "Is that a hazing thing you tell all the new hires?" I can picture it now: I walk into the breakroom and talk to an inanimate coffee machine like I'm missing a few screws.

"I swear it," he says solemnly. "But you don't have to

use it, that's your prerogative. Same goes for the AI in the bathroom, printer, and so on."

Hmm. Maybe I'll test it when there are no people around.

"Now say: Octothorpe, Sawyer Baker, donezo."

With a sigh, I say it, and he explains that before I head home, I'll need to say that phrase in order to lock my workstation.

"I'm going to get some coffee," he says. "Why don't you test it all out for a bit? I'll come back and fix any issues you might discover."

He leaves, and I sign back in with the phrase. I open my email and word processing software, all by using my voice. Then I sign out, log back in, and locate the HR policy on dating to verify what Henrietta told me.

All true, sadly.

Wait, why sadly? That doesn't make any sense. It's not like I—

"All good?" Ishmael asks, reappearing at my shoulder in all his Smurfy glory.

I give him a thumbs up. "All working perfectly."

"Great. Call me if anything breaks. I'm in the company phone book."

I promise that I will, then check my email—and just in time.

As it turns out, I have training in fifteen minutes.

JULIUS IS THE NAME OF THE GUY WHO RUNS THE

training program, and he happens to be almost—but not quite—as distractingly attractive as my namesake.

"I'm sorry you guys aren't getting the usual training experience," he says to me and the only other person in the room. "We don't usually hire new staff in December."

I've heard the usual training mimics *The Hunger Games* and *Survivor*, so I'm actually very glad I get to skip it.

"First things first: let me tell you about Octothorpe."

He launches into the story of how Mr. Nicholas Fonzov, Octothorpe's mysterious CEO, started the company by creating an AI, and what happened after. To put it another way, he tells me what I already know. I also already know the financial concepts he proceeds to teach us for the remainder of the training session.

When the session is over, I head over to the breakroom and look around. No one is here.

Good.

"Octothorpe," I address the coffee machine, feeling like a crazy person. "Sawyer Baker here. Can I have a decaffeinated matcha latte?"

"What kind of milk?" the machine asks in the same chipmunk-like voice that I heard from my workstation.

Damn. Ishmael was telling the truth. I tell the machine to use regular milk.

"Put a cup into the hole, please," the AI says.

Doy. I grab a cup and place it as directed.

"Enjoy." The machine spurts out my latte, and it's decent, though not even close to the yummy one they make in the Starbucks downstairs. But hey, this one is free and saves me a trip down the elevator.

Sipping my drink, I return to my desk just in time to see Jasper get up, collect his stuff, and leave—all without saying the log out phrase.

Sitting at my workstation, I check the time.

Five p.m.

Strictly speaking, it's the end of the workday.

I look around. Unlike Jasper, most of the employees are still working away… which means I will too.

Except there isn't much for me to do apart from signing up for the 401k plan and choosing my health insurance. Turns out, Octothorpe will triple whatever money you put into your 401k, and they also completely cover the cost of the best health insurance plan on the market, one without copays and with access to the best doctors.

I almost want to get sick to test it out.

When I'm done, I catch myself feeling giddy. For someone who's always dreamed of financial independence, things like health insurance and a pension plan are a big deal.

I look around again.

Very few people are left.

Maybe I—

Someone puts a hand on my shoulder.

Startled, I turn.

"Hi, Susan," I say when my heart stops trying to jump out of my throat. "How are things going?"

"Good. How was your day?"

I tell her about the training and strongly hint I'd like to do some real work.

"Here." She hands me a sticky note with a username and password. "That's how you can access the source code repository."

"Wow. Thanks."

"Go ahead, make sure you can get in," she says.

I do so, successfully.

"Perfect," she says. "I can show you the ropes tomorrow."

At my disappointed expression, she smiles. "I can't stay late today. Sorry. Nor should you. Not on your very first day."

"Ah." I guess if your boss says you can go, you go?

I get up from my desktop and and join Susan on the elevator ride downstairs.

As we descend, I learn a little too much about my boss, like the fact that she got divorced recently, and that her ex brought the kids over to her place today, which is why she has to hurry home.

"Well, I'm that way." I gesture toward the Staten Island ferry.

She grimaces. "Staten Island?"

I shrug. "I'm sure I'll be able to move after a paycheck or two."

She nods approvingly. "Have a good night."

"You too," I say and go my separate way.

. . .

As I approach home, I realize I never said "Octothorpe, Sawyer Baker, donezo" before I left the office.

Crap.

I'll have to be more careful.

Wait a second. There's a very familiar minty-green Volkswagen Beetle parked near my place.

"Hi, sweetheart," Mom and Dad say in unison, coming out of the car.

"Hey," Layla says sheepishly, following after them. "Sorry I didn't warn you about this."

"Why be sorry?" Dad demands. "If you had told her, it would've ruined the surprise."

"Please, come inside," I say when I notice one of my designated nosy neighbors watching the gathering with unabashed curiosity.

The last thing I want is for her to ask questions that might make me answer rudely, like "Why don't you look like your family?" or "Why haven't they been over here since they helped you move in?"

Obviously, I was adopted. Layla too. But that doesn't make my parents any less real. In fact, I consider them much more real than the sperm donor who is (or was?) my father, and the junkie who was my mother. As to why they haven't been here, I was too ashamed to invite them to this tiny place. Now, though, with Octothorpe money, I'll be able to afford something much better ... for me and for my parents. And Layla too, if she'll allow it.

"I forgot how much of a dump this place is," Layla says as soon as she steps into my kitchen/bedroom.

I snort. "Didn't you recently ask me how to get rid of bed bugs?"

She darts a worried glance at our parents. "I was asking for a friend."

Ah. Right. She's worried that if Mom and Dad know how bad her living conditions are, they'll insist on giving her money—money they don't really have.

"This place isn't *that* bad," Mom says.

"Yeah," Dad says. "Reminds me of the first place we rented after we met."

They look at each other adoringly.

"Anyway," Mom says. "I brought your favorites." She pulls out a foil-covered casserole dish from a shopping bag, followed by a tin of cookies.

"Wow. Thanks." I rummage under the sink to locate some paper plates and plastic forks before they realize that I only own one ceramic plate, a wooden bowl, and two sets of metal forks and spoons.

"Smart," Dad says. "No need to do the dishes afterward."

As usual, no one is better at finding the silver lining in things than Dad. I bet if a raccoon snuck into this kitchen, Dad would point out how great it is that I don't have to worry about throwing away leftovers anymore.

"So," Mom says when everyone has a full plate. "Tell us about your first day."

I do, and they all take turns telling me how proud they are.

"Now that you have this job, will you finally start dating?" Mom asks.

"Great question." Layla looks like the cat that ate the deep-fried, free-range, organic canary.

I shake my head. "You have it backward. Now that I've got this job, losing my focus would be like using a winning lottery ticket as tinder."

"You're on Tinder?" chimes in Dad—who clearly wasn't listening until this point.

I sigh. "No. I *need* to focus on this job."

"What about Down?" Layla asks. "That's for casual hookups... or so I've heard."

"I'm not *down* for that." I give Layla a look that adds, "And even if I were, why would I talk about it in front of our parents?"

Dad shifts uncomfortably in his seat. "Should we play Uno?"

"I don't have it," I say.

"I have cards." Layla pats her purse. "Regular ones, but we can play Crazy Eights, which is very similar to Uno."

As she explains the rules of the game she suggested, I exchange amused glances with my parents. As long as we've known her, Layla has been obsessed with decks of playing cards, to the point where we all would've been surprised if she didn't have one in her purse today. She's never said it, but I strongly suspect a deck of cards might've been the closest thing to a "toy" that she owned before she was adopted.

What our parents don't know is the dark side of my sister's card obsession. She likes to cheat at cards—something that I've only noticed because of how statistically improbable her poker hands are when I indulge her by playing with her.

Of course, when confronted, she denies the cheating and claims that I'm just a sore loser.

Sure enough, as we play Crazy Eights, I swear Layla doesn't really shuffle the deck when it's her turn, but only pretends to. And then, later, she sneaks an extra card into the discard pile.

Not surprisingly, she wins, over and over, until Mom begs everyone to switch to charades.

I shake my head. "How about we play something that doesn't involve cards at all?" Knowing Layla, she might use her cheating skills to draw easy-to-act-out cards.

"How about telephone?" Dad offers.

Everyone agrees, and soon we're playing our own version, where we start with lines from songs that we don't think the others know. Soon, "Ground Control to Major Tom" turns into "Brown Troll to Major Mom," and everyone cracks up, especially "Major" Mom.

Next, "Is this the real life? Is this just fantasy?" turns into "Is this a real knife? Is this just a fan of tea?"—though I suspect Dad did that on purpose, to make us laugh.

In fact, I think everyone is pretending to be

mishearing, and that's how "Sweet dreams are made of this" somehow becomes "Sweet beans are made of fish."

"We should go," Dad says when there's a pause in the merriment. "Knowing Sawyer, she probably wants to be the first one to arrive at the office—which means she should head to bed early."

I glance at the only clock in my place—on top of the semi-broken microwave.

Shit.

I'm already going to be going to bed late.

Layla yawns, theatrically. "I'd like to go to sleep early myself."

I exchange an odd look with Mom and Dad. Why would the family night owl be sleepy? Did she spend all of last night fiddling with her deck of cards?

Asking this would be futile, especially with our parents around, so I simply thank everyone for stopping by and promise to see them as soon as I've settled at the new job.

After they leave, I talk to my stamps for a few minutes to settle down, and then I head to bed.

Just like the prior night, my sleep is restless, with dreams featuring a certain gorgeous namesake.

6
sawyer

a.k.a. the guy who teams up with Santa's doppelgänger

I **STEP** into the coffee shop and resist the urge to look around.

Who cares if she's here?

I'm here for my caffeine fix, and not to—

"Sawyer," the barista says.

Fuck me.

My namesake floats over to the counter, grabs her cup, then winks at me.

"No mix-up today." As she takes a dainty sip from her latte, her lips draw my gaze—and just like that, my cock stirs.

"Yeah." I shift from foot to foot.

Why am I so fucking horrible when it comes to small talk? It's bad enough that—

"Do you believe in free will?" she says.

I gape at her.

"Is that a no?" She grins. "I guess you're a fate guy? You don't think we have any choices in life, just—"

"I know what free will *is*," I reply. "I just wasn't clear as to why you asked about it."

In my defense, a lot of my blood isn't in my brain at the moment.

She runs her hand through her pixie-cut hair. "You don't like small talk, so I figured you might prefer a deep philosophical question."

Oh. "In that case, *no*. I mean, I think we should live our lives like free will exists, but I'm not sure that it actually does."

She nods solemnly. "I know what you mean." She lifts the cup in her hand. "There was no way I wasn't going to get this matcha today. It was clearly preordained."

Speaking of... "Give me a second." I turn to the barista and order my coffee.

Turning back, I apologize for the distraction.

"No problem," she says. "I was just agreeing with you that the universe is cold and deterministic, and nothing we do really matters in the grand scheme of things. Concepts like moral responsibility are meaningless. We are basically powerless meat puppets dancing to the tune of our genetics and environmental factors, doomed to play out a—"

"I did say we should live as though free will exists," I interject. "If I recall my philosophy classes correctly, my position is called compatibilism."

"Are you sure it's not called illusionism?" she asks.

I shrug. "Could be. It was a long time ago."

"Oh?" she says. "How long ago was that?"

The barista calls out my—our—name again.

Coffee in hand, I turn back to my namesake. "It's been fifteen years since I took that class."

"Wow. How old are you?"

"Thirty-six," I say.

Her eyes widen. "You look way younger."

Thanks? "What about you?"

Shit. Even with my lack of small talk skills, I happen to know you're not supposed to ask a woman about her age. Or weight.

Also, why does this feel like a get-to-know-you chat that happens on a date?

"I'm twenty-two," she says.

Fuck. "You're practically a kid." If thinking about her in a romantic way weren't already insane, this would put the last nail into that coffin.

I was already in ninth grade when she was just born.

Insanity.

"Please," she says. "Twenty-two is *not* a kid."

"Brain development isn't complete until twenty-five," I say and instantly regret it.

She narrows her eyes at me. "You know what? I'm late for work." With that, she turns on her heel and rushes out of the coffee shop.

Fucking hell. I knew talking about age would lead to trouble.

For the rest of the day, I kick myself, wishing that the conversation had gone differently—or better yet, hadn't happened at all.

. . .

THE NEXT MORNING, SAWYER IS GETTING HER MATCHA AS I walk in, so I seize my chance to apologize. Approaching her, I say solemnly, "I'm sorry."

She turns my way. "No need. I looked up the brain development thing, and it's a fact."

"Well, for what it's worth, your brain seems pretty well developed already," I say. "To end up at Octothorpe, you must be pretty good at long-term planning—which is what the prefrontal cortex that's still developing is responsible for."

"Long-term planning might just be my middle name." She turns to the barista and orders my coffee before I can do so.

"Moving on," she says when she turns back. "Do you think time is an illusion?"

I can't help smiling. "Is that today's version of small talk?"

"Big talk." She sips her matcha in that way that turns me on—again. "And… answer the question."

"I'm not sure if I'd say it's an illusion, but it's not as permanent as it feels," I reply. "According to the theory of relativity, time can stretch and contract depending on speed and gravity. What do you think?"

She shrugs. "I think it's a useful construct. Helps us organize our days and whatnot."

The barista informs me that my coffee is ready, and we walk to our building together, chatting the whole way up to her floor.

When I get to my desk, an email from my boss is waiting for me. Apparently, he flew to NYC today and wants to speak with me in ten minutes in the nearest meeting room.

Shit. The meeting request is pretty vague. What could this be about?

I mindlessly sip my coffee and answer a few emails. When it's time, I walk over to the meeting room and wait for Damian.

"I know you don't like small talk and preambles, so I'm going to get to the point," Damian says as soon as he sits down. "Our competition stole AlgoRhythm."

I gape at him. "What?"

"I know. We haven't even finished it yet, and—"

"No. Wait. How can you possibly know this?"

He looks furtively at the door. "What I'm about to say can't leave this room."

I nod solemnly.

"We have a spy at Circumflex," he says. "She has access to their source control repository, and she saw our code submitted. Your name was still there in the comments, and the names of your teammates. They're trying to make it seem like they wrote it in house, but—"

"Then there must be a Circumflex spy here as well," I say.

"Exactly. Someone who works for you or one of the people on the trading platform team. No one else has access to the repository."

I frown. "When was the code stolen?"

"The last comment was dated December sixth."

I blink at him. "That's yesterday."

"Right. And the reason I came to you is that you worked from home."

I raise an eyebrow. "You guys spied on me?"

"Nothing personal. We monitor all work done via VPN, for security reasons. In this case, it proved you're clean."

Should I point out that if I'd really wanted to, I could've gotten that code without anyone knowing—even on a day when I was at home?

"Anyway," he says. "We hired a special consultant to look into this, and I want you to cooperate with him."

"Yeah. Sure." I'm still reeling from this revelation. I mean, Octothorpe has always been on the cutting edge of all sorts of lucrative technologies, which means corporate espionage is something that we do need to worry about, but I always thought that applied more to things like the Longevity Project, or—

"Do you think you can update AlgoRhythm in such a way as to give us an edge over Circumflex?" Damian asks.

I steeple my fingers. "In theory, yes. But what's the point? The spy will—"

"This would be your personal project," Damian clarifies. "Something you will *not* submit into the repository. Something that will not go further than your laptop."

Oh. "Yeah. I can work on that—provided people stop dragging me into stupid meetings."

He nods. "I'll see what I can do about the meetings."

"Great."

He looks at his watch. "Eugene should be here any—"

A man knocks on the door to the conference room.

"Ah. Eugene." Damian waves. "Come in."

Eugene has a bushy white beard and a jolly demeanor that makes him look like Santa in a tailored Italian suit. As soon as he sits down, he says something inane about the cold weather outside.

"Sawyer isn't a fan of small talk," Damian says.

I nod. "I prefer to get to the point."

"No problem." Eugene strokes his beard. "To start, what is to be my cover?"

I'm tempted to suggest he play Santa at the upcoming company party, but that wouldn't give him a good reason to talk to anyone on my team. And our CFO wouldn't want that.

"We could say he's a quant," I suggest.

"Quant?" Eugene arches an eyebrow.

"An analyst who's a wizz at math," Damian explains. "We can say you're helping us come up with a new strategy model. It's a perfect cover, as you'd have a reason to talk to everyone."

"That could work," Eugene says. "I've been told I look like a math or physics professor."

Yeah. Sure. A professor who teaches the physics of flying sleighs to the elves at the North Pole.

"That's settled then," Damian says. "You're a quant."

I scratch my head. "What project are we going to

pretend to have him help with?" Elf motivation? Care and handling of reindeer?

"Sentiment Analysis?" Damian suggests.

At Eugene's blank stare, we take turns explaining that said algorithm would read things like news and social media and then base the trading strategy accordingly.

Eugene strokes his beard again. "That's actually possible to do?"

"For us, yes," I reply with more than a dollop of pride.

"And if anyone asks, what's my role in that?"

Damian drums his fingers on the table. "Just say you're 'building a new model.'"

Eugene nods sagely.

I nod as well. "For the moment, we'll say that you're just learning the ropes and integrating with the two teams. You should be safe for a while."

"I don't need a while," Eugene says. "I'll find your—"

"Don't say the s-word," Damian interjects. "No one can know about this problem. No one."

Eugene nods solemnly—or as solemnly as his jolly demeanor allows. "Got it. Mum's the word."

"You should start now," Damian says. "And if you need me, give me a call."

Translation from Damian speak: "If you bug me, you will get fired."

"Sounds good," Eugene says. "Let's go."

He leaps enthusiastically to his feet, and I show him the floor as I introduce him to my team.

"What about the trading platform guys?" Eugene asks after the introductions are over. "When can I meet them?"

I fight the excitement at the prospect of seeing my namesake. "How about now?"

With jolly steps, Eugene ambles over to the elevator, and I follow.

"So…" Eugene shifts from foot to foot when the doors close. "Did you do anything fun over the weekend?"

I glare at him—purely on autopilot—then sigh. "I'm not a fan of topics like that."

"Ah. Right. Damian said." Eugene spends the rest of the two-second ride in broody silence that makes me feel like I'm now on the permanent naughty list.

Once the doors open to the trading floor, he becomes his jovial self as I take him around to make the introductions.

Hmm. Weird. When we get to Susan—my counterpart on this floor—Eugene gazes at her adoringly, like she's made of cookies and milk.

"It's a pleasure to meet you," Susan says, shaking his hand.

Eugene's cheeks redden. "The pleasure is very much, absolutely mine."

Susan's eyebrow arches, but she continues speaking with Eugene very politely, as though unaware of the metaphorical drool pouring out of his mouth.

"Hey, Susan," I say when I start to suspect that this

introduction will go on until Christmas. "What's the name of the new guy?"

"Jasper Knight." She gestures in his direction. "And before you ask, the new gal's name is Sawyer Baker."

Yeah, like I could ever forget *that*. "Thanks, Susan. Come, Eugene."

Eugene leaves with great reluctance, and I know how he feels. Talking to this Jasper guy will be as pleasant as getting stuck in traffic.

As we approach Jasper, I see Sawyer nearby. Her back is to me, but I know it's her. I'd recognize that hair in a lineup of pixies any day of the week.

"Nice weather last night, right?" Jasper says once he learns Eugene's name. "The game between—"

I tune the rest of it out to keep my sanity. My gaze homes in on my namesake again, and as if she's felt it, she turns my way.

At first, a smile lights her face, but then her gaze falls on Eugene and she pales.

What the fuck?

She leaps to her feet and rushes away.

"Excuse me a second." I don't wait for Eugene or Jasper to reply as I hurry after Sawyer.

Something is wrong. I'm sure of it.

When I catch up with her in the pantry, she's making chamomile tea, and some color has already returned to her cheeks.

"What just happened?" I demand.

"Oh, hey," she says. "What do you think is the nature of reality?"

I narrow my eyes. "Don't try to change the subject."

She cocks her head. "Did we have a subject under discussion?"

"You got scared when you saw Eugene," I say. "Why?"

"Who's Eugene?"

I wave a hand back toward the floor. "The consultant I was going to introduce you to."

She pales again. "He's going to work on my team?"

My jaw ticks. "What did that fucker do to you?" Because whatever it is, I'm going to—

"No. Nothing. It's not something he *did*."

"You expect me to believe that?" I clench and unclench my fists. "Never mind. I'll get *him* to tell me." I'll even enjoy beating the truth out of him.

I start to turn, but she grabs my shoulder. "Don't. I've never met Eugene before."

I turn back, and she snatches her hand away.

"What happened then?"

She furtively looks over my shoulder. "It's Eugene's face."

I frown. "His face?"

"Something *on* his face," she clarifies.

I stare blankly at her.

She sighs. "I have pogonophobia."

Pogo-phobia? Would that be a fear of pogo sticks? I mean, I fell off one when I was a kid, but—

"*Pogono* means beard in Greek," she says, as if reading my mind.

"Oh." I scratch my beardless chin.

"I know how it sounds," she says sheepishly.

I step closer and barely resist enveloping her in a reassuring hug. "Beards *can* be a little creepy sometimes. Rasputin had a weird beard, and there's Bluebeard—who's basically a serial killer from a children's tale. Also, Saruman from *Lord of the Rings* had a beard and turned out to be evil, and so did—"

"But Eugene's beard looks like Santa's," she interjects. "Most people like Santa."

I know I shouldn't, but I grab her hand and squeeze it reassuringly. "Christmas must be a difficult time for you."

She nods. "Growing up, it was hard for everyone around me to compute, but I've been afraid of Santa for as long as I can remember."

I gently squeeze her hand again. "For what it's worth, there won't be a Santa at the upcoming company party." Not after the year we hired one who got drunk and peed on the leg of the chair our CFO was sitting on. Hell, if the CFO knew about Eugene, he'd probably—

"Whew," she says. "I was wondering about that."

"Yeah. Nothing to worry about there."

"But… what about Eugene?" she says.

"What do you mean?"

She bites her lip. "I'll have to be around him."

"He's actually joining *my* team, so he'll be on a different floor." And I'll do my best to make sure their paths do not need to cross, though I'm not yet sure how that's going to be possible.

Someone clears their throat, and it sounds like "ho, ho, ho!"

"Hey, Eugene." I fake my best smile. "Come, we should hurry back to our floor."

"Umm—"

"I want to talk strategy," I say. "Let's go."

He follows reluctantly, and when we get into the elevator, he states the obvious: "I didn't get the chance to speak with that woman in the pantry."

I wave that away. "She's just started at the company, so she wasn't here for the leak." It's *almost* true.

"Ah," he says. "I see."

From there, we're silent until we enter the meeting room that's right next to my office.

"So here's what I think should happen," I say. "I'll invent a project that you're going to be working on and set up some meetings for you. From there, I'll leave it up to you to figure out how to get them to tell you what you need to know."

He nods.

"Oh, and I want the meetings to happen in this room," I add.

"Why?" He tugs at his beard.

Since I can't exactly tell him "to keep your bearded mug away from Sawyer," I come up with the lame, "So that I'm near and therefore in the loop."

His face turns serious. "Damian asked you to keep an eye on me, didn't he?"

Huh. "Whatever I tell you, you're not going to believe me anyway."

He nods again.

We talk some more before I see the guy from IT prowling around the desk that is to be Eugene's, so I call the meeting adjourned.

Until Eugene mentioned it, I took it for granted that he can be trusted and is competent. If he's not, the spy will keep doing what they're doing—and that sucks.

Maybe I could help smoke out the spy in my own way.

They're interested in my team's work, so I could write some new code that doesn't do anything particularly useful, then mess with the source control system so it returns said code as a slightly different version to different people—and then our spy at Circumflex could help us figure out who the mole is based on what version of the code is stolen.

I locate Damian and tell him about this idea.

"Sounds great," he says. "Do that and don't tell Eugene."

Huh. So Eugene is right in thinking that Damian doesn't fully trust him.

"I'll have to figure out how our source control system works," I say. "It will take some time."

"I've already taken care of some of your regular meetings," Damian says.

"Great. What do you consider more urgent—an edge over what Circumflex stole or this?"

"The edge," he says. "But by a small margin."

"Got it. And it goes without saying, but we should

have my team work on something unimportant for now—like maybe that automated documentation tool I've been telling you about."

"Agreed." Damian stands up. "Keep me posted."

I grunt in agreement and head over to my desk to start working.

A few hours later, a window pops up on my screen from the Octo-messenger, the company chat system that I told everyone on my team never to bug me on.

Hi, this is Sawyer.

An involuntary smile curves my lips as I reply:

The window shows your name.

Her reply takes less than a second to show up:

Ah, right. Sorry to bother you. I just wanted to make sure that the bearded guy isn't headed for the elevator at the moment because I'm going home.

I glance at Eugene's desk and find it empty.

Ah. There he is, in the conference room, speaking to his first victim from Sawyer's team.

I return to the messenger window and tell her that she's safe.

Thanks.

I smile again, and then, unable to help myself, I head over to the elevator and press the "down" button.

Just as I hoped, when my elevator stops on her floor, I find Sawyer waiting there, looking worried.

"Just me," I tell her reassuringly.

She jumps inside and mashes the "close door" button, as though Eugene's beard is chasing her.

"Do you think I'm nuts?" she asks as the elevator starts to go down.

I shake my head. "I wouldn't grow a beard even if someone gave me a million dollars. They're too itchy."

"And don't forget how gross they are. I mean, just imagine how much food gets stuck in there. The bacteria that can lead to. And the smell. And—"

The doors open, and she waits for me to walk out first.

I do so and make sure no beards are in sight.

"The coast is clear," I say over my shoulder.

She beelines for the revolving doors, and I pick up my pace to catch up to her.

"Thanks for that," she says once we're outside in the chilly air.

"No problem." I grin. "Feel free to check with me on Eugene's whereabouts whenever you want."

"Thanks." She moistens her lips. "I think I will."

I find myself hypnotized by those lips, and by the vapor she exhales.

How wrong would it be to dip my head and press my own lips against hers? To inhale that vapor?

As if the thought were a magnet acting upon me, I find myself stepping toward her. Our eyes lock, and she seems to sway toward me too, as though feeling that same potent pull.

Heart thudding, I dip my head as she rises on tiptoes, and our lips are but a hair's breadth apart when her eyes suddenly widen and she takes a sharp step back.

"My boat," she blurts. "I'm going to miss it."

"Right." I have no idea what she's talking about on account of the lack of blood in my brain.

"Bye. Thank you." She sprints in the direction of the Staten Island Ferry, which is when the boat comment starts to make some sense.

Fuck.

I almost kissed her.

Right in front of our fucking work building.

What is wrong with me?

Thank fuck she was almost late.

This could've been a disaster of epic proportions.

7
sawyer

a.k.a. the girl who's officially lost her mind

IT'S OFFICIAL. Seeing the Santa guy's beard made me lose the last of my marbles.

I mean, I almost kissed a coworker. On my second day at my dream job for a company that has a zero-tolerance policy for exactly that sort of thing.

What's worse, if the kiss had happened, I've got a feeling it would've almost been worth losing all that money and flushing my career down the toilet.

His lips looked so soft, so inviting, *and* he said he'd never grow a beard.

Wait. What am I saying? Was I really tempted by the comment about beards?

That does it. Now that I have a health insurance policy, I'm going to get therapy for my pogonophobia.

Yeah.

So I'm not tempted to kiss my beardless coworkers, no matter how handsome they might be.

Pulling out my phone, I find a therapist named Dr.

Couch and make a virtual appointment to see her tonight.

"I THINK YOU COULD BENEFIT FROM CBT," DR. COUCH says after I tell her about my issue.

I set my computer more comfortably on my lap as I lean back on my raggedy couch. "That stands for Cognitive Behavioral Therapy, right?"

She nods. "We can also do some very basic exposure therapy, if you're up for that."

My heart rate speeds up. "Does that mean looking at beards?"

"No. We can start with mustaches."

"How about stubble?" I ask.

"Sure," she says, and we proceed with our first session.

8
sawyer

a.k.a. the girl desperately trying to ignore the
fuzzy feeling in her chest

I SHOULDN'T GO into the coffee shop.

My namesake might be there, with his lips and his—

I spot the Santa guy in the far distance down the street, and my heartrate skyrockets.

Shit.

What did Dr. Couch say I should do in this situation?

Santa takes another menacing step, and I dive into the coffee shop—just as the barista calls out the name "Sawyer."

I halt in my tracks.

My namesake waves to me, then picks up two cups and turns my way.

I stare at him, unable to believe my body's intense reaction to his nearness. I mean, my heart is about to jump out of my chest, and I'm flushed in all the places, not to mention—

Wait. I'm not turned on.

I'm scared.

Yeah.

That's my story, and I'm sticking to it.

"This is for you." He thrusts one of the cups into my hand.

"It is?" I look dumbly at the cup.

"It's a matcha latte." He wrinkles his nose. "You know I wouldn't drink something so reminiscent of grass."

"Right." As I take the cup, my fingers brush his, and it takes all my willpower to act nonchalant. "Did you want to talk about our views on the existence of the soul?" I manage to ask.

"In a minute. First, I want to apologize."

"Why?" I blink up at him.

"There was that awkward moment yesterday. Or at least I thought so." His gaze is somber. "It won't happen again."

"Oh." Why do I feel so idiotically disappointed? "Yes. Let's forget anything happened at all." Even if that would require the mind-wiping technology from *Eternal Sunshine of the Spotless Mind*.

"Perfect," he says. "Now about the soul..."

We proceed to discuss our views on this topic and pretend yesterday never happened.

I sip the matcha he got for me as we ride the elevator, and no one kisses anyone the whole time, which is an effort of will on my part.

When I get to my desk, I realize I forgot to lock my workstation again last night.

Crap. When Sawyer told me the coast was clear, I just bolted.

Oh, well. I check my inbox and find it empty. Then I head over to the boring training yet again. Afterward, I peruse some code written by my namesake. By the end of the day, I learn a valuable lesson: one can get disturbingly turned on by how clean and clever someone else's thought processes are.

When I'm ready to go home, I ping Sawyer to check on the location of that-which-I-don't-want-to-think-about.

He's in a meeting. You're safe to go home.

Good.

I run for the elevator, and I'm not surprised to see Sawyer inside, like yesterday.

"Hey," he says.

"Hi. How do you think consciousness works?"

The reward for my carefully prepared question is his devastating smile. "I think consciousness is the result of computations running inside our brains."

"That's it?" I hit the "close door" button.

He shrugs. "What did you expect me to say?"

I tap my temple. "Something about chaos theory? How all the feedback loops of our neurons create the overwhelming complexity that leads to an emergent phenomenon we call consciousness?"

He flashes me that smile again. "I'm not sure I like the idea of chaos happening inside my head."

The elevator doors open before I can reply.

He gestures for me to go ahead.

"Actually, can you go first?" I ask. "Make sure the coast is clear?"

The beard coast, which is the worst type of coast there is on the ocean of nightmares.

"Ah. Right." He steps out and waves for me to follow.

When we exit the building, we stop in the exact spot where the kiss almost happened last night.

"Okay," he says. "You should run for your ferry. It's leaving in ten minutes."

"Right." We did agree yesterday's lapse of reason wouldn't happen again. "Good night."

I run for the ferry, but the red light blocks me from crossing the road without getting killed by a yellow cab.

Unsure why, I look back, just in time to see Sawyer heading back into our building.

Hmm. I thought he was going home…

There's no way he walked me out and then went back to work, right? Maybe he simply forgot something at his desk?

Speaking of forgetting—did I lock my workstation today?

I can't recall, not with that question about Sawyer taking up all the resources of the chaos raging inside my brain. A brain that quickly realizes something else: Somehow, Sawyer knew when my boat would leave. Did he look up the schedule? And if so, why?

My phone rings, and it's Layla.

Ah. Good. I pick up and tell her what happened.

After the obligatory caterwauling, I ask what she thinks.

"He's into you," she says excitedly. "That's all there's to it."

"Nah." And even if he was, it doesn't matter since we can never be.

"He might even be more into you than you are into him," Layla says sagely.

I roll my eyes. "Who says I'm into him at all?" I mean, I'm only into him as much as is normal, considering how gorgeous he is and—

"Your vagina told me," Layla states.

I snort. "And how did that conversation take place?"

"Via queef code," she says. "For example, the letter A is a short one, followed by a long one."

"Moving on," I say with an exasperated sigh. "What's new with you?"

As usual, instead of telling me about a job she wants or a guy she's fallen for, she goes into a nauseatingly detailed account about some difficult sleight of hand with cards that she's just mastered—but hey, talking about anything is better than thinking about Sawyer, so I let her drone on.

"I have to go soon," I warn Layla as I approach my house. What I don't add is that I have a session with my new therapist tonight. I plan to keep this private until and unless I feel some improvement. Otherwise, I'll negatively predispose Layla against therapy, and therapy is something she could use even more than me.

"In that case, let me quickly tell you about the hand

stretching exercises I've been doing," she says and launches into it.

I don't even bother asking which sleight of hand will improve if one flexes one's pinky the way she describes. I don't think I want to know the answer.

"Okay." I unlock the door. "I'd better go."

"Later," she says and hangs up—probably to go play with her cards.

I quickly grab dinner and settle on my couch for a session with Dr. Couch.

Among other things, she talks me into doing a breathing exercise while looking at a picture of Chris Hemsworth with stubble.

"This is a good idea," I tell her after the session. "Somehow, when it's a famous guy, it's easier."

"I'm sure it doesn't hurt that he's very easy on the eyes," Dr. Couch says with a wink.

I arch an eyebrow. "How would Mr. Couch react if he knew about your feelings toward Chris Hemsworth?"

She smiles. "He'd probably have me watch *Thor* every evening—to get me in the mood."

Wow. TMI, and she realizes it because she quickly puts on a professional demeanor and suggests we do a few CBT exercises.

Once we're done, I open my snail mail and nearly jump with excitement.

A stamp has just arrived for my collection. On it is the face of Emma Watson in her role as Hermione Granger from *Harry Potter*.

As usual, my Elvis stamp's signature smirk grows smirkier as I add another woman stamp to my collection—which he probably considers his harem.

I can practically hear him saying, *Well there, darlin' girl, you're clearly a witch, 'cause you've put a spell on me. Thank you, thank you very much.*

The next morning, I can't resist walking into the coffee shop to "accidentally" bump into Sawyer.

He smiles when he notices me, which gives me a jolt of giddy energy that is much stronger than caffeine.

Speaking of caffeine, Sawyer is holding two cups again, meaning he was expecting to see me.

"What do you think about dreams?" I ask in lieu of a hello.

He hands me my cup. "Aspirations and ambitions?"

I shake my head. "I mean the VR-like experiences that happen as you sleep." Ones that have lately turned into wet dreams featuring my current conversation partner.

"Science says that dreams are part of memory consolidation," he says. "I believe they help us process and organize memories."

Hmm. Then why would I dream of him inside me? That's a memory I wish I had.

I mean, no. I don't want that as a memory because—

"What about you?" he asks.

I wave for him to follow me out of the shop as I

explain that I've always believed dreams are just the way our minds make sense of random neuron firings.

He tsk-tsks when we get to the elevator. "Yesterday, you said chaos theory was behind consciousness. Now you tell me dreams are random firings in our brain. What's next? Our memories are our brain's junk drawer to store the cringiest moments of our lives?"

I narrow my eyes theatrically. "Weren't you the one who didn't believe in free will?"

Before he can answer, the elevator doors open to my floor, so I force my feet to drag myself away from him—a task that's becoming harder and harder. Case in point: that very evening, when I almost miss my ferry by chatting with him.

THE NEXT DAY IS A MIRROR OF THE PRIOR ONE. I MEET Sawyer in the coffee shop and talk about something that isn't small—epistemology, in this case. To cool off afterward, I review some code, partake in training, and later—as the highlight of the day—I meet Sawyer in the elevator to discuss qualia.

After our goodbyes, I sneak a peek behind me and see him going back into the office, again.

This proves it.

He really does just walk me out before returning back to work.

Grr. This warm fuzzy feeling in my chest is a bad, bad idea.

I get home, meet with my therapist, and eventually go to sleep, just to have a similar day when I wake up.

This pattern continues until the weekend, then resumes the following week. The only change is that I get myself to the point where I can almost tolerate a guy with a tiny bit of stubble, thanks to all the therapy—but if I got stuck in an elevator with Eugene, I'd still probably backflip the fuck out.

"So," Sawyer says as I'm about to leave for the ferry on Friday of that week. "Are you going to the company party tomorrow night?"

Oh. Shit. That's already tomorrow? How could I forget something so huge?

"I'm going," I say. "What about you?"

"I'm going this time," he says, the words heavy with meaning.

Realizing that I'm holding my breath, I let it out—with an accidental whoosh. "That's… great." Why do I get this weird feeling like he's just asked me to a school dance or something equally silly? "I'll see you there?"

"See you," he says softly, his gaze dropping to my lips.

My heart thumps harder in my chest, as if determined to propel me toward him from the inside. It's all I can do to take a deep breath and step back, mumbling, "I'd better go."

And with that, I sprint for the ferry.

9
sawyer

a.k.a. the guy who can handle his scotch...
mostly

AN ALARM DRAGS me out of the flow state of coding.

Fuck.

The party.

I'm glad I set that alarm.

When I close my laptop, I see Hermit's slitty eyes glaring at me.

"Ah. Right. I need to feed you."

The cat exudes annoyance the whole way to the kitchen and until the food is in his bowl.

"All right," I tell him. "I'm going to a party. See you later."

He looks up from the food long enough to give me a "who cares what happens to you?" stare.

Fine. Whatever.

I shave carefully, making sure not a single hair is visible to prevent potentially grossing out my namesake. Shaving twice a day like this has actually become a ritual, and I kind of like the nearly constant smooth-skin feel.

Next, I put on my best suit, style my hair, and run to get a cab.

"So cold out, right?" asks a guy whose name I can't recall as soon as I step into the so-called "Rainbow Room" at Rockefeller Center.

"Hey, Sawyer," says someone else. "How's your Saturday going so far?"

Fucking hell. This is exactly why I usually skip this event each year. In fact, what possessed me to torture myself this time?

"Ah, there you are," says a familiar voice.

I turn. It's Sawyer, but unlike I've ever seen her. Her pixie hair is adorably mussed, and she's wearing a cocktail dress that hugs her curves in the most—

"Can you gentlemen excuse us?" she murmurs to the two assholes before she grabs me by the elbow and tugs.

I let her drag me away and hope the tent situation in my pants isn't too noticeable.

"Thanks for the save," I say. "And... you look amazing."

"Thank you." She bats her eyelashes at me and then blushes. "I'll be honest... I only saved you as a means to an end."

"Oh?"

She gestures into the distance. "See that guy by the bar?"

I nod grimly. He'd better not be her date, or he's dead.

"He's got sideburns, which means I'd really appreciate it if you got me a drink."

Fine. He gets to live. "Of course. What can I get you?"

She pulls a twenty out of her purse. "A beer. Domestic?"

I back away from the money. "You realize this is an open bar." And even if it weren't, the day I take her cash is the day I talk about the weather to everyone I meet.

She grins. "Open bar? In that case, I'll have a single malt scotch—the most expensive one they have."

"Got it." I head over to the bar and get two glasses of The Macallan 25-Year-Old.

"Here." I hand her the glass. "This was aged for longer than you've been alive."

She rolls her eyes. "This again? Are you going to tell me how behind my prefrontal cortex is compared to yours?"

I shake my head and raise the glass. "To our prefrontal cortices."

She clanks her glass to mine and takes a huge swig.

I arch an eyebrow. "You know you're supposed to sip this, right?" To demonstrate, I take a small sip of mine.

She shrugs. "It tastes great. Try it."

I take a big gulp, and it does taste good like this, but

still, not as good as sipping. "I'm glad my parents can't see me right now," I say as I take a cleansing sip.

"Why?" She teasingly takes another big gulp. "Is everyone in your family an expert on drinking this stuff?"

"I'm not sure if I'd go that far, but my dad definitely enjoys sipping scotch and having a cigar from time to time."

"Your dad sounds rich," she says.

"He's actually only second-generation wealthy. It's my mother's family who come from so-called old money—and they're proportionally snooty, of course."

"Oh." She bites her lip. "That's cool." Looking away for some reason, she takes a small sip, the way I did.

I observe curiously. Is it my imagination, or does she seem a bit down all of a sudden? "Like it?"

She meets my gaze. "Yeah, it's pretty good. But as far as social lubrication goes, chugging is way better."

I grin. "So do you have a new conversational gambit tonight?"

Her face brightens. "What do you think about the way technology is changing humanity?"

Huh. "I think it's a mixed bag, but with more good than bad. Our company alone is working on profound advancements in medicine, education, and communication—and the list goes on."

"True. On a more personal note, I love that I can speak to a bearded person over a video chat that supports filters."

"Exactly. Speaking as someone who likes solitude,

the video chat technology is a godsend, as it allows me to work from home."

She swirls the amber liquid in her glass. "You like solitude?"

"I do." Then I surprise myself by adding, "But I'm also enjoying *not* being alone at the moment."

Her eyes widen, and she downs the remainder of her drink while I stare at her, mesmerized by the movement of her slender throat as she swallows.

My voice is a little hoarse as I ask, "Want something else?"

She looks at my glass. "After you're finished."

I gulp the rest of my drink. "More scotch?"

Perching on a nearby barstool, she nods.

I get us refills and take a seat on the stool next to her as we resume discussing the pros and cons of technology.

"Another?" she asks when our glasses are empty.

I go to the bar and, to save a return trip, get four glasses.

"So, to sum up: you're very pro-technology," Sawyer says.

I hand her one of the drinks. "I'm not sure I'd use the word 'very.' Not when I happen to think that technology might explain the Fermi Paradox."

She grins. "As in, where are all the alien civilizations out there?"

"Exactly. It's possible that once a civilization invents sufficiently advanced technology, its ultimate destruction is inevitable."

She scoffs. "That's a pretty dark way of looking at it. It's just as likely that alien civilizations choose to remain hidden out of safety reasons or ethical concerns."

"True. Life might also be rare, but—"

"We might lack the technology to detect the alien civilizations," she interjects. "Or—"

"Ladies and gents," says the emcee. "Can I get everyone's attention?"

I sigh. This is the most boring part of the party, where upper management gives speeches. Sawyer, however, seems fascinated by all the slideshows and corporate talk, and I find that the scotch helps me tolerate it as well. Especially once I get us a few more refills.

After what feels like a year, the emcee comes back on and invites everyone to the dance floor, at which point club music starts blasting.

"Want to dance?" I shout at Sawyer over the pounding beats.

She grins and jumps down from her barstool.

I get to my feet also and realize that my legs are a bit unsteady.

Fuck. How many scotches was that? That asshole waiter took away the empty glasses, so I have no idea.

Too many, I guess, but then again, given the way everyone is gyrating on the dance floor, I'm not the only one who might have overindulged.

"Let's go over there," Sawyer murmurs into my ear. "Away from anyone with facial hair." She points to a clearing that is free of people, one smack in the middle of the dance floor.

"Good idea." Unsure of what is possessing me, I take her hand and lead her onward, trying to ignore how soft and delicate her palm is.

"Here?" I ask when we're in the spot she chose.

She looks up at me through thick lashes. "Perfect."

What an apt word. She *is* perfect.

Reluctantly, I let go of her hand. "Let's dance?"

In answer, she begins to move her body to the rhythm—while I just stare, rooted to the spot, blood rushing down south.

Hips swaying, Sawyer wags her finger at me.

At first, I wonder if she's chastising me for the huge hard-on that she's just caused, but no. She dances over, rises on tiptoes, and whispers in my ear that I should also dance.

Ah. Right.

I start moving to the music, following the beat.

With a huge grin on her face, Sawyer sways and shakes her hips next to me—and the rest of the world seems to disappear.

10
sawyer

a.k.a. the girl who smells like stamps

IT'S OFFICIAL. I'm drunk, and dancing like this was a bad idea.

Watching Sawyer move to the music causes some seriously impure thoughts—and by "impure," I mean triple X-rated.

Quick. Distraction.

Turns out, this is easy. The rest of the company is as drunk as I am, if not more so. Case in point: The guy who's been training me is doing the robot, and near him, my manager, Susan, is moving like a chicken. All the while, nearby, Ishmael is performing the Smurf dance. The worst of them all are probably Henrietta and Harlan from HR, because they're grinding on each other like two teens who've discovered dry humping for the first time.

Is this even allowed? I thought there was a strict policy against fraternization.

Is HR exempt?

Ah. Right. They're married, which is an exception to the rule.

The thundering beat stops, and the sadist—I mean DJ—puts on an oldie but oh-so-goodie: Elvis's "Can't Help Falling in Love."

Everyone around us shifts into slow-dance positions, and before I can blink, Sawyer is holding me close to him, one hand on my waist and the other enveloping my hand.

Oh, my. We sway to the music, and I feel just like a Hershey's Kiss near an active volcano—super melty.

Sawyer leans in to whisper into my ear. "You're an amazing dancer."

I am? "You're not bad yourself." Which is unfortunate both for my sanity and the integrity of my panties.

"You smell very nice," he murmurs. "Like flowers."

I let my eyebrow ask the obvious question, but when he doesn't seem to reply, I say, "Which flowers?" And how is it plural?

He bends down and inhales my neck, which might be the most sensual moment of my life.

"Lavender." He twirls me. When I'm pressed against him again, he adds, "Chamomile too."

I can't help but breathe in *his* intoxicatingly woodsy scent, one that also reminds me of—

"Oh, and you also smell like stamps," Sawyer says.

I stiffen. "Do I?"

Come to think of it, he kind of, sort of, also smells like stamps. I just couldn't place it until this moment. In his case, I find the idea pleasant, sexy even, but—

"I realize how crazy that sounds, but you do, and it's amazing." He sniffs my neck again, an action that is quickly becoming my favorite thing in the world. "There's a sweetness to the adhesive aroma of the back of a stamp that's unmistakable, along with the cozy, library-like notes to the paper."

Wow. If he needs a backup career, he can always try poetry. "I own a lot of stamps," I admit. "I'm a philatelist, though I didn't realize that would lead me to smell like said stamps." Despite how prettily he describes it, I'd rather smell only like flowers.

His eyes widen. "I'm a philatelist too."

What? "No way." How could we have known each other for this long without talking about something so huge?

"Yeah," he says. "I've been collecting stamps for years."

"Me too." I breathe in his scent again, which makes my head spin very pleasantly.

"I can't believe it," he says. "We talked about free will, consciousness, and other universal questions, yet didn't touch on the most important topic of them all: stamps."

I moisten my lips. "I'd love to show you... my stamps."

He stares devouringly at my mouth. "I'll show you mine if you show me yours."

Once again, I feel a powerful pull toward him, like that of a licked stamp toward an envelope. He seems to feel it too because he leans in just as I get on tiptoes… and his lips smash into mine like a perforator machine into a sheet of uncut stamps.

Everything inside me goes wild. The kiss is fierce and tender in equal measure. It's everything I've dreamed about, except multiplied by a thousand.

The song fades away, and with it the rest of the world. All I'm aware of are Sawyer's delectable lips and then his ultra-clever tongue, as well as his large hand that perches on the low of my back and—

Faintly, I hear gasps around us.

Weird.

Now that I think about it, even with eyes closed, I can feel myself being watched by a multitude of eyeballs.

To my huge disappointment, Sawyer halts the kiss and gently pulls away, which is when I realize that the music has stopped, and everyone on the dance floor is staring at us judgmentally.

Fuck. Fucking fuck. What did we just do?

My cheeks burn like they've been slapped by everyone around us. Heartbeat skyrocketing, I touch my swollen lips.

Yep.

Sawyer and I just kissed in front of the whole company—upper management included.

Somewhere in the distance, Henrietta charges

through the crowd like a linebacker through a defensive line.

Oh, no. No, no, no.

I'm not getting fired here and now, in front of everyone. Getting caught making out is humiliation enough… for a lifetime.

I turn on one of my high heels and run.

11
sawyer

HOW CAN life take such a sharp turn?

One moment, I'm enjoying a transcendental kiss, and then in an eyeblink, I find myself in the biggest clusterfuck ever.

The whole company has stopped to gape at the two of us, like a bunch of fucking peeping Toms.

I snap my attention back to Sawyer just as she turns and sprints away.

Fuck.

I glare at the judgmental expressions all around me. If I had the time, I'd smack some sense into these fucks for making Sawyer feel like she needed to run. As is, I just chase after her, but she's so fast I only manage to catch up outside.

"I'm going to wake up," I overhear her mutter to herself. "This is a dream. It has to be."

"I'm afraid that it's not," I say, touching her shoulder. "Though it sure feels like a nightmare."

She waves her phone at me. Her voice is shaky and filled with tears. "Where is that fucking Uber?"

I shrug helplessly.

"How are you so fucking calm?" Her voice rises. "Do you realize what's just happened?"

I exhale, loudly. "We've violated the non-fraternization policy, and in front of too many witnesses. Our jobs are forfeit."

"Yeah. Our futures, too. Our financial independence. Our—"

Her phone dings, and so does mine.

I check the screen. A meeting request from Henrietta from HR, and from Damian.

No agenda for said meetings, but I know what it is: my termination, and Sawyer's too.

Hey, at least they're not doing it over email, so there's that.

When I look up, Sawyer is looking at her inbox in confusion. "My manager and Henrietta want to talk to me on Monday," she says. "Maybe not all is lost?"

I sigh. "I just got the same type of requests from my manager. I'm afraid such meetings mean all *is* lost."

"No." She clenches and unclenches her fists. "They can't. It was just a kiss."

"An amazing kiss," I say. "One that was almost worth it."

"Stop being cute," she says. "This is serious."

"I know. Believe me. I was this close"—I show an inch's worth of space between my thumb and index finger—"to my first batch of stock options vesting."

A car stops next to the curb. Sawyer checks the license plate, yanks at the door, and jumps inside. On a whim, I hop in after her.

"What are you doing?" she demands. "I'm riding to the ferry."

"And I'll come with. Misery loves company and all that."

"Again, you are way too cool with all this," she says, her voice shaking again.

I drag in a breath. "What do you want me to do?"

"Scream. That's what I want to be doing."

"So scream."

She lets out a half-hearted yell, and the Uber driver gives me such a worried look in the rearview mirror that I decide to triple his tip.

"Better?" I ask her.

She shakes her head. "There has to be something we can do."

"There is something *I* can do," I tell her as an idea occurs to me. "I'll tell them I was drunk, and that I forced that kiss on you. That way, only I will get into trouble, and you can—"

"No." She shakes her head vehemently. "I can't let you do that. That's too serious. And besides, no one would believe that for even a second, not with the way I had my tongue on your spleen."

Hmm. "There's another idea… but it's crazy."

She grabs my arm and gives it a hard squeeze. Her gaze is imploring. "Tell me."

"Married people are allowed to kiss—or do whatever they want…"

Her eyes widen. "You can't mean what I think you mean."

"Give me a second." I take out my phone and do a couple of internet searches, feeling more and more optimistic as I scan the results. "There's a 7:30 p.m. flight to Vegas leaving from JFK," I say without lifting my gaze from the screen. "Given the three-hour time difference, we'd land around 10 p.m., which means we can still put *today* on the marriage certificate. And there are plenty of chapels open 24/7."

When I finally look at her, her pupils are the sizes of dimes. "We're going to get married over a kiss? Like in Victorian England?"

"It would be a marriage on paper only," I clarify.

"Right," she says. "Or as Victorians would say, 'a marriage of convenience.'" She gives the last words a stiff-lipped British accent.

I shrug. "Do you have a better solution?"

She purses her lips. "Even if we do get married—and that's a big if—can't they fire us regardless? They can rightfully point out that we kissed and therefore broke the rule *before* the marriage. Also, how could we have dated before ending up married without breaking that stupid rule?"

I place my hand on hers. "Look, I'm not a lawyer, but I'm pretty sure they *can't* fire a married couple over a kiss. Not even if the sequence of events was kiss and marriage afterward. As to how anyone dated or whatnot, that is moot after the marriage as well. But if you're worried about all that, an argument can be made that we first met before you got this job. The coffee shop might have camera footage to prove it. Who's to say it wasn't love at first sight? We could have easily kept things platonic after that until we were sure we wanted to get married, and then tied the knot when the time seemed right, close to the holidays. Regarding timing—and mind you, I don't think we *need* to be dishonest—but we *could* lie. According to what I've read, Vegas chapels don't list the time of wedding on the marriage license, only the date, which means we can say we were married *before* the kiss… assuming we make that flight."

She pulls away the hand I was touching and taps the Uber driver's shoulder. "Sir, a change of plans. Take us to JFK."

The driver gives me another weird look in the rearview mirror.

"Please," I tell him. "I'll pay you double what the app says, especially if you can get us there promptly."

He nods and makes a sharp U-turn.

"I meant promptly and safely," I clarify. Turning to Sawyer, I ask, "So… are we doing this?"

She covers her eyes with both hands. "Can I decide once we're in front of the Elvis impersonator?"

I smile wryly. "What if it's a Johnny Cash impersonator?"

She shakes her head. "I still need you to behave proportionally to the solemnity of the situation."

"Marrying me is that bad?"

She rolls her eyes. "You're much wealthier than I am, so you should be the one concerned."

"I'm not. Something that we should also bear in mind is: if we get fired anyway, we can always annul the marriage."

She sighs. "But what if we're not fired? How much would we have to commit to this farce?"

Hmm. "Depends."

"On what?"

"On how much Octothorpe wants us gone." If at all.

"I doubt they want you gone," she says. "You'd be difficult to replace. Me, on the other hand—I haven't done anything useful yet."

"They can't fire you and keep me," I say. "And besides, they're already invested in your training, not to mention all the hassle of recruiting. That's not nothing. I'm sure they'd rather you stay, all things being equal."

"Still," she says. "If we go through with this insanity, there are a lot of logistics to figure out… Like what do we tell our families?"

Fuck. I guess I still have too much alcohol in my system to think straight. I haven't thought of my parents at all, but yeah, they'd have thoughts on me getting married, let alone eloping in Vegas.

"My parents can't keep a secret to save their lives," Sawyer says. "Which means I'll have to tell them this is for real. If they spill the beans one day, we'll not only get fired, but Octothorpe could raise fraud charges, or something else draconian."

Hmm. "My parents are also blabbermouths."

"Well, that settles it," she says. "We tell everyone this is real."

"With one caveat," I say. "At work, our story is love at first sight—the first sight being that day in the coffee shop." And hey, it was lust at first sight for me, so if anyone pulls up that footage, the story won't be hard to believe. Hard being the operative word here. I rein in my unruly thoughts and continue. "When we talk to our families, I think we should say we got very drunk and flew to Vegas, where we got hitched. Now we're just looking to see if it works out."

"You're pretty good at this," she says. "This way, our families won't have too high of expectations."

"Exactly," I say.

"And they will not be too disappointed when we get divorced."

I scratch my head. "About that... You realize that if we don't get fired—which I don't think we will—we will have to stay married for a while."

She gapes at me. "Would we? Can they really penalize us for a divorce?"

"If it makes it look like the marriage was fraudulent, then yes. But if it happens after a reasonable amount of time, then probably not. The safest bet is to stay married until our options vest."

"Whoa. That's... years." A long minute passes before

she says, "It'd probably be worth it. I mean… we'd be billionaires at the end."

"Hopefully. But maybe yours was a good idea. We should hold off on committing to this until we're in front of that Elvis."

She nods solemnly. "Still, for the moment, let's assume we'll get married."

"Let's," I say.

"Where are we going to live?"

Fuck. I wish there were a magic way to sober up and think clearly so I could grasp every implication. "My place? That's obviously negotiable, of course, but —and please don't take offense—you do live on Staten Island."

"No offense taken. In fact, I was going to move as soon as I got my first paycheck."

I smile. "And now you'll move sooner." Wait. Why am I so cool with this? My Fortress of Solitude is about to become The Hut of Nonstop Chatting.

"Where do you live?" she asks.

"Battery Park City."

She whistles. "You walk to work?"

"Unless I'm in a rush, in which case I cab it."

"I bet you also get to sleep in longer."

"Compared to Staten Island? I bet."

"Wow." I can see she's getting really excited about the improved commute. "Your place it is. Now something related… We need to learn more about each other."

I cock my head. "Do we?"

"To pass as a married couple? Hells yeah. We can't have another stamp collecting incident."

I can't help but snort. "You mean how we ended up kissing as soon as we learned about the other's philatelistic tendencies?"

She blushes, and I want to peck each cheek, which is crazy.

"What college did you go to?" she demands.

"Hold on. I need to get us those tickets."

She covers her mouth in shock. "I can't believe you haven't. What if they're not available anymore?"

"There were a bunch of open seats a few minutes ago."

"Just get them," she hisses. "Now."

"Thanks. I feel like I'm married already."

She rolls her eyes.

I pull out my phone and purchase two tickets in first class.

"There." I show her the electronic receipt. "We're good."

"Whew," she says. "So… your college?"

I grin. "I think it's pretty telling that you consider such a question so important for a dating tête-à-tête."

"Fine then. What do *you* think we should learn about each other?"

I shrug. "Not that."

"Nice. Super helpful. What else should we not talk about? I imagine putting such a list together will be as fun as proving a negative."

"Fine. Here's one practical thing," I say. "Are you

allergic to cats?" Or worse, does she think the fur on their faces looks too much like a beard?

She shakes her head. "My parents have a cat, Chairman Meow, and we get along as well as any typical siblings. Why? Do you have a cat?"

I nod. "His name is Hermit."

"Hermit? Does he live in a cave?"

"No, but he does like his solitude, like me."

She frowns. "Look, Sawyer, if you really value your solitude, what are we doing?"

Great question. "We don't exactly have a choice."

"We do," she says. "Just not a very appealing one—unemployment."

"Yeah. No. You're not weaseling out of this marriage so easily."

"How big is your place?" she asks.

"Big."

"Perfect," she says. "That means I can stay out of your way."

"Thank you. We will iron out such minutia as we go."

"Yeah," she says. "With the money that we'll save by not getting fired, we can get a huge house somewhere in the suburbs, with separate entrances."

I don't know why, but I hate the direction this conversation is taking, so I change the subject by saying, "Harvard."

"Huh?"

I groan. "My college degree. I went to Harvard."

"Oh. Wow. I can't believe it. I thought there was an

ancient curse that forces every Harvard alumnus to namedrop their alma mater every chance they get."

"To ward off that evil curse, I slept with a salt circle around my bed while living at the dorms," I say with a grin. "And there was always a horseshoe hanging over the door and a clover leaf in my pocket during class."

"No rabbit foot talisman?" she asks. "That's what I had to use at MIT."

I shake my head. "Too many vegans at Harvard for such a talisman. But I did wear one of those thingies with an eye on it."

"Wait. Wouldn't vegans mind you wearing an eye even more than they would a foot?"

The Uber stops, so I don't get a chance to answer her carnivorous question.

I pay double as agreed, and then we rush inside the airport where—thanks to our first-class tickets—we get priority screening.

"We have to run," Sawyer pants when we're through security. "Our flight is almost done boarding."

I'm skeptical, but I join her in a jog, and it's a good thing that I do because they close the gate right behind us.

When we settle in our comfy seats, Sawyer blows out a relieved breath and grins, patting the armrests. "I could get used to this."

The flight attendant rushes over to us. "Would you like a glass of champagne?"

"Yes," we say in unison.

"As I was saying…" Sawyer leans back. "I could definitely get used to this."

The champagne arrives, and she sips hers so sensually I feel jealous of a crystal flute.

"So…" I shift in my seat. "Do you recall that expression about the order in which you're supposed to imbibe alcohol of different concentration levels?"

She salutes me with the champagne. "It's 'Beer before liquor, never been sicker; liquor before beer, you're in the clear.' So… if liquor is scotch, and beer is champagne, we're safe."

"Okay, but still, let's not overdo it."

She shrugs. "The more we drink, the less we have to lie to our family."

"There's some logic to that, but if we're too drunk, we might forget all the get-to-know each other information that you're so eager to share."

She sips her flute slower this time. "Good point, and a great segue: what was your last longest relationship?"

Fuck. I knew I wouldn't like this game.

"Her name was Delilah." I grimace. "I thought she was the one. She thought differently. It sucked. I don't care to repeat the experience."

Sawyer sets her glass down and looks at me with a sympathetic expression. "I'm sorry. I didn't realize that was a sensitive subject."

"It's not… anymore." Or if it is, just a little bit.

"For what it's worth," she says conspiratorially. "In the Bible, Delilah was a major traitor."

Huh. "Are you very religious?" Our philosophical conversations made me think otherwise.

"I'm not *not* religious, but I also don't go to church every Sunday. What about you?"

"Similar," I say.

"Great. The more we have in common like that, the more realistic this union will seem."

So, for the next few minutes, we look for similarities in our backgrounds and interests and come up with a few besides our obvious shared interest in computer science and finance. Turns out she loves puzzles, including the Rubik's cube, though perhaps not with the same ardor as I do. Also, we both like staring at clouds, so, thanks to the full moon, we spend a little bit of time doing exactly that, our cheeks almost touching as we crowd the tiny window by her seat.

"This is so relaxing," I say after a couple of minutes of cloud gazing. "I might fall asleep like this."

She pushes me away. "You can't." She closes the little window and turns on the reading light above my head. "There's a lot more to learn about each other."

"Right." I rub my eyes in order to wake myself up. "Tell me what your longest prior relationship was like."

She gives me a palms-up shrug. "Nothing to tell. I haven't dated much—was too focused on getting the Octothorpe job."

Alcohol must be to blame for the degree to which this information pleases me. "Okay," I say. "Is there anything that you need to tell me? Something that your husband has to know?" I can't fathom what such a thing would be, but—

"Yes, actually." Her expression darkens. "There's something I've debated telling you, but it's very private."

"Oh?" I know I shouldn't feel hurt by her words, but here we are. "Is it more private than what I told you about Delilah?"

She sighs. "Fair point, but yes. More. I think."

I gently squeeze her hand. "Sorry. You don't have to tell me something that would make you uncomfortable."

"No. I do. At least a part of it," she says. "My family wouldn't believe that I'd marry someone without telling him."

"Oh."

"But this is it," she says. "Forget putting off our decision until we're in front of Elvis. If I tell you this, we get married. Full stop."

"Deal," I say solemnly. "Especially considering that I've been sure about marrying you since you told me that you can solve a Rubik's cube." Or was it when I learned that she collects stamps?

She inhales a big breath. "When I was four years old, I was adopted."

12
sawyer

"OH. WOW," my husband-to-be says. "Thanks for sharing that with me."

I gulp down the remnants of my flute. "I haven't shared anything yet." Because I'm struggling to get the words out.

The truth is, I don't even like to *think* about the time before I moved in with the Bakers, who are now my parents. I haven't even talked about this with my therapist, and that's her main purpose.

Sawyer rests his hand comfortingly on my elbow.

Ah. That's nice. His palm exudes warm strength, which helps me squeeze the words out. "This has to do with my life before the adoption." I know my voice is coming out very small, but I can't help it. "Back then, I lived with my junkie mother… who is no longer on this earth."

He doesn't say anything, just squeezes my arm reassuringly.

"There was no father in the picture. In fact, I don't think my mother knew which of the many candidates he was."

Another squeeze.

"Anyway," I say. "I only remember bits and pieces. We slept in the park more than once—and there was a time when I got frightened by the ramblings of a smelly guy with a dirty beard, which might be the root cause of my pogonophobia."

"My god," he whispers. "I'm so sorry that happened to you."

I swallow and keep my voice level. "I don't recall the day that she overdosed, or my time with CPS. There was a foster family, and they were nice, I think, but what I remember very clearly is my first day with my parents, the Bakers. They already had Layla, my sister, and we became best friends from the moment we met. So, anyway, it all worked out in the end. I couldn't ask for a better family."

He nods solemnly. "They sound amazing. I'm glad I'll get to meet them."

"That's right. You will." I'm still adjusting to that fact. "My sister might just lose her mind when I tell her I'm married." And then shit a brick when she sees just how hot my new husband is.

"My mother might lose her mind also," he says.

"Because she's old money, and I'm the furthest from it?"

He frowns. "No. She's not a snob about it. I meant she will lose her mind in the best possible way... She dreams of grandchildren. In fact, I might as well warn you: she will ask about our plans for said grandchildren, and maybe how fertile you are in general."

Can anyone blame my ovaries for clapping excitedly as I take a second to imagine what such hypothetical children would look (or smell) like? Amazing smile, woodsy scent, and a chiseled jawline if it's a boy who obviously takes after his dad. A girl with a pixie haircut and a fresh stamp collection if—

"No, don't get upset," Sawyer says. "I'll talk to my mom ahead of time and warn her that we plan to wait when it comes to kids—and that pushing you might just delay things."

"I'm not upset." There's no way I'm telling him where my mind actually went. "My sister is just as likely to ask something inappropriate." I don't even know what it will be, but if she ties playing cards into it somehow, I wouldn't be surprised in the slightest.

He smirks. "I'm sure I can handle whatever your sister throws my way."

Huh. "Famous last words."

He chuckles. "So… what else should we know about each other?"

"How about you tell me more about your family, and I tell you about mine."

He agrees and tells me all about his parents' very amicable divorce, as well as how happy they allegedly are in their solitude. Despite how convinced he sounds, I'm a little skeptical, especially in light of the fact that his mother might be dating, and his father was inquiring about said dating.

When it's my turn to share, I tell him about how much my parents clearly love each other, then mention my concerns about my sister being a card cheat.

"So… you think she does it for money, or for the thrill?" he asks after I'm done talking about Layla.

"Money," I say with a confidence I don't actually feel.

"And she wouldn't accept money from you instead, right?"

I shake my head. "She's too proud for that."

He scratches his chin. "Maybe you could lose some to her in a card game?"

Huh. "That's not the worst idea. Once I get my paycheck, I'll see what I can do."

"Great. What else should we learn?"

"My parents might ask about your finances," I say sheepishly. "Like if you have any outstanding debts and the like."

He waves that off. "That's totally fine. I don't have debts, and I have a high net worth, at least on paper. I'll make sure they feel that you're financially secure, and you can decide what to tell them when it comes to how we share responsibilities… so long as in reality, I pay all the bills."

"Wait, why?"

He shrugs. "To appease my conscience."

"What do you mean?"

"I have more to lose here than you do. As in, I'm

more attached to Octothorpe. So... I'm getting the better end of the bargain in this marriage."

"You couldn't be more wrong if you tried." I wave the flight attendant over to get more champagne. "With your experience, an Octothorpe competitor would snatch you up in a second, but less so with me, especially if they caught wind of my getting fired shortly after I started."

The flight attendant comes over with our drinks. Sawyer waits until she leaves before he says that we can agree to disagree.

"This is all moot anyway," he says. "I own my penthouse, and it's not like I'd charge my wife rent."

"All the more reason we should split things like grocery bills and the like."

"No." He folds his arms across his chest. "I won't take your money. This isn't negotiable."

"Fine." As in, I can table this discussion for a later day. "But while we're still on financial matters... we should do a prenup."

He sips his drink with a frown. "Is that to protect you or me?"

I roll my eyes. "I don't have anything. You're the millionaire in this marriage."

"Technically, I'm a billionaire—again, purely on paper," he says.

Wait, what? A billionaire already? How many Octothorpe options does he own?

"Then you should definitely demand a prenup," I say, trying to hide my envy.

"Nah. I don't think you're in this to take half my stuff."

I'm not, but… "I don't want you to worry about this later."

"I won't," he says. "Unless… do *you* want one? I mean, you are pretty clever, so if you plan to file a patent that would make you—"

"No. I'm not worried about becoming richer than you." Not with that head start.

"In that case, please, can we drop it?" he says. "It's ruining our special day."

"Special day?"

"Do I sound like a groomzilla?"

"Totally. You sound like you've brought a stopwatch with you to ensure every wedding moment is timed to perfection."

He nods. "The Elvis—or Johnny Cash—will have to do some breathing exercises before he can officiate the ceremony in the exact rhythm that I require."

I shift in my seat. "Jokes aside, are we taping the ceremony for our families?"

"Sure."

"Then we should write some vows. Maybe something that sounds like it was written while we were drunk?"

"We are drunk. Anything we write will sound like it should."

Good point. We write the vows, in which we promise each other, among other things, to never lick the stamps in the other's collection and to face all of life's *perforations* together as a team.

"If you want to sound more drunk, change 'philatelic partner' to 'phallic partner,'" he says with a wide grin.

And just like that, images of his cock pop into my head. "No. Not when our work might see the video," I tell him.

"Ah. Right. Parents as well."

"That reminds me," I say. "Do you have any siblings?" He hasn't mentioned any, but with his love of solitude, a sibling might be a painful memory that he's blocked out.

"No. I'm an only child. I'm glad you couldn't tell."

Oh, I could totally tell, at least in hindsight, but I don't tell him that and opt to ask about his taste in music instead.

"Anything that sounds like a puzzle for the ears," he says. "Classical avant-garde artists like Stravinsky, some electronic music, some jazz. What about you?"

"I like Radiohead. Also, the Beatles, which I listened to growing up."

"Oh, I like them both," he says animatedly. "Radiohead especially, particularly their later albums, with experimental sounds and more complex structures."

How is he getting more perfect? "What's your favorite Beatles song?"

"*I Want to Hold Your Hand*," he murmurs.

What a coincidence. I suddenly want to hold his

hand also, but I don't, for reasons that I'm too drunk to recall at the moment.

"With that song, the Beatles set a new standard in using polyphony," he says in a professorial tone that should ruin my mood but doesn't.

I smile mischievously. "Nice try, buster. No polyamory in our marriage, thank you very much."

He snorts. "Polyphony is a musical texture where two different melody lines are combined. As far as I know, it has nothing to do with opening a marriage."

"Are you sure that's not what Polythene Pam was about?" I ask.

"No. That's about a plastic-wrap-eating fetish. I think."

I waggle my eyebrows. "This probably won't come up with our families or work, but it's something I figure your wife should know: do you have any fetishes?"

He smirks. "I'll tell you mine if you tell me yours."

I make the mistake of glancing at his fingers and, of course, get barraged by images of them going inside me. "Is it a fetish when you like someone's hands?" Because I do. His. I would so, so much, like to have them all over me, in me, and—

"Yes." He flexes and unflexes his hand. "It's called quirofilia."

I blush. "Now tell me yours."

"Pygophilia," he says.

I arch an eyebrow. "For someone who didn't know

what pogonophobia means, you sure like to throw around Greek-based words."

"That's not a coincidence," he says. "After that snafu, I brushed up on Greek-based words."

Is it a fetish when you find it sexually appealing when someone does their homework? "So, what is pygo?"

"The buttocks," he says conspiratorially.

"That's it? You're basically saying you're a butt guy —just like countless millions of your fellow males."

He shakes his head. "I like the way butts look in jeans. I don't think it's *that* common."

"I bet it's second most common, right after liking the way butts look in yoga pants." Also, note to self: start wearing more jeans, especially once we move in together.

"To be honest, I like yoga-pant-clad butts also," he says.

Second note to self: wear yoga pants as well.

The flight attendant comes over and asks if we want more champagne, and we both say that we do.

For the rest of the flight, as we sip our drinks, we continue to learn about each other, from minor things like each other's favorite breakfast, to major, such as where we see ourselves in five years. Allegedly, this is all for the purpose of our pretense, but in my case, I devour every morsel of information greedily, like I can't get enough. He also seems genuinely interested in me, and after we land and take a limo that he's hired, we continue both the quid pro quo and the champagne drinking.

"What kind of a theme would you like for your wedding?" asks the host when we enter the so-called chapel.

I narrow my eyes at his outlandish outfit: a Xenomorph costume, from the *Alien* franchise. "Not sci-fi," I say, doing my best not to slur my words.

"And no dragons," Sawyer says, and hiccups.

Shit. I can't remember how much alcohol I've consumed at this point. "He's not a dragon," I whisper loudly.

"I know." Sawyer gestures at the poster nearby. "They have a *Game of Thrones* theme."

"Yeah. Why would anyone pick that theme? Have they not seen the Red Wedding episode?"

"Do you have a stamp-related theme?" Sawyer asks.

The Xenomorph furrows the front of its cranial carapace. "*Harry Potter?*"

"How is that related to stamps?" I demand.

"There are letters from Hogwarts in the series," the Xenomorph screeches. "Letters mean stamps."

"Not when they're delivered by owls," Sawyer says.

"Oh." The Xenomorph looks like it's considering its violent method of procreation. "How about *Charlie and the Chocolate Factory?*"

"Chocolate?" I ask. "Very Valentine's Day… I think it could work."

"But how is that related to stamps?" Sawyer interjects.

Huh. Maybe he *is* a groomzilla?

The Xenomorph purses its mandibles. "Willy Wonka mails the golden tickets?"

"I'm pretty sure one finds the golden ticket in a chocolate bar," Sawyer retorts.

The Xenomorph's insectoid eye twitches. "Do *you* have any suggestions?"

"Can you do *The Grand Budapest Hotel*?" Sawyer asks.

"I guess." The Xenomorph looks like it's about to spray us with its acid blood. "I could borrow some porters from the next-door hotel and—"

"What's the connection to stamps?" I ask Sawyer. "I've never seen that movie."

"A stamp is part of the plot," he says. "As soon as we move in, we must watch it, together."

Danger. Danger. Do not picture yourself curled up on a couch, cozying up to him and feeling like—

"Give me a few minutes." Looking like it's about to lay an egg, the Xenomorph departs, and my husband-to-be asks a question that yet again highlights how unprepared we are for this matrimony business: "Are you keeping your last name or taking mine?"

13
sawyer

a.k.a. the guy who needs a very cold shower

SHE GAPES AT ME. "I can't believe I didn't think about that."

"Yeah. Same here… but you do need to decide."

She scratches her chin. "If I take your name, there will be two Sawyer Worthingtons at Octothorpe."

I shrug. "So?"

"You don't think it might get confusing?"

"I don't care." That is, I don't care about anyone's hypothetical confusion. I do care which path she takes here because a part of me wants her to have my name. It's silly, I know, but it's there. For what it's worth, that same part of me wants to claim her in any way it can, so obviously, it can't be trusted.

"I think I should probably take your name," she says.

"Yeah?"

"It will make our fiction that much more believable," she says.

I smile. "So would a tattoo of my name on your lower back." Which sounds oddly appealing.

She rolls her eyes good-naturedly. "I guess 'merely' taking your name will have to suffice."

Before I can reply, the chapel host finally comes back, and he is dressed like a mustachioed concierge in purple livery.

"Where did he change?" Sawyer whispers. "And is there a Xenomorph outfit just splayed out outside?"

I grin and watch the guy join us. With him are a couple of porters, their outfits not an exact match with his.

"Welcome to the Grand Budapest Hotel," says the "concierge." "Thank you for choosing us as your wedding destination."

Turns out, he's also going to officiate the wedding, and the porters do not mind capturing the event using our phones. Once we are all situated in front of the tiny altar, the ceremony finally begins.

"Dearly beloved," says our concierge officiant. "Ladies and gentlemen, esteemed guests—"

I tune out the rest because my heartbeat is thudding heavily in my chest. The key moment of this charade approaches: the part where we'll be told that we are now husband and wife and instructed to kiss. Given that the ceremony is being recorded for proof, this kiss needs to be pretty realistic and—

"—and please always remember: 'Rudeness is merely an expression of fear,'" the officiant says, sounding like he's wrapping up. "And so, by the power vested in me by the State of Nevada, and with the elegance befitting the Grand Budapest Hotel, I now pronounce you husband and wife." He turns to me. "You may now kiss the bride."

I wrap one arm around Sawyer's waist and cup her face with my other hand.

Our eyes lock, and we lean toward each other.

Her gaze is filled with so much warmth that she'd get an Oscar if the category "Best Fake Kiss for Family" were a thing.

Slowly, almost teasingly, she rises on her tiptoes as I lean down … and our lips meet again.

Fuuuuck.

I thought the kiss that got us into this mess was the best one in history, but it has nothing on this all-encompassing, passionate, explosive, whole-body experience.

Her lips are soft and her breathing shallow as her tongue dances feverishly with mine. And I don't know how, but I can feel her smiling, which causes me to return the smile even as my cock hardens uncontrollably and—

Someone clears their throat, loudly.

Shit.

It's more than one throat.

Reluctantly, I let go of Sawyer and step back as she blinks dazedly, touching her kiss-swollen lips.

The officiant clears his throat again. "Why don't we finish up the paperwork now? There's also your bill."

Right. I do what is needed purely on autopilot, and

once I'm done, I turn to see Sawyer looking over a video of us that was taken with her phone.

The paperwork has cooled me down enough that my voice sounds almost normal as I ask, "Does it look believable?"

Sawyer's cheeks turn a pretty pink color. "Do you mean the kiss?"

I nod as I take my own phone from one of the porters and tip everyone.

"Sure," she says over a hiccup. "Believable is one word you could use." Under her breath, she mutters something about "X-rated" being the other.

I agree with her. That kiss *was* more arousing than all the porn I've ever seen... combined.

"What do you want to do now?" I ask after I take a deep breath to combat the unwelcome return of my hard-on. "Should we take a red-eye home or catch a flight first thing in the morning?"

"The latter," she says. "Though if you don't mind, I'd like to leave later in the day."

"Why?"

"Because we're in Vegas. I want to see the Strip. Particularly, the fountains at Bellagio. And I want to take pictures at the Eiffel Tower. Not to mention—"

"I understand. We can fly tomorrow afternoon." I take my phone and make the arrangements with the cat sitter.

"Thank you," she says when I look up from the screen. "Bear in mind, the pictures we take will add to the verisimilitude of our story."

Ah. Right. For a second there, I forgot about our charade.

"Let's check out the fountains on the way to our hotel," I say. "They look better when it's dark."

"Great idea."

"Where would you like to stay?" I ask. "We could try the Bellagio, or the Paris Hotel, which is across the street, or—"

"It's just one night. We should save money and stay at a motel."

I give her an incredulous look. "Did we not just have the conversation about how I'm a billionaire?"

"On paper."

"I also make seven figures a year in cold, hard cash." Or its digital equivalent. "Either way, we're going to the most romantic hotel on the Strip, and I'm renting us their best honeymoon suite."

Her eyes widen. "The honeymoon suite?"

"Verisimilitude, remember? What if our employer hires a private detective to investigate this visit?"

She scoffs. "That's unlikely."

I shrug. "Bedbugs *are* likely at a cheap motel."

She scrunches her nose. "Fine. In that case, let's stay at the Paris."

AS WE STROLL TO THE BELLAGIO FOUNTAINS, I WORRY that Sawyer might be upset by the copious amount of Christmas decorations, but she just quickly looks away from any depictions of Santa. Otherwise, she takes such joy in our surroundings that she reminds me of a hyperactive kid who's had a few cappuccinos before being teleported to Disneyland.

On my end, I'm just glad that I'm still drunk. It's the only way I'm able to tolerate all the people who try to strike up inane conversation with me just so they can hand me some stupid flyer.

We get to the Bellagio just as the fountain show begins to the tune of "Silent Night."

Hmm. The last time I saw this show, the song was "Can't Help Falling in Love" by Elvis—something that I will now associate with this marriage.

"Majestic, isn't it?" Sawyer whispers reverently.

I nod. "It's a work of plumbing art."

She snorts. "You make it sound like those 'Oxidation Paintings' by Andy Warhol."

"I'm not familiar with those."

She drags her gaze away from the fountains. "He created them by having his assistants urinate on canvases coated with copper paint."

I snort. "And here I was thinking *my* boss asks me to do weird stuff on occasion." Like finding that spy. "Urinating on a canvas is on another level." But in the same ballpark as some of the stupid meetings that I occasionally attend.

Sawyer looks back at the fountain. "Speaking of weird—am I crazy, or do these fountains look sad?"

"No. Good art is supposed to make you feel things."

She smiles. "I don't know if it's the alcohol, the talk

about those paintings, or these fountains, but the thing I feel the most is nature's call."

I give her my elbow. "How about you go take care of it while I book us a room?"

She loops her hand through my elbow, and we head for the lobby of the Paris Hotel like the married couple that we are.

Once we reach our destination, I go to the front desk and ask for a room.

"We're fully booked," the receptionist says apologetically. "Between Christmas approaching, that concert, and the UFC fight, every hotel in town is at max capacity."

I take all my remaining cash from my wallet. "Can you just please check thoroughly? Maybe your best honeymoon suite is available for just one night?"

Pocketing the money, she clickety-clacks on her computer, then says, "You'd have to check out at eleven, at the latest."

"No problem." Sawyer and I will be busy doing touristy things in the morning, so we can give up our keys before we leave.

Sawyer returns just as the concierge hands me the room keys.

I smile at my new wife. "Do you want to go back to the fountains?"

She shakes her head. "I'd rather catch up on sleep and wake up earlier tomorrow to get a head start on our tour of the Strip."

"Deal." I give her my elbow again, and she oohs and

aahs the whole way to the Versailles Tower and then to our suite—which is so romantic and gorgeous it impresses even me.

"Wow," Sawyer says, looking down at the Strip from the giant window. "The view is gorgeous."

"Yeah." I scan her delicate shoulder and swan-like neck. "Gorgeous."

She drags her gaze from the window and scans the room as if searching for something, then reddens. "There's only one bed." She gestures at the rose-petal-covered four-post behemoth in the middle of the room. "I guess that's another thing we didn't think through…"

"It's not a problem. I can sleep on the floor." Or on a couch—if there is one somewhere deeper inside this massive suite.

She takes a step toward me. "No. That's crazy. We can share the bed."

I also take a step forward. "Bad idea."

"Why?"

Her lavender scent pleasantly caresses my flaring nostrils. "We've had too much to drink. I'm not sure if I can be a gentleman."

In fact, I know I can't be. We're not in bed, and she's completely dressed, but I'm feeling a severe lack of gentlemanliness.

"You seem pretty sober to me," she says, and as if to highlight how unreliable her judgement is, she hiccups.

"Sober or not, it's a bad idea," I say, not sure whom I'm convincing at this point.

She sighs. "We're about to move in together."

"Right." I think I see where she's going.

"Do you have two beds at your place?"

I shake my head.

"Do you plan to purchase an additional bed?"

I shrug. "I guess we have another entry on the never-ending list of things we didn't fully think through."

"Here is what I think." The way she puts her hands on her hips is beyond sexy. "We have to be prepared for a scenario in which Octothorpe hires a private investigator to look into our marriage."

As proof that our employer can easily do what she's just suggested, Eugene's bearded face comes to mind.

"So," she continues. "We can't sleep in different rooms, or in different beds. It would be suspicious as hell."

Hmm. "You have a point, so I guess we'll sleep in the same bed… when we move in together."

"No." She moistens her lips. "That same private dick could bribe someone here at the hotel to see some footage from some hidden camera."

Why did she have to say the word "dick?" It makes mine stand even harder at attention. "You make another good point." It was all too easy to bribe the woman downstairs to get this room.

"That settles it." She walks over to the giant bed and unceremoniously sweeps all the rose petals to the floor. "Do you want the right side, or the left?"

"Lady's choice." At the moment, I sleep in the middle of the bed, as nature intended.

"The right side," she decrees. "Now, who takes the first turn in the shower?"

I arch an eyebrow. "You're not afraid it will look suspicious to the hypothetical detective if the two newlyweds do not shower together?"

Because if this marriage were real, that is what would happen: I'd cover every inch of her with soap and then—

"No. Everyone knows that the consummation of a marriage takes place in bed."

If she wanted to make that sound nonchalant, she needs better control over the delicious pink hue that floods her cheeks.

"All right. You go first," I say. "Meanwhile, I'll get us the tickets back." And otherwise try to occupy my mind before I do something stupid, like kiss her again.

Nodding approvingly, she scurries away. As promised, I get the tickets and then futilely try to calm myself by playing word games on my phone, followed by mathematical puzzles.

All too soon, I hear soft footsteps and look up to see my wife wearing a hotel robe.

"Done," she says. "You can go."

"Okay," I say but do not move an inch.

"Umm... Can you go... now?"

"Right," I reply and still don't move.

"Please, Sawyer. I want to get into bed, but I don't have any pajamas with me."

Fuck me. Is she saying that she's going to sleep naked?

I think she is—and I thought I'd go insane while imagining her sleeping in a bra and panties.

Turning my back to her to hide the full effect that this conversation has had on me, I force my legs to waddle forward in the vague direction of the bathroom. Once I'm inside, I strip and get under the hot water. My top priority is to fist my cock to take the edge off.

But wait. I shouldn't. It wouldn't be appropriate. Sawyer is just beyond a thin wall, and I'm not sure I can do this without making some sort of animalistic grunt that she could overhear and correctly interpret.

Then again, maybe I could bite my tongue?

No.

This is a good test of self-control. Though it'll be so difficult it might just require drastic measures.

Feeling inspired, I dial down the hot water and wait for the calming chill of the cold shower.

There. The intensity of my erection subsides, though the desire to run over to that bed and have my way with my new wife is somehow more intense.

Well, there's no way that is happening, so all is well.

When I'm done showering, I locate a robe, put it on, and tiptoe back inside, praying that Sawyer is already asleep, and that she's firmly on her side of the bed.

"Hey," she says. She *is* on her side of the bed, but her eyes are very much open. "How was it?"

Cold as fuck. "Great."

"Sweet dreams," she says.

Not likely. "Same to you." I climb under the blanket and close my eyes.

And wait.

And wait.

In the far distance, a car honks.

Sawyer turns.

A car alarm blares.

Damn it.

I turn onto my left side and wait.

Nope. Sleep eludes me.

I turn onto my right.

Even worse. I can vaguely see the curve of her hip jutting from under the blanket, and now I'm more awake than an overcaffeinated rooster greeting the dawn. Oh, and speaking of cocks, mine is harder than ever.

"Are you asleep?" Sawyer whispers.

I don't answer, figuring it's better to pretend that I am.

"Sawyer," she whispers and pats my side of the bed under the blanket. "I heard you moving."

Fuck me. Her slender hand lands on my hard cock.

14
sawyer

a.k.a. the girl who's blaming the alcohol

WOW.

Wow. Wow.

His cock is amazing, hard and velvety and—

"What the hell are you doing?" he demands.

What *am* I doing? "Sorry," I say breathlessly. "Is that… what I think it is?"

What? That is the dumbest question in the history of—

"Yes," he growls, and it sounds pained.

Under my hand—which is still on his cock—there's a twitch, or a seismic event.

"Why… is it like that?" I whisper.

I mean, there's no way that my new husband is as turned on as I am. Or that if he is, it's because of me. No way he couldn't sleep because he—

"My brain sent a signal to that region," he grunts. "That signal caused the arteries to relax and dilate."

Yeah. Right. "This is the exact opposite of relaxed."

"You'd better pull that hand away."

Ah. Right. I'm still gripping him, and I can't seem to let go.

"If I keep doing this… will that help you sleep?" How is it that my questions are escalating in stupidity?

"Help me sleep?" He turns my way, and despite the dark, I see the heat in his eyes. "If you keep going… I'm not sure I can be responsible for my actions."

I scooch over to his side of the bed, cock still in my hand. "Maybe I don't want you to be responsible."

Oh, fuck. What am I saying? What am I doing? Can I blame this on alcohol? I mean, I did have a lot, right?

And why am I stroking him up and down?

This is so, so wrong. And so, so hot. And so, so irresp—

"Fuck it," he growls, and before I can so much as blink, he's on top of me, his lips covering mine.

Oh, yes. I'm not sure if this was my intent when I grabbed his cock, but this is exactly what I want now.

What I need.

This kiss is fierce. Claiming. Carnal.

Freed from my hand, his cock presses firmly against my sex, which causes liquid heat to pool inside me, along with a gnawing need that I've never felt before.

He nibbles on my lip.

I full-on bite his—and taste copper.

He frees my lips, but then his mouth zeroes in on my neck, kissing, sucking, and licking it until I'm covered in gooseflesh and want him inside me so badly I'm about to scream.

"Please," I gasp instead.

He kisses the front of my neck, then my collarbone. His voice is a dark rumble. "Please what?"

Is he going to make me say it?

No. He kisses me again, his tongue penetrating my mouth in a semblance of that which I was just begging him for.

That's it.

I can't take it anymore.

I reach down and grasp him again, figuring if a picture is worth a thousand words, then guiding his cock inside me should be worth a cool million.

He pulls away from the kiss, his eyes wild as they meet mine. "Are you sure?"

My answer is to guide him further, my sleek wetness making the journey effortless despite his very impressive length and girth.

"I'm clean," he grunts, looking like he's straining with the effort not to go into some sort of beast mode.

"Me too," I manage breathlessly. "And I'm on the pill." Though having said that, some distant part of me can't believe that I—a person who plans every detail of her life many years in advance—could forget something as critical as a talk about STDs with my husband.

"You feel so fucking good," he growls as he slowly enters me, going deeper and deeper until I feel his heavy balls against the sensual nexus between my ass and pussy.

"Yes," I gasp. "More!"

"Fuck." He pulls out most of the way and then thrusts into me again, his pace intensifying until he's pistoning into me with everything he's got.

I rake my nails down his back and squeeze my eyes shut as a cry escapes my lips. That cry echoes around the room as though we were inside a canyon. As the tension grows, I cry out again, and the sounds reverberate together.

"Come for me," he orders raggedly—and I'm all too happy to oblige.

My whole body contracts and releases in a wave of white-hot sensation that washes over my nerve endings like a tidal wave, and he grunts, "Fuck," as my climax makes the walls of my pussy squeeze around him and pulse.

Panting, I grab his butt and pull him deeper into me. "Come, please."

For a moment of bliss, what seems impossible happens—his cock hardens more. Then I feel the warm jet of his release, which sends an orgasmic aftershock through me just as he growls my—our—name.

As we separate, a wave of sleepy contentedness overtakes me, so I'm only partially conscious when he gets a warm cloth to clean me up. By the time he puts me into a spooning position, I'm a total ragdoll.

"Hopefully, you'll sleep now," he murmurs into my ear.

"Right," I mutter back and fall into a slumber so deep that if Leonardo DiCaprio were to do his *Inception* thing on me tonight, we'd end up in Limbo.

. . .

I wake up to a headache, yet I feel paradoxically cozy and warm.

The cause of the latter is easy to figure out. I'm held in a spooning position by my new husband, his hands massaging my breasts as though they were two balls of dough that he wants to turn into fluffy bread, like brioche or challah. Despite said massage, he appears to be asleep, so I gently extricate myself, grab a robe, and sprint into the bathroom.

The headache intensifies with the movement, and when I look in the mirror, my face looks puffy, and there are circles under my bloodshot eyes.

Oh, and did I mention the hickey on my neck?

Everything Sawyer and I did last night comes back to me with a vengeance, along with the memory of why my head hurts and why I look like a cadaver.

I have a hangover.

Shit. Shit.

We got so drunk that we accidentally consummated our new marriage.

How stupid was—

There's a light knock on the door.

"Are you okay?" Sawyer asks in a deliciously male, rumbly voice.

"Yeah. Great. Never better." If I were Pinocchio, my nose would pierce the mirror, and maybe the wall behind it as well. "What about you?"

"How about we talk once you're out of the bathroom?"

Hmm. Sounds a little ominous.

I quickly brush my teeth and put on yesterday's clothes before extracting the makeup kit from my purse to make myself as presentable as possible under the circumstances.

When I open the door, Sawyer is standing there as expected. Sadly, most of his body is hidden by the stupid robe. Even with said body covered, I can see why my drunk self succumbed to temptation: he smells deliciously woodsy and his face brims with health and vitality, unlike mine. Even his hair is sexily tousled, like he's either just gotten up or just had sex—both of which are true, actually.

"You wanted to talk?" I ask, but the words sound too raspy for my liking.

"Let me just change and use the facilities for a moment," he growls.

Ah. Right. I get out of his way and pace the suite as I plan the upcoming conversation from every angle.

Which is why, as soon as he comes out, I blurt, "I'm fine if you want to get an annulment."

His expression darkens. "Look, Sawyer, I realize last night was a mistake, but an annulment will not—"

"I'm not saying I want one," I clarify. "I just thought that you might."

His frown smooths out. "Oh. No. What about you?"

"I still don't want to lose my job." For obvious, normal, reasons, like financial security, of course. "I do agree with you about one thing: what happened *was* a mistake."

His lips tighten a bit, but he nods. "Don't worry. It won't happen again."

"Agreed." I ignore a weird tightness in my chest that is clearly hangover related. "What happened wouldn't have happened if it weren't for the alcohol." Right?

He gestures around the room. "The romantic atmosphere didn't help."

That works on guys? "Being naked in bed also didn't help."

"Definitely," he says grimly. "I'll invest in some pajamas as soon as I get the chance."

Oh, my. He always sleeps naked? The images, the yummy images... "Great idea. I already own pajamas, but I could get uglier ones, or purchase some khaki-colored granny panties if you'd prefer."

His eyes gleam. "I think it's best that we don't talk about panties in general."

"That can be our family motto." I pull out my phone and do a quick translation into Latin. "*De subligaculo non loquimur.*"

Finally, there's a crack is his too-serious expression. "Subligaculum—those were the loincloth-like undies worn by gladiators, right?"

Using my phone, we learn that they weren't just for gladiators. Actors, athletes, and dancers wore them as well. Then, as if ready to change the topic, my stomach rumbles in the most unladylike manner.

So much for feminine mystique. Now he's probably

wondering what other digestive surprises I might spring on him.

"Let's feed you," he says, not looking put out in the slightest.

"Okay… hubby."

He arches an eyebrow as he opens the door for me. "We're picking terms of endearment already?"

I step into the hallway. "It would be suspicious if we didn't."

"In that case, what do you think of Sawyerina?" he asks.

I snort. "She sounds like the daughter of the Jigsaw killer from the *Saw* franchise. The one who became a ballerina and lost her right pinkie toe in a—"

"Sawyerette?"

"She sounds like a Smurf. Or the wife of Ishmael Tickle—which might be saying the same thing."

He grins as he summons the elevator. "He *does* look a tiny bit like a Smurf."

"Sure, if by 'a tiny bit,' you mean a fuck ton."

"Where do you want to eat?" he asks.

I shrug. "Any suggestions?"

"They have a huge buffet downstairs. There are buffets in all the hotels, for that matter."

"A French buffet sounds great."

"Good choice," he says. "If we don't eat at a buffet at least once, Las Vegas will deny that we even came here."

I mock frown. "Are you trying to wriggle out of the terms-of-endearment conversation?"

He smiles crookedly. "What do you want to be called?"

"That's not how this works."

The elevator doors open, and he lets me go in first. "Let's try going at it from a different angle. I don't like 'hubby.' What else might you call me?"

I frown. "Saw?"

"I thought scary movie references were off the table."

Right. "Sawford?"

"Sounds more like a last name."

Hmm. "This is hard."

He snorts. "Hard. Now we're getting somewhere."

I roll my eyes. "You really want me to call you something like 'hard?'" It would be justified, of course, but—

"No. How about Solver?"

My frown deepens. "Why?"

"Because I like puzzles?"

I shake my head. "Not cute, nor romantic. How about Key?"

He cocks his head. "As in the 'key' piece that fits into the puzzle that is your heart?"

Said heart squeezes, like an idiot. "You're right. That's the kind of saccharine that might give everyone who hears it a case of diabetes."

"But doesn't that make it perfect? We want them to think we fell instantly in love."

Which we didn't. "If you're 'Key,' what would I be?"

"*Locky*," he says, and I know he's faking the

tenderness with which he says it, but I love my new nickname instantly and never want him to call me anything else.

"Sure," I say as nonchalantly as I can. "*Locky* could work."

"That settles it… Locky."

Is it normal for a hangover to make your heart skip a beat? "So, Key, what are you craving?"

Just as I finish asking, we enter into a buffet that looks like a French village, and I gape at the giant spread that could *feed* a village, or maybe a dozen of them.

He stares at my lips a second too long before pointing at a large blackboard. "They have crepes made to order. 'La Caprese' looks good."

While he waits for his crepe, I get a sample of as many items as they have on display. When I pick up a piece of brioche, I can't help but flush—it reminds me of the earlier boob massage.

We find a nice table and settle in, which is when I realize that I'm hungrier than a bear who's just crawled out of hibernation.

"This is good," Sawyer says about midway through his crepe.

"Can I trade you?" I gesture at my plate.

With a smile, he cuts me a chunk of his crepe and takes one of my macaroons in exchange.

"So," I say. "What are you into besides stamps and puzzles?"

He halts the path of his fork to his lips. "Wordle."

"That's a puzzle of sorts."

"What about pangrams?" he asks.

"What's that?"

"The quick brown fox jumps over the lazy dog," he says.

"Huh?" The sentence sounds familiar, but I can't place it.

"That's a popular pangram," he explains.

"I still don't get it." Is it a bad poem? One that doesn't rhyme?

"A pangram is a sentence that uses every letter of the alphabet at least once. I like and collect them, and do my best to come up with new ones."

"Ah. In that case, it still seems puzzle adjacent."

He looks so disappointed that I can't help but add, "But interesting."

His eyes light up. "They really are."

Yeah, right. But hey, I like seeing him happy, so I ask, "What are some of your favorites?"

"Farmer Jack realized that big yellow quilts were expensive."

"Those darn quilts," I say in my best farmer accent.

"The jay, pig, fox, zebra, and my wolves quack," he says with a smile.

"Wow. That's a quacking zoo."

"Here's another one: Five quacking zephyrs jolt my wax bed."

I snort. "Isn't zephyr a gentle wind?"

"It is. I do prefer pangrams that make sense, like, 'My girl wove six dozen plaid jackets before she quit.'"

I grin. "Is that a hint?"

He shakes his head. "I don't need anything woven. Thank you."

"Any others that make sense?"

"Brown jars prevented the mixture from freezing too quickly." He cuts his crepe. "We promptly judged antique ivory buckles for the next prize."

I steal the piece he just cut from his plate. "I think you're maybe stretching the idea of 'make sense.'"

"True, but they make *more* sense than perfect pangrams."

"Perfect?" Like my new husband?

"Pangrams that use each letter only once."

"Ah. Want to hit me with one of those?" I can't even imagine how cryptic it will sound.

He grins. "Mr. Jock, TV quiz PhD., bags few lynx."

"Huh?"

"Yeah… There's also, 'GQ's oft lucky whiz Dr. J, ex-NBA MVP.'"

"I think both of those stretch the meaning of the word 'sentence,' as well as the word 'word.'"

"Maybe. But there's no perfect pangram that *does* make sense."

I smack myself on the forehead. "I remember where I've seen 'The quick brown fox jumps over the lazy dog.' It was when I changed fonts on my computer."

"Yep. It's popular. People also use it to learn to touch-type, to check if every letter on the keyboard works, and so on."

He continues telling me all about pangrams for

quite some time, and I realize I have favorites: "When zombies arrive, quickly fax Judge Pat," and "Waxy and quivering, jocks fumble the pizza."

"I'm full," he announces after finishing a crème brulee.

I stuff another éclair into my mouth and swallow almost without chewing. "Full was a half hour ago for me. Right now, I'm bursting."

"Sounds like we should take a nice stroll down the strip."

We do just that, heading outside to gawk at the Volcano at the Mirage and the theme of the Excalibur. After that, we selectively go inside some hotels and do a few uber-romantic things, like the gondola ride at the Venetian and a stroll in the gardens at the Bellagio. Throughout the whole adventure, we take copious pictures, and I totally feel like I'm on vacation with a boyfriend—or more accurately, like I'm on my honeymoon.

An alarm on Sawyer's watch starts to blare. He glares at it, then looks up at me, apologetic. "We have to grab a cab now if we want to make our flight."

"Of course," I say, doing my best to hide my disappointment.

"Unless… we could call the office and tell them that we've gotten married. And that we're on our honeymoon now."

I gape at him.

"There's no way they'd fire us before we got back," he says defensively.

"But they could. And knowing that would ruin any fun to be had here in Vegas."

Also, given how our first night went, it would be foolish for me to share a bed with him again. Right now, if we head home, we can tell ourselves last night was a fluke, and that what happens in Vegas stays in Vegas.

"You're right," he says. "We don't want a vacation with this sword of Damocles hanging over our heads."

"No." But it would've been nice. "Let's go."

WE SHARE TIDBITS ABOUT OURSELVES ON THE WAY TO the airport and during the flight. After we land, Sawyer calls a moving company, and then we get a cab and continue chatting. By the time our cab stops next to my place, I know more about Sawyer than any other person outside of my family. Hell, given how secretive Layla has been lately, I might—

"You don't really have to move in today," he says. "We can tell HR that we have a plan for—"

"No. Moving in will make our marriage more of a *fait accompli.*"

"*Fait accompli?*" He arches an eyebrow. "Is that the French breakfast buffet talking?"

I roll my eyes. "Touché."

He grins. "Let's get you packed."

He exits the car and holds the door for me.

I lead him to my door and warn him to set his

expectations low because I rented the place before I had my current job.

As soon as we walk in, I wince at the dinginess. Then I spot a small laundry hamper and in it an assortment of my panties.

Shit.

How did I forget about that?

"Turn away," I order, then quickly snatch the hamper and, in a panic, hide it inside the refrigerator.

My husband's smile is teasing when I turn back. "A lot to unpack there. Did you put your panties in there because otherwise they'd be too hot for my eyes? Or did you just take our family motto a little too far?"

"You were supposed to turn away," I say sternly. "Also, our family motto is *we don't talk about panties.*" I gesture at the fridge. "That was hiding, not talking. If anything, *you* just broke the family motto."

He mockingly places his hand on his heart. "*De subligaculo non loquimur.*"

In a sullen silence I don't really mean, I grab a suitcase from behind the couch, stand in such a way that he can't see what I'm doing, and then move my panties from the fridge into the suitcase.

Turns out, it's just in time.

The movers have arrived, and I definitely don't want them handling my underwear.

Speaking of... "I want you to go out and wait with the movers," I say.

Sawyer agrees, and as soon as he's gone, I place my stamps into the suitcase (because they're precious) and then my massager (because it doesn't get used on my neck).

I zip my suitcase and walk over to the front door to open it. "You can come in now." I nod at the suitcase. "This one is coming with me."

"Sure," says the head mover. He scans my meager possessions dubiously. "Are you bringing everything or leaving some stuff?"

By his tone, I can tell he left out "by the dumpster."

I shift from foot to foot. "I'm not sure."

"How about you bring everything?" Sawyer suggests. "You can discard whatever you don't need later."

"Won't that make the cost of the move higher?" I turn to the head mover guy and add, "No offense."

"No offense taken," the head mover says, but I can tell he is lying.

"Sorting things means this will take longer." Sawyer looks at his watch. "I think our priority should be to get as much sleep as we can before work tomorrow."

He's got a point. It's already nine-thirty in the evening. I usually start to unwind at this time. By the time we complete the move, it will be late into the night.

"There's something else," Sawyer says. "We still haven't told our families about our situation."

I can't believe something so monumental slipped my mind. "I need to call them. Now."

"Exactly." He faces the head mover. "Go ahead and get everything into the truck."

I take out my phone. "I'll be outside." Layla is about to caterwaul so loudly I fear it will deafen my new husband and the movers.

"Good luck," Sawyer says.

Yeah. My ear drums are going to need it.

I step out and dial my sister.

"Hey," she says, "How are you?"

"Are you sitting down?"

"No."

"Sit. I've got something huge to tell you."

"You're scaring me."

"Oh, it's not bad news. Something wonderful actually."

I hear some rustling, and then she announces that she's in her lounge chair.

"Remember my namesake, the guy from my job that I told you about?"

Her chair creaks, and I can picture her sitting up. "Are you talking about the guy who may or may not be more into you than you are into him?"

"Yeah. Turns out, we *have* been very much into each other, so…" I seek the right words, but they don't come.

"You fucked him?" my sister asks in an awed voice. "I didn't think you had it in you. His dick, I mean."

"The correct term would be making love, under the circumstances, but that—"

The caterwauling is as bad as I feared it'd be, so much so that I pull the phone away from my head to avoid permanent damage.

When she calms down, I clear my throat. "That was premature, considering what I'm still going to tell you."

There are a few seconds of stunned silence on the other line, and then she says, "You guys have done it twice already?"

"No. Something more permanent."

Another silence. "You're a couple?"

"You're warmer."

Another stunned silence. "It's too soon for you to know you're preggers. Unless this has been going on for much longer than—"

"It's not that, but—"

"What. Did. You. Do?" She enunciates each word.

"We went to the company party together," I blurt out. "Then one thing led to another: we got drunk, flew to Vegas, and got married."

There. Like ripping off a Band-Aid—just one that was attached to a demented banshee.

At first, the stunned silence lasts a good minute. Then there's a nervous chuckle. "If this is your idea of a joke, it lacks a punchline."

"I'm serious," I tell her. "Hold on." I text her a few pictures from the reception and then more from our stroll. "Check your phone."

"All right." I can hear her fondling the phone, and then she caterwauls and squeals and produces a sound that only dogs have a name for. All this is so loud that despite the fact that we are currently located in different boroughs, I strongly suspect I'd hear her if I hung up.

Speaking of hanging up, she does just that.

I stare at my phone worriedly. Did I break my sister?

No.

I mean, maybe.

She's calling back via video.

"Hey," I say as I accept.

She looks at me with narrowed eyes. "Say it again, and look straight at the camera."

I sigh. "I got married. His name is Sawyer Worthington, and as of last night, so is mine."

15
sawyer

a.k.a. the guy with big news

I VIDEO CALL MY MOM.

As soon as she picks up, I smile reassuringly. "I have some news that will make you very happy."

She's only pestered me about this very thing on a daily basis for the past few years.

"Hi, mom," she booms, mimicking my voice. "How are things with you? How was your weekend?"

I wave away the nuisance that is all that small talk. "Trust me, you want to hear this ASAP."

She takes a seat in her favorite chair. "Okay, you've got me. I'm dying of curiosity."

"I got married," I announce triumphantly.

Mom blinks. "What?"

"Locked down the ball and chain, jumped the broom," I say with a grin.

She blinks faster. "Whom did you marry?"

"Ah, right, I haven't mentioned her before. Her name is—"

"That's right, mister," Mom exclaims, narrowing her eyes sternly. "You indeed didn't tell me anything at all."

"I didn't want to jinx it."

Mom gasps. "Is she pregnant?"

"Who?"

She rolls her eyes. "Your wife. Who did you think I meant? Oprah? Dolly Parton?"

"No. Sawyer is not pregnant."

"Wait." Mom brings her face closer to the camera. "Sawyer… Are you having a mental breakdown? I always knew you worked too much."

With a sigh, I launch into the prepared story about how Sawyer and I met in the coffee shop thanks to our shared name, and how we flirted until the party happened—then boom, Vegas wedding.

"So… that's her place?" Mom peers exaggeratedly at my surroundings.

"About to be her former place. She's moving in with me today."

"Where is she?" Mom's eyes dart from mover to mover. The underlying question of "Does she actually exist?" is obvious.

"One second."

I step outside just as Sawyer says, "I got married. His name is Sawyer Worthington, and as of last night, so is mine."

Mom gasps. "So she *is* real."

Sawyer turns her phone my way. "Dear husband, please say hi to my sis."

"Hi." I smile broadly. "Dear wife, please say hi to my mom."

"Hi, Mrs. Worthington," Sawyer says just as I say, "Hi, Layla."

That's the sister's name, right?

Mom shakes her head vehemently. "Please, call me Claire… or Mom."

"Hello, mom-in-law a.k.a. Claire," says Layla with a heavy dose of snark. "Did you know these two were tying the knot?"

"I did not… Layla, was it?"

Layla nods.

"Do you understand any of this?" Mom demands.

"No," Layla says. "I mean, how drunk do you have to be to get married in Vegas?"

"Not very," Sawyer says. "Not when the groom is this hot."

I grin cockily. "Or the bride."

On our phone screens, Layla and Mom look dubious, so, purely for verisimilitude, I give Sawyer a kiss on the lips.

I meant to go for a quick peck, but it doesn't seem like we're capable of such a thing. In an eyeblink, the kiss turns scorching, and I find myself getting hard despite my mother's presence on the phone.

I drag myself away because Layla produces a blood-chilling screech reminiscent of the one Hermit made when they tried to weigh him at the vet's office.

"You okay?" I ask my sister-in-law.

"Kind of." Layla clears her throat. "Claire, I no longer think this is a prank."

"Yeah," Mom says with giddy excitement. "I'm finally going to be a grandmother."

At that, Layla repeats the screech, and when she stops, Mom mutters something about hoping that said grandchildren do not inherit whatever that was from their aunt.

"They can't," Sawyer says. "Layla and I do not share any DNA."

The sisters then quickly explain that they were both adopted by the Bakers.

Mom nods approvingly. "I haven't met the in-laws, and I already like them—that's a great start."

"They're awesome," Layla and Sawyer say almost in unison.

"Then it's settled," Mom says. "The whole family is henceforth cordially invited to my Christmas party."

Shit. I completely forgot. "That's three days from now."

"Exactly," Mom says.

"I'll need to speak with my parents," Sawyer says. "They invited me over to their house for Christmas."

"Give me their numbers," Mom says. "I'll invite them."

"I haven't told them I'm married yet," Sawyer says.

Everyone stares at her with different degrees of incredulity.

"I'll do it now," she says guiltily. "I'll text you their info after."

Mom magnanimously agrees, and my wife and I hang up to look at each other.

"That went surprisingly well," Sawyer says.

I wipe a bead of sweat off my brow. "Yeah. Sure. 'Well' is exactly how I'd put it."

"I think doing it together helped," she adds.

I nod. "How about we call your parents next, and then my dad?"

"Sure. But stay out of the camera at first."

"Deal."

Looking like she's about to walk the plank, Sawyer starts a new videocall.

"Hi, Mom," she says rather mournfully, all things considered.

"Hi, sweetheart," says a kind voice that brings to mind chocolate chip cookies and warm milk. "How was your weekend?"

"Eventful," my wife replies, setting a record for understating the case. "Which is why I'm calling."

"Did something happen?"

"No. Nothing bad, anyway. Can you get Dad? I want you both to hear this."

"Thomas!" my mother-in-law shouts. "Come! It's Sawyer."

"Hi, sweetheart," says a man's voice after a minute. "How was—"

"I got married," Sawyer blurts out.

"Good job easing them into this," I mouth.

There's a deafening silence from the phone.

"Would you like to meet my new husband?" Sawyer asks.

The silence continues, so she drags me into the reach of her phone's camera.

"Hi, Mr. and Mrs. Baker," I say. "I'm your new son-in-law."

Sawyer's mother looks like a capybara—purely in a cute, warm, and fuzzy sort of way. Her father reminds me of Luigi, of *Super Mario Brothers* fame, except he's missing the signature mustache, and he's wearing a tiny bit less green.

"Oh. My. God," Mrs. Baker whispers. "And please, call me Mama."

"Why?" Sawyer asks.

"And me, Papa," says Mr. Baker.

"Again, why?" Sawyer says.

"No, honey, it's okay," I say. "Hello... Mama and Papa."

"Tell us everything," they demand.

"Oh, crap," I say. "I didn't tell my mom about Vegas."

Speak of the devil, one who also wears Prada... My phone rings, and it's my mom, demanding to know the details about the wedding.

"Locky, sweetie, do you want to take this one?" I croon.

"Sure, Key."

"They have nicknames," the Bakers say in unison.

"His ex didn't get a nickname," Mom mutters.

She's talking about Delilah, and it's not exactly accurate to say that she didn't get a nickname—more that I never gave her one. My mother did, though—she's called Delilah "harpy" ever since the breakup.

"Anyway, let me tell you how it all happened," Sawyer says conspiratorially. "I walked into this coffee shop, you see, and…"

She proceeds to tell the story we've concocted, and I'm glad I had her take the lead on this: she's clearly a much, much better liar than I can ever hope to be. Almost scary good, actually. She talks with the conviction of someone who actually *did* fall for me that day.

When Sawyer finishes, Mom wipes an errant tear off her cheek and my in-laws clap.

One of the movers sticks his head out of the door. "We're ready to load the truck."

"Ah, we'd better go," Sawyer says.

"Wait!" Mom shouts. "I want to invite everyone to the Christmas party."

"How about you call each other and set that up?" I say, then rattle out Mom's number to the Bakers.

"Can you talk now?" Papa asks, presumably addressing my mom.

"Sure," Mom says.

"Calling in a sec." Papa looks our way. "Good luck with the move."

"Thanks."

I hang up, and so does my wife.

"Whew," she says. "Done."

"Lucky. I still need to call my dad."

She puts a reassuring hand on my shoulder, which feels amazing.

The movers come out and load the boxes into their truck. Once we're following them in a cab, I videocall Dad.

"Hey," he says. "I was just about to call you."

"Oh?"

"Your mother texted and asked what I thought about 'the amazing news.' When I asked what news, she suggested I talk to you."

"Right. So… I got married," I tell him.

"You did?"

"Yeah." Should I show him my wife now?

He sits up in his favorite chair. "That's wonderful. I'm very happy."

I blink at him. "That's it?"

"What do you mean by 'it?'"

"You're not going to demand to know how it happened, or who she is, or why I never mentioned so much as dating?'"

Dad shrugs. "I figure you'll tell me all that I need to know as soon as you feel ready."

Wow. No wonder he and Mom split. They couldn't have reacted more differently if they'd tried.

I point the camera at Sawyer. "Dad, this is Sawyer—yes, we're namesakes."

"It's very nice to meet you, Sawyer." Dad winks at me. "Good job, son."

All right. I guess saying embarrassing shit is something Mom and Dad still have in common.

"Hi, Mr. Worthington," Sawyer says.

"Oh, call me Roger," Dad says.

"Roger that… Roger," she says.

Dad grins. "So maybe *you* can tell me how the two of you met?"

Once again, she tells the story, and this time, her lying seems even smoother and more believable—and that's perfect because my dad can always somehow sniff out when I'm fibbing, something that was particularly inconvenient when I was a teen.

"Well," Dad says when she's done. "You two seem like a perfect couple. May you have many happy years together."

Something about the way he says that tightens my chest and makes me wish we weren't lying. I'm picturing our future clearly for the first time, and I can see that our "break-up" will deeply disappoint everyone.

"Are you going to Claire's Christmas party?" Sawyer asks.

Dad frowns. "She invited me, but her new—"

"You have to come," I say. "Sawyer's parents will be there."

"Oh. I see. Do you know if Claire wants me there?" he asks.

I cock my head. "Did she send you a card with an invite?"

"Yes, but—"

"Was it gold plated as usual?"

"Yes, but—"

"The card is a strong hint that she wants you there."

"Gold plated?" Sawyer asks with a raised eyebrow.

"Yeah," I whisper back.

"But hold on," Dad says. "The new boyfriend might be there."

I sigh. "And who is that?"

He shrugs. "I don't know. I asked you to look into this, remember?"

Ah. Right. "I don't think she has a boyfriend, but if she did, she wouldn't invite him to that party."

"Well, all right then," Dad says. "I'll see you there."

With that, we hang up, and then we each call our friends to give them the same news.

"Whew," Sawyer asks after we hang up on her childhood friend who moved away. "I'm tired—and we haven't done the most difficult thing of them all."

The car stops, as if to punctuate her point, and I realize we're home.

"What exactly is the most difficult thing of them all?"

She leans in. "Changing our relationship status on all our socials."

16
sawyer

a.k.a. the girl getting aroused by Caprese skewers

WE ENTER the lobby of Sawyer's swanky building and take the elevator to the top floor.

"Welcome home," my husband says as he opens the door.

I step in, and at first glance, the place looks like a penthouse that's even swankier than the building.

The furniture inside is sleek, stylish, and pretty minimalist, with the only exception being a lush armchair a few feet away from us.

"Ah, you're back," says a female voice.

Hmm. "Who is that, *honey?*" My voice is sweet, with a steely edge.

"Linda, the cat sitter," he replies.

A woman walks out, garbage bag in her hand. An annoyingly pretty young woman who doesn't seem to be pleased to see me.

"Hi, Linda," I say with a smile so fake I might just fool a polygraph machine. "I'm Sawyer, Sawyer's wife."

A lot of emotions flit through Linda's eyes—disappointment and curiosity definitely among them. But then she takes on a resigned expression and doesn't ask anything, only tells Sawyer that the bag she's holding contains the old contents of the kitty litter.

"Yeah. Okay. I'll Venmo you shortly. Thanks."

Wow. Given the dismissive way he said that, I might not have to worry about Linda. Still, as soon as she leaves, I inform my husband that his cat sitter has a crush on him.

"No, she doesn't. We worked together for almost a year. I'd know."

I sigh. Men are so clueless sometimes. "What was she supposed to do? Get naked and—"

I'm interrupted by a knock.

Ah.

The movers.

"Take the boxes into the guest room for the moment," Sawyer says and shows them the way.

He's got a guest room? In what world does someone living in New York have a spare room just to accommodate guests?

Before I can voice this question, a giant cat darts over to Sawyer's legs and rubs himself on them.

It's an exceptionally fluffy, blue-eyed creature with gray fur and a face so flat it would make an ironing board jealous.

"Hey, Hermit," Sawyer croons, looking down.

"I thought you said he's a loner," I say. "That he couldn't care less if you're home."

Sawyer crouches and scratches his furry charge under the chin. "He is a loner. This is just his way of telling me that he prefers me to Linda. Or that he's happy I'm home."

"Yeah, no. Sorry to tell you, but Hermit's alleged loner status is just a cat being a cat." Case in point, the supposedly antisocial cat prances over to me, takes a sniff, and promptly purrs.

"Weird," Sawyer says. "He likes you… immediately."

I sit on the floor and give the cat a nice scratch, blinking slowly whenever those feline eyes meet mine.

The purring intensifies, reminding me that I'll need some sort of a private cupboard to hide my "massager."

"Seriously, you're amazing with him," Sawyer says.

I grin. "The only thing I remember about the foster family I stayed with before the Bakers is that they raised cats. They taught me this slow-blinking trick." I demonstrate.

Sawyer slowly blinks at his cat. The cat's tail swirls slightly at the tip.

"That's a sign of happiness," I tell Sawyer, pointing at the tail. "That's something else I recall."

"It is? He does it all the time."

I slowly blink once more. "Sounds like he's a happy cat."

"I hope you're right." Sawyer gets his phone out. "I'm going to update my socials."

I wait for him to do so. It takes him only a minute.

"Pet the cat," I say sternly, then update my own profiles, which seems to take a hundred times as long.

"Why is that taking so long?" Sawyer asks.

"I'm uploading all the pictures," I explain. "Not to mention—"

"All done," says the head mover before Sawyer can reply.

The cat hisses at the intruder.

"Thank you," Sawyer says, then pays the guy and tips his colleagues. "Now," he says to me. "How about a tour?"

"Sure."

"Want to check out the guest room first? To check on your stuff?"

I nod, and he leads me through a sleek corridor lined with paintings that, on closer inspection, turn out to be jigsaw puzzles. They're lit up by some sort of smart gadgetry that turns on the ambient lighting automatically as we approach.

The guest room we enter is larger than my old place —with the boxes containing my things looking rather sad and small in it.

"You really call this a guest room?" I ask.

"Yeah. Why not?"

I gesture toward the cat trees, the plush floor bed, and the robotic mice scurrying around the floor. "This should be called Hermit's room."

Sawyer snorts. "I sometimes call this apartment the Fortress of Solitude, but my mom calls it the Fortress of Feline-tude."

"Your mom is right."

"Don't tell her that. I'll never hear the end of it."

"Okay." I spot what looks like a Chihuly glass sculpture. "You know, this place seems expensive even for an Octothorpe employee."

He shrugs. "We get paid nice bonuses. After the first one, I bought this place with a mortgage, and after a few more, I was able to pay it off early."

"Are you sure you're a billionaire just on paper?"

He smiles. "Did we fly to Vegas on my private plane?"

"Good point." Still, he's clearly wealthy enough that if he did lose his job, he'd be fine… as in, he didn't *really* need to marry me, and he absolutely should've gotten a prenup.

"Want to see the kitchen?" he asks.

"Please." I'm actually starving.

He leads me there, and as expected, everything is modern and minimalist, with state-of-the-art appliances and sleek countertops.

"Are you hungry?" he asks.

I nod. "Maybe I could slap together some sandwiches for us?"

Hopefully, I won't mess that up too badly. I probably should've warned my husband not to expect any cooking from me. The last time I tried to make something, I burned the water.

"That's boring," he says. "How about I make us some Caprese skewers?"

"Sure." Whatever those are.

He approaches the fridge and pulls out cherry tomatoes and some sort of white balls—probably mozzarella. He then snips a few leaves off of a nearby basil plant, and as the name had implied, he takes out some skewers.

Wow. The way he navigates the kitchen and the presence of the thriving basil plant implies that his skills in this arena are way beyond mine.

Yep. I watch in fascination as he assembles the dish by threading tomatoes, basil leaves, and cheese on each skewer as though it were a small puzzle that he's trying to solve. The result is gorgeous, like the chef himself, and the process makes me weirdly turned on.

Huh. Maybe next time I need porn, I'll just turn on a cooking show. Come to think of it, some of them even sound fetishy, like *Barefoot Contessa*.

The porn continues as Sawyer expertly drizzles some balsamic glaze and olive oil and sprinkles salt and pepper over his creation. By the time he hands me a skewer, saliva has pooled in my mouth, mimicking the situation in my panties.

"Taste it," he says.

I do, and as the flavor explodes on my tastebuds, I close my eyes in pleasure.

The balsamic glaze is heavenly on my tongue, the tangy sweetness a perfect complement to the rich cheese, the acidic warmth of the tomatoes, and the earthiness of the basil.

Oh, shit.

I just moaned, didn't I?

When I open my eyes, Sawyer is staring hungrily at my lips.

"Sorry, did you want me to share this?" I offer him the skewer with just one tomato left.

"No," he says huskily. "I'll make more."

I have no idea why, but knowing how sensual the skewers taste just makes his cooking even more sexy. He makes a bunch, then splits them equally between us and pushes a plate my way.

"Bon appétit," he says.

His classy words prevent me from attacking my food and grunting as I devour it, cavewoman style. Instead, I eat like a civilized person, except for the part where I stare inappropriately at my fake husband's lips throughout.

"Can I do the dishes?" I ask when we're finished.

He gets up and puts the two dirty plates into what turns out to be a fancy dishwasher. "How about we let the machine take care of it?"

I stand up too. "Sure. It's not like this is how the Skynet scenario will start. Giving machines too much to do."

He starts the dishwasher, then sets a small bowl of cat food on the counter. "Hermit, come eat your dinner."

The cat appears as though out of thin air and attacks the food with the gusto I almost applied toward mine.

"Is he part Cheshire cat?" I ask.

"Cheshire Cat is the name of a specific cat," Sawyer says. "It's not a breed."

Damn it. Even his correcting me doesn't dampen my libido. What would it take? Nose picking?

"We should resume the tour," I suggest.

Wait. Am I making it sound like I want to see the bedroom? I mean I do, but I don't want him to think that, nor do I think going there is a good idea given my current, turned-on state.

To my relief—or disappointment?—the bedroom isn't where he leads me. He shows me the home theater, followed by the living room—and yes, people this rich apparently need both and know the difference between them. Afterward, he shows me his amazing home office, and I make a mental note to design something like that for myself one day.

"I saved the best for last," he says when he leads me to the next room, one he calls his study.

Intrigued, I step in and notice that the air here is drier and cooler. It must have a separate climate control system from the rest of the penthouse.

Then I spot the framed stamps, and it clicks.

"That's right," he says with a knowing smile. "This is where I keep my stamp collection."

I rush over to the first frame. "Wow. Is that—"

"Yes," he says proudly.

"And you own this?"

"Yep."

"Those Octothorpe bonuses must be insane," I say.

"They are."

I point at the famous misprint. "You realize that this, right there, is why you don't have a private plane, right?"

He chuckles. "The ongoing expenses for stamps are a bit lower than for private jets."

I walk over to another framed stamp. "Are they all ancient misprints?"

"Yes."

I peer at another frame. And another. "These are wonderful."

"Thanks." He walks over to a large album. "Want to see more?"

I nod enthusiastically, and he shows me the whole collection, which only makes me want him more—something I didn't think was possible.

"Can I see yours?" he asks.

"Sure," I say breathlessly and leap to my feet. "Be right back."

I retrace my steps to the guest room, get the book out, and sprint back.

"Here." I open the first page, showing my new husband the stamps, and I can almost imagine Stamp Elvis's smirk.

Hey, girl. Congrats on your nuptials, but why didn't you have one of my impersonators do the dirty? Thank you, thank you very much.

Then I can almost imagine Marylin winking at me.

Hi, sweetheart. Of all the juicy twists and turns in your life, this one seems to be the most delectable. He reminds me of my ex-husband Joe when we first met, and you have the same sparkle in your eyes that I did.

Considering the conversation is imaginary, I let the Blond Bombshell continue in her assumption that my marriage is real. Nor do I correct any other stamps that opine on my marriage as I flip the pages. Instead, I tell Sawyer about each of my favorites—and he listens intently and enthusiastically, which makes me want to jump him all the more.

"And last but not least," I say as I get to the end, "Ruth Bader Ginsburg."

Congrats, dear. Sometimes life takes unexpected paths, and that is okay. Just stay true to your principles, and all will be well. Here is what my mother-in-law told me on my wedding day: "In every good marriage, it helps sometimes to be a little deaf."

"This is an amazing piece," Sawyer says. "I'm sure you know this already, but I've read that it was based on an oil painting by—"

I kiss him because what else is a reasonable response to him knowing *that?* Unlike our other kisses, this one is tender, at least at the start. Soon, however, he's deepening the kiss, and I feel very melty, so much so I almost drop the stamp book.

Suddenly, he pulls away. "I'm sorry."

"No." I touch my lips dazedly. "I kissed you, so if anyone should apologize it should be me."

"Still." He looks at something behind me, and his eyes widen. "Did you realize it was this late?"

I follow his gaze.

Shit. It's one-fifteen in the morning.

I leap to my feet. "We have to get up in four hours."

"More like six," he says. "Don't forget: you now have a much shorter commute."

"Still, given what we have to do tomorrow, we need as much sleep as we can get."

"You're right. Let me show you our bedroom."

My heart pounds faster as I follow him into a huge room with a California King bed that I do my best not to think about and a bathroom that features a jacuzzi and a waterfall-style shower.

I swallow, doing my best not to look at him. "Okay… who showers first?"

"Usually, I'd say 'ladies first,' but today, it might be best if I start. That way, I can make the bed while you're in the shower and hide under the blanket—I didn't get a chance to get those pajamas we discussed."

"All right." Keeping my face placid is a feat worthy of an Oscar. Because holy fuck, he's just hinted he's going to sleep either totally or mostly naked.

I flush at the images racing through my mind as he continues to stand and look at me instead of going to the aforementioned shower.

"It's fine," I tell him as normally as I can. "Go ahead and shower, please."

His smile is crooked. "I was waiting for you to leave the bathroom."

Ah. Right. I wasn't waiting to see him naked, I pinky swear.

Face flaming hotter, I spin on my heel and hurry

out. And I'm not sure if he's teasing me or what, but he takes off his shirt just as I'm closing the door, allowing me to catch an eyeful of delicious muscles.

Okay. I have a problem. I'm too wired and turned on to sleep.

Could I use my "massager?"

No.

Maybe.

Feeling like a perv, I locate the guest room and rummage through my stuff until I find what I'm looking for.

Gripping the device, I glance at the door. There's a lock on it, so maybe if—

With a loud meow, Hermit materializes out of thin air again, rubs himself on my leg, and looks askance at what I'm holding.

I wince. "Hiiii…"

His reply is to purr louder than any machine.

"My neck is sore." I wave the massager guiltily. "I can't exactly apply *you* to my neck, can I?"

Hermit purrs even louder and looks ready to be wrapped around my neck like a shawl, if that is what's medically required.

"Actually, my neck is feeling much better. Thanks." I pet the puss, which leaves my pussy very jealous.

Reluctantly hiding the massager, I locate my favorite pajamas and frown: there's a hole in the top and a weird stain on the bottom. My second favorite also has a hole, this time on my butt.

Should I wear one of these and hope he doesn't notice in the dark?

No. It might be better to wear the nightie I got at Victoria's Secret. It has no holes, which is great, but it's not the most modest item that I own. It's red, lacy, and sheer with spaghetti straps and copious mesh on the bottom. Then again, my husband still has no pajamas and will sleep in the nude tonight. What's good for the goose is good for the gander. Once the gander gets himself pajamas, this goose will reciprocate by getting herself granny panties.

"Good night, kitty," I tell Hermit and slow-blink at him.

When I open my eyes, he's gone without a trace.

All right. I glance at the massager again, only to shake my head in defeat. I know without a shadow of doubt that the cat will reappear if I so much as touch the device.

I get back to the shared bedroom and sit on the edge of the bed, facing the bathroom door—but not because I hope to get a good view of my husband, should he come out naked.

Nope. The thought hasn't even crossed my mind.

When the door opens, Sawyer isn't naked. And I'm not disappointed. At all.

He's wearing a robe. Which shouldn't be sexy in any way, but the sight of his strong calves and large, masculine feet does to me what an overdose of Viagra would probably do to a teenage boy.

"My turn," I squeak. "Please be covered when I get back."

Though I'm not sure if it would help to cover him in twenty dirty potato sacks at this point.

"I left a robe in there for you," he says. "Sorry if it's a little big."

Did he say "big" intentionally?

"No problem." I sprint into the bathroom and close the door, then lean against it, panting a little.

After a minute, I brave the warm shower, then turn the water cooler, just in case I spontaneously combust or something.

When I'm done, my body feels clean, but my mind is not even close. Putting on the sexy nightie only makes matters worse, and I wish I'd gone for the holey pajamas.

Oh, well. I brush my teeth, cover myself with a robe, and tiptoe out of the bathroom.

There's a nightlight on, but as soon as I reach my side of the bed, Sawyer turns it off.

"Good night," I mutter, taking off the robe to place it on the nightstand.

He mumbles something unintelligible.

Weird. Is saying "good night" an example of the small talk that he so hates?

I'll ask tomorrow. For now, I turn away from my all-too-nice-smelling bedmate and close my eyes.

Sleep doesn't come.

Not even a hint of sleep.

I turn to my other side.

He turns too—away from me.

What feels like an hour passes and I still can't sleep, so I roll onto my back.

He does the same.

"You up?" I whisper.

No answer.

My hand twitches, as if possessed by a demon. The urge to touch him is so strong I have to grit my teeth to deny it.

I turn to face him instead.

He turns my way as well, and despite the darkness, I can feel him looking at me.

"You *are* up," I say accusingly.

"So are you."

"Why aren't you sleeping?"

"Probably for the same reason as you." His voice is low and husky.

My heart rate picks up, and I scoot closer to him. "Because you're worried that despite our charade, we're going to be fired tomorrow?"

Or rather today, given the time.

He scooches forward, so we're almost touching. "No one is getting fired," he growls. "I won't let that happen to you."

And that's all it takes.

In an eyeblink, my hand is on his shoulder, his hand is cupping my face, and our lips lock, our tongues intertwining in an intricate dance that makes all sorts of dirty promises.

17
sawyer

a.k.a. the guy with no self-control

OH, fuck. I can't stop myself. Again.

I straight-up devour Sawyer's lips, reveling in the taste and scent of her, in the way her slim, warm body fits against mine, her arms wrapping passionately around my neck as I stroke her sleek curves, unable to get enough of her silky skin.

And that's not all that's silky. What exactly is she wearing?

I have just enough rational willpower left to flip on the lamp—to regain sanity, I tell myself—but the moment I lay eyes on the slinky lace-and-silk number wrapping her mouthwatering figure, I'm a goner.

Distantly, I'm aware of fabric ripping, and then her rosy, taut nipples are exposed, luring me to suck, lick, and gently nibble them.

Her moan is a reward for my ministrations, and it causes my cock to harden almost painfully.

"I want you inside," she breathes.

"Not yet, Locky," I murmur into her nipple, then glide my tongue down her smooth belly, lower and lower, until I'm face to face with the mesh material of her lingerie, which I move aside to give my mouth access to her deliciously velvety core.

She gasps.

I smile into her folds, then give her budding clit a luxurious lick.

She moans.

"That's right." I look up and meet her gaze. "You are going to come all over my tongue."

Her eyes widen but she doesn't respond, just flushes crimson over her face and breasts and then nods.

"Good girl," I murmur and flatten my tongue against her clit just as she buckles into me and does exactly as she was ordered, with a scream.

"Now, can I get your cock?" she pants, reaching for me.

"Get on all fours," I say hoarsely.

I have to see her ass in this lingerie if it is the last thing I do on this earth.

She moves into the position but a little too slowly, so I help her, and the sight of her on all fours leaves me momentarily speechless.

"Fuuuck," I groan when my ability to speak returns. "Your ass is otherworldly hot."

She looks over her shoulder. "Just to clarify, my ass isn't where I want you, no matter how otherworldly you think it to be."

Nodding, I rip the mesh part of the lingerie like

some sort of savage and then finally, wonderfully, lose myself in her silken depths. I go in and out slowly, teasing us both and kneading her ass with my palms.

"Faster," she moans. "Harder. Please."

Her begging is the end of me. I lose control completely as I thrust into her with everything I've got, and then I continue to piston in and out at breakneck speed, holding on to her ass like a lifeline.

My balls tighten as my release begins to build.

Her moans grow louder, more desperate, and then she comes, screaming our name and squeezing her walls around my throbbing cock.

That's it. With a guttural grunt, I find my release.

Afterward, things happen in a blissful haze. I hug her as we catch our breaths. A quick cleanup and we get back into bed, and this time, sleep comes instantly and is as deep as the philosophical questions Sawyer utilizes in lieu of small talk.

AN ALARM BLARES.

I wake to find Sawyer in my arms. My hand is on her breast—but in my defense, hers is on my erect cock.

Fuck me.

I extricate myself and turn the alarm off.

She's still sleeping, soundly.

"Hey," I whisper.

Nothing.

"Sawyer." I gently shake her. "We have to go to work."

Nope.

Fine. I get up and go to the bathroom.

I'm just finishing shaving when Sawyer stumbles in sleepily.

"Why didn't you wake me up?" she asks, yawning.

I catch her gaze in the mirror. "I tried. I swear."

She looks down at my midsection and blushes. "Why are you still not wearing any pants?"

Great question. "Sorry about that. If you could do me a huge favor and go feed Hermit, I'll make sure to be decent by the time you return."

"Where is the food?"

I cover my toothbrush with toothpaste as I tell her, and she pitter-patters away, but not before I catch a glimpse of her hypocritically naked behind.

The rest of my routine is done in a horny haste, and then I dress with the speed of a military man—and finish just in time for my wife to return.

"The cat is fed," she says as she walks in, and I'm not sure if I'm relieved or disappointed that she's dressed as well.

"Perfect. Thank you." I let her do her thing while I order us some breakfast and arrange a ride to work.

Today, every minute counts.

"We should talk," she says as we sprint out of my place.

I jam the elevator button. "About last night?"

She nods. "It was just a fluke. Right?"

"Exactly." I let her enter the elevator before I join. "It was just a way to help each other fall asleep."

"And we didn't even have proper sleeping attire," she adds.

"Good point." I get my phone out. "I'll order something for myself right now."

"Great idea. I'll do the same."

The whole ride, we keep our noses in our phones, though I'm not sure if she's shopping for granny panties the whole time or just avoiding talking about last night.

"Got it," she says when we're almost at our destination. "And it's hideous."

"I got a pair of baggy PJs. With rushed shipping, they'll be at my place by tonight."

"So that's settled. Now we just need to *not* get fired —which would render the clothing moot."

Fuck. Until this moment, I hadn't thought of losing my job in terms of losing this marriage as well, but now that she's put it like that, I feel an odd heaviness in my stomach—which is obviously hunger.

"Everything will be fine," I say. "You'll see." Though I wish I were as confident as I sound.

The car stops. A scooter is already waiting right across from our coffee shop, and the driver is holding our breakfast orders.

"What's this?" Sawyer asks when I thrust her bag into her hands.

"Breakfast banana split and a matcha latte," I say.

She blinks at me. "You remembered my favorite breakfast?"

"Well, yeah." I remember everything she's told me about herself.

As we walk to the elevator in our building, I munch on my breakfast burrito, and she pulls out her latte and takes a big sip. While we wait for the elevator, she gets her dessert/breakfast out and greedily dips her spoon in it.

The elevator comes and we step inside. Just as the doors are closing, someone shoves a large hand into the quickly disappearing crack.

Ugh. I hate when people do this. Just get the next one.

The elevator doors open back up, and Henrietta from HR steps in.

At the sight of us, her sturdy jaw almost drops.

"Sawyer...s," she booms. "How... was your weekend?"

"I'm glad you asked," I reply, and this is the first time in my life I'm happy to be asked that inane question. "We got married." I give my fake wife an equally fake smile. "You saw us kiss, so I doubt it's a surprise."

Henrietta's eyes widen so much her signature glasses fog up.

"A Vegas wedding," Sawyer chimes in. "If you can believe it."

Henrietta either can't, or she's having a bowel movement after a weeklong fight against constipation.

The elevator stops on the floor where Sawyer's team—and HR—reside.

"Go ahead," Sawyer tells her. "I'm heading up with my husband."

Nodding robotically, Henrietta lumbers out, and as soon as she clears the doors, I jab the "close door" button.

When we're alone again, Sawyer asks, "How do you think that went?"

I look around furtively. "I think she's happy for us."

With my eyes, I try to remind Sawyer that we're at work, and thanks to the AI controls that no one uses, there's someone—or something—always listening.

"Can I borrow your phone?" I ask.

She unlocks it and hands it to me. I navigate to her contacts and do something no husband has probably had to do for his wife *after* the wedding: make sure she has my phone number.

When we reach my floor, I text myself from her phone and add her to my favorites.

In that moment, I get a notification that my meeting with Henrietta has been rescheduled.

I show that to Sawyer and then text her:

That probably means our little encounter did go well.

It's either that, or HR needs more time to figure out what to do with us.

18
sawyer

a.k.a. his wife's beard-guard

THE ELEVATOR DINGS, and the doors open to reveal Eugene waiting for us.

Fuck. Did his beard get bushier over the weekend?

Jaw twitching, I put myself between him and Sawyer, and when he waves and starts to say something that starts with an H—either "hello" or "ho, ho, ho!"—I give him my least friendly stare.

It works. Swallowing the rest of what he was about to say, he joyfully jogs away, an echo of jingle bells ringing in the air mingled with the crunch of fresh snow.

When I turn to Sawyer, she is still pale, like she's just seen a ghost from a twisted version of *A Christmas Carol*, one where a spirit possesses the creepy doll from *The Conjuring*.

"Sorry about that," I say. "I shouldn't have brought you to this floor."

"It's fine. I shouldn't have reacted as I did. I'm in

therapy for this very reason. I just didn't get much sleep last night."

"Why don't I take you to your desk?" I press the close-door button.

"You don't have to. I'm fine."

"I insist." And not because I want to parade her around to stake my claim.

Nope.

Not the reason.

She nods resignedly, and we descend back to her floor. Proudly, I lead her all the way to our destination, ignoring curious glances from every cubicle.

"All right," I say when she's safely sitting in her chair. "Text me or ping me on the messenger if you hear from HR."

Still looking a little dazed, she nods and unlocks her workstation.

I'm reluctant to leave her, so I stay as she opens her inbox and checks her email.

"Huh," she says. "My meeting got rescheduled too."

"See?" We've gotten a reprieve, at least.

"Okay, you go," she says. "You probably have a ton to do."

Dragging myself away, I start walking, and it takes all my willpower not to flip off what's-his-name when he looks at me with unabashed curiosity.

As I reach the elevator, Susan steps out of it, her nose in her phone.

"Ah, hey," she says with a smirk, spotting me. "I hear congratulations are in order?"

That confirms it. After learning about our marriage, Henrietta spoke to Susan, Sawyer's manager, and probably my manager as well.

"Thank you," I reply. "Now, if you'll excuse me, I've got to run."

By now, Susan knows me pretty well, so she doesn't seem to take offense at the brisk dismissal, which proves that a reputation for hating small talk can actually come in handy on a rare occasion.

When I get to my desk, I review the last thing I worked on before the weekend: a promising avenue in the project that will give us an edge over Circumflex.

But wait. I will likely have to talk to Damian, and he will no doubt ask about the other idea I had: the bullshit code that will look different depending on who requests it from the source control repository. As I'm not a fan of multitasking, I haven't worked on this as much as I maybe should have.

Well, I can fix that now—assuming I can banish the images of what I did to Sawyer last night, and the night prior.

Fuck.

Focus.

With a huge mental effort, I review what I've done thus far and pick a route that I think might be the easiest—using environmental variables, like LOGNAME or UID.

Yes. I explore this as I finish my burrito, and I'm about to test what I've come up with when someone clears a scratchy throat right next to my ear.

I turn with a frown. "Hello, Damian."

Damian gestures at the conference room that doubles as his office when he's here. "I know you want me to skip the pleasantries, so let's go."

I follow him to the conference room, though I'm a little bit confused. The glass walls of the room seem to be covered in some metallic material that wasn't there last time.

When we get inside, I theorize that someone used double-stick tape to glue kitchen foil to all the windows and walls.

We sit down, and I arch an eyebrow at Damian.

"One second." He takes out some kind of gizmo from his back pocket, then sets it in the middle of the desk and presses a button.

A white noise emanates from the device, and I've got a feeling that if I were a dog, I'd be really uncomfortable from the other sounds the thing might be making.

"Now we can talk," Damian says.

I gesture around the room. "Why the stealth?"

"Officially, because we have a spy," Damian says. "But unofficially, I wanted to make sure whatever is said in this room stays in this room."

"Okay." I poke a finger at the foil. "Is that what I think it is?"

"Aluminum foil," he confirms. "It's five thousand per pound at the moment."

Did he buy a ton of this stuff? Or is that just a statistic he had handy? "Should we make hats from the stuff too? To make sure no one is listening to our thoughts?"

"Har fucking har," he says. "You clearly haven't spoken to anyone on the InsightVision project."

My eyebrow arches higher. "Octothorpe is working on mind reading technology?"

"Multiple teams," he says. "But the InsightVision people are the closest. Their lip-reading AI can look at your body language and facial expressions and make pretty eerie guesses about your mental state—and that's just the beginning."

Damn. Either Damian's developed paranoia, or our Big Brother CEO is very close to "watching you."

"Anyway," Damian says. "First and foremost, I want an update on the projects you're working on."

Ah. Good, no dismissal yet. I tell him I'm pretty close on both fronts, and he doesn't seem to notice that I'm exaggerating in the case of one of them. "Oh, and," I say in conclusion, "it goes without saying that meetings with HR and other distractions will set me back."

"Oh. Right. About that." He looks around furtively. "That was well played, getting hitched."

"Played?" I fold my arms across my chest. "I don't know what you mean. We're in love."

He nods approvingly. "Good poker face there. You might just get out of this shit with your stock options intact."

I don't even reply. I just wait for him to continue.

"You're not the first to get into this conundrum," he says. "Or to solve it the way you have."

Oh? "Who else?"

He glances at the wedding band on his left hand. "That's unimportant. What is important is that it usually works, but not always."

"Well, it should work in our case, considering we're really married, and married people can kiss at the company party and all that."

Damian strokes his chin. "Did you go to Nevada or Utah?"

"Utah?"

"In Utah during the pandemic, you could get a marriage certificate online, conduct the ceremony virtually, and get married right away without a waiting period," he says. "I don't think they've rolled any of that back yet. Oh, and they also don't put the time of marriage on the certificate."

"You know a suspicious amount about this topic," I say.

He glances at his ring again. "I know a lot about a lot of things."

"To answer your question, we physically flew to Vegas and got married *there*."

"That's perfect," he says. "Seriously, well played."

I sigh. "Are you saying we're not in trouble?"

He grimaces. "I wish I could say that, but I can't. Not yet. HR is deliberating—and probably checking on… things."

I take my phone out. "Have they looked on our social media?" I flip through a few of the images.

Damian nods approvingly. "Hers has a trail too?"

I nod. "She was as excited as I was to let the world know about the happy occasion."

He takes his phone out, then curses. "The aluminum blocks the signal, but I'm sure you two aren't idiots."

"No. We're not."

He pockets the phone. "You should've called me as soon as that shit went down."

"You mean me kissing my wife at the party? Or us getting married?"

"Either. Both. Not knowing the full picture, I went above Henrietta's head and got people involved who didn't need to be involved. She's probably pissed."

"What was I supposed to consult with you about? How to talk to my new in-laws? How to consummate the marriage?"

"Oh? Did you seal the deal? That would be perfect. How likely is she to be knocked up? Because a kid would—"

"Do not ever talk about my wife like that." I unclench my fists.

He raises his hands. "Hey. I'm on your side. I swear."

Yeah. Right. Translation from Damian speak: "You're useful to me, but if you weren't, you'd be gone in an eyeblink."

"Tell HR that if they make Sawyer uncomfortable, I'll make sure they regret it."

He nods. "Will do, though I'll make it sound nicer than a threat."

"How?"

"I'll just ask legal what is safe to ask when it comes

to your marriage," he says with a smirk. "And, of course, I'll copy HR on that email. I bet the answer will be, 'Do not ask a single thing.'"

Yeah, that does sound like the legal team. The approach we usually take with them is that it's better to innovate first and ask for forgiveness later, if necessary.

"When will we know the verdict?" I ask.

He shrugs. "HR isn't exactly famous for efficiency."

"Fine. Is there anything else?"

"No. Get back to the two projects—and let me know when either is finished."

Translation from Damian speak: "Finish something so that I can squeeze the last bit of usefulness from you."

19
sawyer

a.k.a. the girl who could use a cooking lesson

AS I PRETEND TO WORK, I can feel the eyes of my coworkers boring into my back, and I can almost hear the whispers floating in the dusty office air.

I wait and wait for any update, but even after what feels like hours, nothing comes from HR—or Susan for that matter.

I ping Sawyer via the messenger, and he tells me the same is true on his end.

Fine. I load up some code that Susan suggested for me to become familiar with and force my brain to concentrate on the characters that are dancing a jig on my screen.

Nope. This would be difficult to do even if I got a good night's rest and didn't have a mind-blowing sexual experience with my *fake* husband. As is, this might as well be the code for a quantum computer, which uses qubits—items of information that can exist in a superposition of 0 and 1, like the dead and alive

Schrödinger's cat. Or like me, who's in a superposition of having a job and being fired.

After a while, Sawyer messages me, asking if I want to get lunch.

Are you sure we should?

We've never done that before, and—

It would be suspicious if we didn't.

Seeing the logic in his words leaves me oddly disappointed. I guess I wanted him to ask me to lunch because he missed me, not just to keep up our charade.

We head over to the Italian restaurant down the street and realize too late that we are seated near Jasper. Oh, well. We pointedly reminisce about the weekend in Vegas loudly enough so he can overhear, with me being genuinely excited to have experienced it all, and my husband faking it rather well.

After Jasper pays for his meal and leaves, I ask Sawyer if his pajamas have arrived.

"Yeah." His eyes drop to my collarbone. "What about yours?"

I check the status of my order. "Not yet, but everything should be there by the time we get home." And it's the kind of getup that will turn any cock within a thousand-mile radius limp.

On the way back to the office, Sawyer tells me about the oddball meeting with his boss, and we hypothesize whether said boss got married under circumstances similar to ours.

"It might explain why he never goes to the company holiday party," Sawyer says. "He might not want to show up with his wife and remind people of what happened."

"Could be," I say, nodding gratefully when he lets me go first into our building and pushes the heavy revolving door for me.

Reaching the elevators, we wait for what seems like ten minutes. Then, just like earlier, as we walk in and are about to get going, someone shoves a weathered hand into the crack of the closing doors.

When the person enters, I freeze in place, eyes focused on the disgusting pube-like growth sticking out of the bottom of his face.

Sawyer swiftly puts himself between me and the interloper and glowers at him. "What the hell, Eugene? You couldn't wait for another?"

"Sorry, I'm late," the terror replies, and his beard warps his voice to sound like that of the devil himself—which makes sense, given that the ultimate evil is often depicted with the most dreadful thing in the natural world: the beard of a goat.

To my horror, the terror matches his sinister words by smashing a pudgy finger into the door-close button.

"What the fuck?" Sawyer demands as the doors close.

"Sorry," the evil one says. "Like I was saying—"

Sawyer presses the button for the second floor, which is where we instantly stop.

"Out," he growls in a tone that seems to cut any further arguments short. "You will take the next one."

As if hit by a tsunami of holy water, the bearded one

slithers away, leaving me with my back against the wall, faint and panting.

Distantly, I'm aware of doors closing and the elevator starting to move again, which makes me see white spots.

I must look as bad as I feel because Sawyer jabs his finger angrily at the emergency stop button.

The elevator halts.

Strong arms envelop me in an extremely comforting embrace, and I melt into them, doing my best to even out my frantic breathing.

"I'm sorry," Sawyer croons.

I drag in a shaky breath. "This isn't your fault." I press my fingers to his chin. "You're always silky smooth."

"It's a little bit my fault." He hugs me tighter. "I think if I were faster with certain projects, that asshole would not need to be here."

Oh, please. "This isn't even about that guy. Not really. It's all the stress of not knowing what HR will do to us, and the lack of sleep, and—"

"I'll talk to those assholes," he growls.

"Who? HR?"

He nods, eyebrows furrowing.

"Don't. Please. If you grumble at them, it could make our situation that much worse." Assuming that it *can* get worse. "In fact, I feel better already." Having his arms around me works better than any therapy or drug.

"I'm taking you home," he decrees.

"No. You've got work to do. So do I."

He sets his jaw stubbornly. "We can work from home."

I fight the urge to kiss those firmly pressed lips. "I don't even have a company laptop."

He waves that away. "IT can remedy that in a few minutes." With that, he releases the stopped elevator and takes us two floors up to enter the homebase of Ishmael Tickle and his coworkers.

"This place looks more like a hardware warehouse than Smurf Village," I whisper to Sawyer as I step over a disconnected router.

He doesn't full-on smile, but his eyes sparkle—which is a nice change from the gloomy concern during the elevator incident.

It takes a few minutes before Ishmael is handing me a shiny new laptop—a relief, as I was afraid that he'd been given instructions not to provide me with anything on account of my being fired.

As we return to the elevator, I finally verbalize what bothers me the most about Sawyer's work-from-home idea. "HR might want to see us."

He shrugs. "They can wait till tomorrow."

I shake my head. "I don't want to delay this torture until tomorrow. If I'm not fired, I need to know ASAP."

He sighs. "Are you sure you're feeling better?"

I nod.

"Fine," he grits out. "We can work in the office—but only because I don't want you to keep stressing about the job."

The way he says the last bit makes me remind him not to "talk" to HR, whatever that entails.

"I promised that I wouldn't, so I won't," he says.

"Fair." The elevator stops on my floor, but I find it difficult to leave.

"Let me walk you to your desk," he says, as if reading my mind.

I know I shouldn't, but I let him. Then he seems to not want to leave, but I urge him to do so and then regret my insistence as soon as he's gone.

Oh, well. I get back to reviewing the code and waiting for the HR verdict—which still hasn't arrived by the time people start heading home.

A messenger window from Sawyer pops up around six p.m.:

Want to go home together?

I refresh my inbox. Nope. No news on my employment status—and my manager seems to be gone for the day, so it's extremely unlikely I'll have the resolution I had hoped for today. I reply to my husband in the affirmative, and then we take a nice romantic stroll home by way of Battery Park.

Two boxes are waiting for us when we arrive—the sleepwear that is meant to prevent another... incident.

Picking up the boxes, Sawyer opens the door for us.

As soon as we step in, the allegedly solitude-loving cat appears out of thin air with his tail held high and slightly curved at the tip. He proceeds to gently headbutt both of our legs while he purrs like a bubbling brook, exuding friendliness, calm, and serenity as only a feline can.

"He likes you so much," Sawyer says, sounding annoyingly surprised.

"Why wouldn't he?" I mockingly narrow my eyes. "Am I not likeable?"

Sawyer puts a hand on his chest. "If you were any more likeable, even the cat from *Cinderella* would be besotted. Not to mention, rainbows would follow you around, and plants would start blooming as you pass near them, and—"

"Fine, you're forgiven—provided I can feed this one again." Doing so in the morning was the only consolation prize for having woken up with barely any sleep.

"Be my guest," Sawyer says. "Assuming he's okay with it."

"Are you?" I slow-blink at Hermit.

The cat nuzzles himself against my leg and meows.

"I'll take that as a yes," I say.

Sawyer mutters something about miracles as I stride to the kitchen and get the food out, the way I did this morning.

Hermit attacks the meal like his distant cousin, a hungry lion.

"Well, he's happy," Sawyer says. "Now, what about you?"

I blink at him. "What about me?"

"What should I make for you?"

I shake my head. "You cooked yesterday. It's my

turn." That would be fair in a real marriage, but in a fake one, it's doubly so.

Also, his cooking was on par with his being naked, as far as turning me on was concerned, so if we really mean to avoid doing things, it's best that either I cook, or he does without me watching.

"It's really no trouble," he says. "I'm used to fending for myself."

"But you're not by yourself."

He cocks his head. "All right. What's for dinner?"

I shrug and rummage through the fridge, looking for easy but tasty options.

Hmm. There's cheese, and there's bread.

"Do you like grilled cheese sandwiches?" I ask Sawyer.

"Who doesn't?"

I shrug. "Someone lactose intolerant?"

"I'm not so unfortunate," he replies. "And thus I love grilled cheese, as well as any variations on that theme, like pizza, quesadillas, Croque Monsieur, and on and on."

"Perfect. Grilled cheese it shall be." I mean, I've never made one before out of fear of burning down the house, but seriously, how difficult can it be? I have a Bachelor's of Science from MIT; I should be able to figure this out… right?

"Can I help?" he asks.

"No." Probably. "Why don't you go change, relax, and I'll call you when dinner is ready?"

Not if, *when*.

"All right," he says. "I guess I can get on my laptop and finish this one thing I was working on."

"Yeah. Show Octothorpe that at least one of us is useful. Great idea."

"I'm sure you're useful," he says. "Or will be as soon as someone gives you the chance to shine."

"Thanks." I'm going to make him the best grilled cheese that anyone has ever grilled.

He leaves.

I take out the bread and butter, my confidence already waning.

No.

I can do this.

If I recall anything from watching *Barefoot Contessa* that one time, the lady loves her butter—and she has a TV show, so she must know what she's doing. To that end, I add a layer of butter to four slices of bread, on both sides.

No. More butter. And a little more.

There. Now I need to glue cheese to one side.

I think.

There's a huge selection of cheeses in the fridge, some that I don't even recognize the names of.

I scratch my chin. Which one should I use?

I taste a little of each of them. Some are sharp. Some very salty. The moldy-looking one is earthy and mild. The one that looks like it's already melted is creamy and silky.

You know what? I bet you get the best of all worlds

if you mix a little bit of each of them. The flavors will be subtle and stuff.

Yeah.

I chop up the ones that are choppable, then add in the spreadable cheese as a way to glue the pieces together.

Hmm. It doesn't look that appetizing, but it doesn't matter—it's all going to melt anyway and become a lot more cohesive-looking in a moment.

Yeah.

Now for the trickiest part of them all.

I locate a skillet and fire up the stove.

Do not burn this.

Do not.

No matter what.

Repeating that simple mantra, I wait until the pan looks hot and then plop the sandwiches on it.

Crap.

Hissing, the butter melts instantly, and the whole thing looks chaotically greasy.

Whatever. As soon as the cheese melts, I'll pour some of the extra grease out.

But the cheese mix refuses to melt—or at least, to melt evenly. Some parts of it melt too quickly and spill into the skillet to join with the butter as they hiss at each other. Other parts look lumpy, but most of them just slowly sit there, waiting for something, like a cat you're foolishly trying to teach dog tricks.

Speaking of cats, Hermit jumps onto the counter and peers into the skillet with a dubious expression.

"Hey," I say sternly. "I realize you're curious, but need I remind you about the relevant proverb?"

Hermit wrinkles his nose and jumps away—and that is when a heavy, black smoke rises from the skillet.

Shit. Shit. Shit.

Coughing, I turn off the heat, but it's too late.

A smoke alarm begins to blare.

"Sawyer, are you okay?" my husband shouts.

"Yeah, sure!" I rush to the window and open it to get fresh air.

What the hell? At first, it seems like it's starting to rain, but then I realize it's the sprinklers—which I guess this fancy building is equipped with.

Sawyer strides into the room and worriedly checks me from head to toe. "You're okay."

"I'm so sorry," I say, my face burning hotter than the skillet. "Your stamps… they'll be ruined."

"No." He walks over to a nearby wall and presses something that seems to shut off the sprinklers and the alarm. "Only the kitchen got wet." He points to the floor. "Thanks to the tiles, it's no big deal."

Hermit waltzes in, steps into a puddle, and lifts his paw in disgust, looking like he strongly disagrees with the "no big deal" statement.

"Sorry." I glance at the skillet and wince. The soggy, lumpy mess looks like a piece of charcoal, and it's wet on top of that. Time to fess up. "I should've told you… I'm not very good in the kitchen."

He smiles. "That's fine. Let's get you dry, and I'll

take a stab at…" He frowns at the skillet. "What *was* that supposed to be?"

"Grilled cheese."

"Ah." He grabs a wad of paper towels. "I have a secret recipe for that one. Give me a few minutes."

"Okay."

Feeling horrible, I head over to the bathroom to dry myself and change. By the time I get back to the kitchen, the place is dry, and no sign of my cooking efforts remains—except a huge dent in my pride and self-esteem.

Meanwhile Sawyer is whistling under his breath as he slices just one type of cheese—mozzarella, by the looks of it.

"That's cheating," I mutter under my breath. "I probably could have succeeded if I'd just used one type of cheese."

He grins over his shoulder. "Sure, but there's no way you know my secret recipe." Matching actions to words, he slices double the bread I'd expect for an open sandwich, and then I see why: it's not an open sandwich.

He's trapping the mozzarella, arugula, and tomato between two slices.

Then he goes into the fridge again, takes out some prosciutto, and fries it until crispy. Then he grills the bread in the resulting fat until the cheese melts.

Which is some kind of cheating, definitely.

He sets two plates where all of this is combined into the most gorgeous sandwich I've ever seen—which makes sense, seeing how it was made by the most gorgeous man I've ever seen, who at this point looks downright edible to me.

"Taste it," he murmurs.

He's talking about the sandwich, right?

I take a bite, close my eyes, and moan out loud in pleasure. I'm not even ashamed of it—his creation is *that* good.

When I open my eyes, he is staring at me with his eyes heated. "If that is going to be your reaction, I'll have to cook every day."

I bite the sandwich again, to save myself from blurting out something inappropriate, like, "If you cook like this every day, I'll start sounding like that scene from *When Harry Met Sally*."

He must pick up on some of my thoughts because he grips his sandwich a little too tightly.

The rest of the meal takes place in a sexually charged silence, and afterward, I insist on cleaning up.

To cool off, if nothing else.

"And you're sure I can't help?" he asks.

"Yes. It's the least I can do."

"All right." He takes his plate, rinses it, and I have to give him a glare to prevent him from sticking it into the dishwasher. "I said I want to clean up," I grumble. "Don't put it away."

"Right. Right. Just habit." He takes the cat's bowl and washes it.

I put my hands on my hips. "What did I just say?"

"That's cleaning up after my cat, not us."

I sigh. "Is there something else you can do for now?"

He strokes his chin. "I could use a workout."

"Oh." The images. Oh, the gleaming-muscle images.

"Should I wait for you?" he asks. "It's mostly body weight stuff, like—"

"No, thank you." I've already made a fool out of myself today, no need to do so twice.

He turns to leave. "Suit yourself."

And now he's somehow wearing a suit in my head as his muscles gleam—and the fact that this is a physical impossibility doesn't seem to bother my fantasizing uterus in the slightest.

I start to clean, frantically, but it doesn't dampen my libido.

I blame the weird domesticity… and the stress. Because stress causes horniness, right?

I'll have to ask my therapist about that.

Once I finish cleaning, I go look for Sawyer.

When I find him, it's as if a new set of sprinklers goes off, the one in my panties.

His shirt is off, but that's only half the problem.

Using a contraption above the door, he's doing a pull up, and his back is absolutely rippling with delicious muscles. Yes, gleaming muscles.

No suit, though.

And I'm okay with that.

This is a thousand times hotter than in my imagination.

My palms are sweating, and I'm pretty sure I'm

panting. Or at least my breathing is way elevated. As is my heart rate. And body temperature.

Am I ovulating?

No, can't be. I'm on the pill.

Then again, women do get pregnant on it, and I bet this is how. Some men must exude such extreme sexiness that it cancels out the hormones—and I don't care if that's not medically accurate.

Right now, I feel like I'd ovulate even if I were nine months pregnant with triplets.

Hermit materializes out of thin air, looks askance at me, then at his human, then back at me with a judgy expression.

The cat is right. I shouldn't be watching this.

Tearing my eyes away, I slink into the climate-controlled study and look at stamps… for ten minutes, that is. After said minutes, I get very curious about the rest of the workout, so I retrace my steps—and just in time to see Sawyer do pushups, which make his earlier pullups a G-rated movie to this triple-X porn.

Would it be so wrong if I were to lick just one bead of sweat? Or nibble on just one of his triceps? Or lie down so that when he descends for his pushup, his cock enters my—

He jumps to his feet, panting and sweaty and disturbingly virile.

"I'm headed to the shower," he says. "I want to go to bed early—to make up for last night."

"Great idea," I manage to squeeze out. "I think I'll go to bed early too." Even if I don't feel a tiny bit sleepy.

Picking up his shirt, he strides away, leaving me salivating and disturbed.

As he showers, I unpack the outfit I purchased and wince.

Are things so bad that I have to resort to this?

Well, at least for today, I must wear it since I don't have anything else.

I head over to the bedroom, sit on the edge of the bed, and stare at the door.

When it opens, Sawyer comes out wearing a pair of pajamas—and I'm not disappointed at all. I swear.

Also, if the idea behind these pajamas was to make him look less sexy, it's a failure.

He clearly didn't take this project as seriously as I did.

"Tomorrow, I'll let you shower first," Sawyer says when he spots me. "I was just sweaty and—"

"Say no more." Please. Or else I can't be held responsible for my actions, and those of my pussy.

He smiles and walks up to the bed. Before I do something that I'll regret, I clutch the heap of clothing to my chest and slink into the bathroom.

Fuck me. It smells like soap and naked skin in here.

No. Must calm down my libido. Must think unsexy thoughts, along the lines of IRS audits and root canals.

Nope. Either IRS audits and root canals are sexier than they seem, or my problem transcends such minutia.

Somehow, I get myself clean—in body, if not mind

—and then I put on my outfit, feeling beyond like an idiot.

When I come out, the nightlight is on, and Sawyer is staring at me, eyes wide.

"What the hell is that?" he asks.

With a sigh, I look down at the scratchy monstrosity. "I wanted to get an unsexy outfit."

And this *is* that, for sure. The top is puke green and has balloon sleeves—and balloon everything else. It's made out of a frumpy bag-of-potatoes material that hides anything feminine—or human—about my upper body. The pants—and I use this term loosely—are baggy and include every color of the rainbow. They make me think of M.C. Hammer getting murdered by an evil clown.

Sawyer gives me a thorough once-over. "I don't think there exists an outfit that would make *you* unsexy," he says gruffly. "All this thing has accomplished is that it makes me want to save you from it, by—"

"Well, don't," I say, and wish I meant it. "It's a bad idea, remember?"

"Right." He watches me walk to the bed, my outfit crinkling and rustling, like rotting leaves under the feet of John Wayne Gacy.

Once I'm in bed, Sawyer turns off the light and says, "Sweet dreams."

"Yeah. Sure." I close my eyes and do my best not to scratch the parts of my skin that come in contact with my "pajamas."

One would think that after a sleepless night like last night, I'd fall asleep immediately, but one would be wrong.

I toss. I turn. I consider stripping off the top—or bottom—a million times, but I don't because I know the scratchy material is only a small part of the reason I can't fall asleep.

The much bigger reason is on the opposite side of the bed, breathing evenly and smelling much too yummy for it to be legal.

"Trouble sleeping?" he whispers after an excruciating half an hour.

"No," I mutter. "I'm totally asleep. You're dreaming this conversation."

"You seem uncomfortable."

Yeah, no shit.

Ugh. Maybe I do need to take off this monstrosity.

With a huff, I sit up. "Don't look," I warn, though I'm not sure why.

It's pitch black in the room.

"I'm not looking," he says, but his voice sounds suspiciously husky.

I start to wriggle out of the pajamas, but it's weirdly difficult. Somehow, I'm caught in one of the balloon sleeves.

Crap, I think it's choking me.

"Help," I gasp out, struggling in earnest—and then I feel a strong tug and hear a loud tearing sound as my husband comes to my rescue, doing what every girl who's ever read a bodice ripper dreams about.

In a moment, I'm completely naked.

Which is weird because I didn't even feel him do anything to my pants.

"Are you okay?" He sounds concerned. And oddly out of breath.

Before I can answer in the affirmative, his hand brushes over my face and collarbone. My nipples immediately stand at attention.

"Um…" How do I answer him? I'm not choking anymore, but I am on fire. Everywhere, but especially where he's touching me.

"Sawyer, you're not answering me." The concern in his voice deepens, and a second later, a soft light comes on.

We stare at each other—me fully naked, he clothed in his all-too-sexy pajamas. And then—and I will swear in a court of law that I have no idea who reached for whom—we are somehow locked in a full-blown, open-mouthed kiss.

I tug off his pants, releasing his gorgeous cock, and then I'm grabbing onto it like a lifeline.

He hisses and draws back. "You're fucking amazing." Frantically, he strips off his pajama top, even as he asks, "Are you sure about this?"

I stroke him up and down, then bend to lick the precum beading on the tip. "What do you think?"

Grunting something unintelligible, he manhandles me in the most wonderful way, until I find myself on my side, like we're about to spoon, only it's not spooning that we end up doing, but forking.

Forking fiercely.

Forking fast.

Forking hard.

Forking until I come thrice—a new record. Then, during aftershocks from number three, Sawyer thrusts extra deep and shoots his own release inside me, which makes me come a fourth time.

And just like that, I'm sleepier than a sloth after a five-hour marathon. I'm semi-conscious as we clean up, and as soon as my eyes close, I'm completely and utterly out.

20
sawyer

a.k.a. the guy who might like his wife

I WAKE up before the alarm, with Sawyer in my arms.

The events of last night come back to me vividly, and my already stiffening cock goes completely hard.

Down, boy. She's asleep, and besides, we have to go to work.

Yeah. Sure. Cocks are famous for listening to reason.

Fine. Whatever. This isn't the first—or even the hundredth—hard-on I've gotten in Sawyer's presence, and it won't be the last. Ignoring it, I shimmy out of our embrace and softly slide off the bed.

As I brush my teeth, I can't help dwelling on everything, until finally, I admit it.

I'm officially sleeping with my fake wife.

And I like it.

A lot.

And I like her.

A lot.

The door squeaks open.

"You didn't wake me again," Sawyer says sleepily as she walks into the bathroom... *naked*.

I spit out the toothpaste. "I figured I'd wake you after I brush my teeth."

She glances at my erection and sighs theatrically. "You realize that—to slightly paraphrase Britney Spears—oops, we did it again."

I hand her her toothbrush. "Yeah. I guess we did." And I doubt any pajamas, no matter how ugly, would prevent another incident. Maybe a medieval chastity belt would do the trick, but even then, neither of us can be trusted with the key to the thing.

"We shouldn't have," she says.

"Isn't that from that same song?"

She snorts. "Doesn't make it any less true."

I look hungrily at her pebbled nipples. "How can this be wrong when it feels so right?"

She squeezes toothpaste onto her brush. "Is this a talk-in-songs morning?"

"It's true."

She gestures at my dick again. "Please get dressed. I can't talk like this."

Huh. "I bet I find it much *harder* to talk to you when you're naked than vice versa."

"Out. Now."

With a sigh, I leave and get dressed, then feed Hermit and order us a cab, as well as some breakfast.

I return to the bedroom to find Sawyer already dressed.

"We need to run," she says.

We rush out in a companiable silence, and once we're in the cab, I remind her that she wanted to talk.

"Right." She bites her lip, which messes with my concentration. "I think we keep playing with fire, doing what we're doing."

"Oh?"

"We can't have a relationship," she says. "Or anything like it."

"We can't?"

I'd call what we already have a relationship, but clearly, she doesn't agree.

"If we do and then decide to break up, it would be extremely awkward, to say the least."

The way I feel currently is pretty awkward, so—

"Speaking of awkward," she says with a weak smile. "I hope you're ready for the Baker clan tonight."

Oh, fuck. With everything, I forgot today is Christmas Eve.

"If you're ready for my mom and dad, I'm ready for yours," I counter.

"Don't forget my sister," she says. "You, at least, are not bringing any siblings along."

Her phone rings. "Speak of the devil." She picks up and in hushed tones tells Layla that she can't speak right now.

By the time she hangs up, we've reached our destination, so I decide to shelve the conversation until a more opportune time.

"There." I point at the food delivery guy loitering in the lobby. "That's our breakfast."

We both grab our food, then go to the elevators and ride to our respective floors.

Wow. It's a ghost town on my floor. I love this time of the year, especially this specific day when so many of my staff take the day off, giving me the chance to actually get some work done.

But first things first. As I devour my blueberry muffins, I order last-minute Christmas presents and have them delivered here to the office because I'm not sure if Sawyer will want to go to the party straight after work.

Speaking of Sawyer, a message from her shows up on my computer screen:

Nothing from HR, and I don't think Susan is in today.

Could she be right? I go into the HR system where such things are kept and confirm that yes, Henrietta is out, and so is Susan—along with a million other people.

I reply to Sawyer with that information.

Sawyer's comeback is instant:

Unbelievable. Now we have to wait until Thursday to learn our fate?

Thursday?

I think you should be prepared not to get the answer this year.

She replies with a dramatic crying emoji, but I can tell she wanted to use expletives instead.

In answer, I say:

There is nothing to worry about. No one would dare fire you for kissing your husband. That's the kind of story that ends up on the news.

There. No doubt someone at the company will read these messages, and this will hopefully remind them that if they do the unthinkable, I've got enough money to hire a fancy law firm, as well as a PR company, to maximize headaches for everyone involved.

But I can also work this from another angle. I'll finish the high-profile corporate-spy projects to show how indispensable I am. Since a sub project of this has to do with leverage over Circumflex, Damian would no doubt explain to HR that if they were to fire me, I could easily go to work for Circumflex, and render said leverage obsolete. Relatedly, if I use my stratagem to figure out who the spy is, I can choose to only share that information *after* our continued employment is assured.

With this extra motivation, I dive back into work. I'm so focused I lose track of time and find Sawyer's message about lunch confusing for the first second that I see it.

Shit.

It *is* lunchtime already. I reply that I'd love to join her, and then we meet in the elevator and agree on Thai food.

"Anything I should be aware of when it comes to tonight's festivities?" Sawyer asks when our Pad Thais arrive.

I sigh. "Grandchildren might come up."

She grins. "What's our answer to that?"

I shrug. "That we'll get around to it… one day."

She nods. "A day far, far away."

"Exactly."

She twirls a nest of noodles onto her fork. "Do you actually want kids… eventually?"

"Yeah. Two."

Her eyes widen. "I want two as well. I *loved* having a sibling."

"I was an only child and loved the associated solitude—so that's not why," I say. "I just think that having a sibling can teach one better social skills." At least that's one of my theories as to why mine are subpar.

"All right. Two kids it is. Do you want a boy and a girl?"

I shrug. "It's not like you can control that—at least not without involving fertility technology."

She rolls her eyes. "People can't control winning the lottery, but they play and want to win."

"Fine. If I had a magic wand, I'd want a boy and a girl. Happy now?"

She grins impishly. "Your *wand* is magic, and it makes me very happy during… the child-making practice."

I nearly choke on a peanut someone forgot to crush for my Pad Thai. "Is that a way to talk when you want to keep things platonic?"

"Good point," she says. "Let's talk about something else. Something safe."

"Sure. Do you also lose your umbrella after only using it once?"

Her grin widens. "I do, actually. Also, before disappearing, it likes to flip inside out on me during the gentlest of breezes."

"I hate that. One once flipped on me when a nearby guy sneezed."

"That guy was probably also the person who stole it after you used it," she says sagely. "I bet he was part of a secret society that is behind this umbrella conundrum."

"I bet they go to the Umbrella Academy."

Sawyer sips her Thai iced tea. "Is that where Mary Poppins got her MBA?"

"No," I deadpan. "I think she got her MBA at Hogwarts."

"Ah, right. She was in Gryffindor. Back when Hagrid was there, and they bonded because they were both into umbrellas—she flew on her black one, and he hid a wand in his pink one."

I arch an eyebrow. "Why did that sound dirty?"

She shrugs. "Because of the word 'pink?' Or maybe because we discussed your *wand* a few minutes ago?"

I chuckle and get back to the mystery of umbrellas, and we manage to stay on that topic all the way back to the office.

"Do you want to go to the party from here?" I ask just as she's about to leave the elevator.

She glances at her image in the reflective surface on the back wall. "Do I look okay?"

"You look amazing," I say earnestly.

"In that case, we can go straight there."

I nod, and she sashays away, leaving me hard, again. Oh, well.

I ride to my floor, and the front desk lady tells me I've received a few packages.

Good. Gifts are covered.

I get back to coding and lose track of time again, but thankfully, a message from Sawyer reminds me that we have a party to go to. She also asks if the coast is clear. That refers to Eugene, who's actually out today—no doubt busy planning his milk-and-cookie-motivated breakings-and-enterings later tonight. I tell her that she's got nothing to worry about on that front, and that I'm about to meet her shortly.

Once she comes down to the lobby, I notice she's holding something behind her back. I can guess what it is, and thank heavens I've come prepared for this very eventuality.

"Hey." She smiles shyly at me.

"Hi." I take the box designated for her from the shopping bag that I'm carrying and offer it to her on the palm of my right hand. "Merry Christmas."

Grinning, she takes out a box from behind her back, snatches my offering, and places hers in its place. "Merry Christmas to you too. I wasn't sure if this particular greeting counted as small talk."

I resist the urge to kiss her. "No. Maybe. But not from you."

And it's true. Somehow, she's become like my family in that I can tolerate some small talk from her.

"Great," she says. "My Plan B and C were kind of lousy. I was either going to ask about your thoughts on the commercialization of Christmas, or how you think Santa Claus reflects our views on the concept of deservingness."

I nod. "We can discuss either of those issues once we're in the Uber… if you wish, that is."

She shakes her box. "I wish to know what's inside this."

I glance at my own box. "Me too, but we'd better wait before opening them."

She pouts. "How come?"

I sigh. "Mom will make a big deal about opening presents toward the end of the party."

Sawyer eyes the box curiously. "Can you just tell me what's inside?"

I tsk-tsk. "Can you tell me what's in mine?"

She shakes her head. "You'll have to wait until the official gift-opening ceremony."

"Right back at you."

She fakes another pout—or at least I think it's fake. "Fine. Let's go. The sooner we get to the party, the sooner I can open my box."

We sprint for the ride that I summoned and then discuss Sawyer's conversational gambits labeled B and C from earlier, as agreed. Something about the topic must grate on the nerves of the driver because he gives us dirty looks from time to time, especially once we exit.

"My score on Uber is about to get lower," I say

when the car departs. "And this time, it's *not* because I snapped at the driver for trying to make small talk."

"Don't worry, Key," Sawyer says conspiratorially. "I still have a five-star rating, so if anything, we can use my phone to summon us rides."

Someone clears their feminine throat nearby.

Turning, I freeze.

"Hi, Sawyer," Delilah says in that signature breathy voice of hers.

Fuck me. I should have been prepared for this possibility, even if it was remote. I met Delilah because her family and Mom were neighbors, and it seems like they still are.

She must be here for the holidays, same as I am.

"Hi… Delilah." I grab Sawyer's hand. "Sawyer, this is my ex-girlfriend." When Sawyer gives my hand a reassuring squeeze, I add, "Delilah—this is my *wife*."

Delilah looks us over, her expression difficult to parse. "I saw that post about your nuptials," she says. "Still, I didn't expect to run into… the happy couple."

"The *very* happy couple," Sawyer says. "And it was a pleasure to have met you, but we have to run."

With that, she drags me into Mom's building by the hand.

Once we reach Mom's door but before I ring the buzzer, Sawyer lets go of my hand and faces me.

"Are you okay?" she asks softly, looking up at me.

"Yes. I'm fine." Surprisingly, this is true. "I'm okay." Better than okay.

I'm completely and utterly over Delilah.

"Good." Sawyer smiles. "I mean, I'm glad."

"Me too." More than glad, actually. Seeing Delilah like that has given me an epiphany: I thought I'd cared a lot about my ex, but the way I feel about Sawyer is different.

Stronger.

Deeper.

And we've only just met.

So... was Delilah right to break things off? Could she have picked up on the fact that I didn't care about her enough?

And while we're asking questions, do I really prefer my solitude as I've been saying, or was that just something I started feeling after Delilah left? I certainly do not feel that way with Sawyer. Living with her is actually better than—

"Are you sure that you're okay?" Sawyer shifts her weight from foot to foot.

"Yes. Sorry." I shake my head, clearing it for now, because I won't get a chance to process this, let alone talk with Sawyer about it, anytime soon. "Ready to go face the music?"

"Yeah. Sure. Let's unleash the dogs of... merriment."

With that, she bravely rings the doorbell.

21

sawyer

I'M GLAD THAT CLAIRE—OR should I call her Mom?—takes her time opening the door. It gives me a chance to rein in my jealousy.

And yes, I am jealous. More jealous than I've ever felt in my life. The fact that Delilah clearly hated me at first sight—no doubt because she's jealous too—doesn't help… much. I'm not a violent person, but I was an inch away from smacking her too-pretty face or pulling out her shampoo-commercial-perfect hair.

Oh, well. I'm just glad it is not possible to turn green from jealousy. Otherwise, I would be the hue of Hulk, Yoda, Kermit, Shrek, and the Wicked Witch of the West combined. Or—more apt for this time of the year—the Grinch.

"Hi, Sawyer," Claire says as she opens the door. "Come inside."

"Which of us are you referring to?" my husband asks with a grin as we step in.

"Ah. Right." She hands us each a pair of slippers—and they look to be our respective sizes, which makes me wonder how she knows mine. "You two are going to need nicknames within the family, ASAP."

"You can use ours." Sawyer puts on the slippers. "She's Locky."

"And he's Key." I try on my pair and confirm it's a perfect fit.

Claire nods approvingly. "I remember those now." Over her shoulder, she yells, "Did you hear the nicknames, Ronald?"

Sawyer frowns. "Did you say Ronald?"

"That's me," says a man in the distance, and as he walks over, my husband and I look him over—not that there's a lot of him, given his miniature height.

With his striped suit, he initially makes me think of a zebra, but then I realize that he reminds me very much of the Hamburglar, and it's not just thanks to his outfit. The bags under his eyes are reminiscent of a mask, and his name is Ronald, which primed me to think of McDonald's mascots.

"Ronald," Sawyer says, his frown deepening. "Are you a distant relative that I'm just meeting for the first time?"

"No. I'm Claire's lo—"

"Friend," Claire interjects. "Claire's—I mean, my—friend."

Hmm. Is he the friend Sawyer's father was wondering about? And what was he going to say? Lover? Lo-llipop? Lo-bster?

"I… see." Sawyer's left eye twitches. "Well, nice to meet you… Ronald."

Wow. He sounds as enthusiastic as I was when I met Delilah a few minutes back.

Sawyer turns to his mother. "Is Dad here?"

Maybe it's just me, but the question appears imbued with meaning.

"Not yet. It's just your grandmother, Ronald, and I."

Grandmother?

Before I can voice this out loud, a loud yapping contradicts Claire's words—and then a white fluffball of a creature runs over, wags its tail at me, and growls at Sawyer.

"Hi, Q-Tip," Sawyer says, sounding even less enthusiastic.

"Hey, now," Claire says. "Is that a way to talk to your brother?"

"That is no brother of mine," Sawyer grits out through his teeth. "That's a semi-sentient pom-pom."

A second dog runs over, identical to the first in every way except for being a quarter of the size and therefore a lot closer to looking like an actual Q-tip.

I have no doubt that if Q-tip—the dog—could speak, he'd call this creature Mini-Me.

"You got another one?" Sawyer asks, looking horrified at such a prospect.

"No. This is your nephew—Ice-Q," Claire says. "As part of my negotiations for Q-Tip's stud services, the bitch's parents agreed to visiting rights for the holidays with a puppy of Q-tip's choice."

At the mention of the word 'stud,' Q-tip stands straighter—as straight as a ball of fur can.

"There's too much to unpack there," Sawyer says. "And I'm not sure I want to."

"Where is everyone?" asks a new voice that is equal parts haughty and ancient. The speaker floats in on a cloud of Chanel No. 5, and she looks exactly like what I was already imagining—a hybrid between Cruella de Vil from *101 Dalmatians* and the Dowager Countess of Grantham from *Downton Abbey*. From the Manolo Blahniks she's wearing on her dainty feet (no sign of slippers here) to the pearls on her surprisingly (expensively?) youthful neck, she exudes snootiness and richness.

She smiles widely at Sawyer, and you can tell that in her long life, her face has not deigned to contort itself in this way very often. "Snickerdoodle. I heard you've finally settled down." She looks at me with a lot less warmth. "You're the wife then?"

"Hi, I'm Sawyer." I extend my hand.

"A man's name," the grandmother says as she wrinkles her nose. "But mostly feminine otherwise." She snatches my proffered hand and peers at it. "Good bone structure too." She drags me closer, and before I can blink, she lifts my chin with her bent index finger and turns my head this way and that, making me feel like a horse she's debating on buying.

"Do you have any Romanov blood in you?" she asks, still holding my chin captive.

I stare at her. "Are you talking about Scarlett Johansson's character from *The Avengers*?"

She releases my chin. "Was that impertinence?"

"No, Mother," Claire says. "Not everyone knows that the Romanovs are the Russian royal family."

"You do not get to speak to me today," the grandmother says and nods at the Hamburglar. "A plumber? You've brought shame upon this family. Shame."

Wait, she thinks I'm part royal? That might actually be a compliment.

Of course, there's no way my birth mother was in any way noble, more like the exact opposite of that. As to the sperm donor who was my father, who knows? It's unlikely that he was somebody, but it's feasible.

The doorbell rings again.

It turns out to be Mom and Dad.

Claire gives them slippers (which also magically happen to be their sizes) and introduces them to her burger-thieving friend, the dog and his progeny, and then her mother.

"Bakers?" Sawyer's grandmother examines my parents closely. "Are you from Scarsdale?"

My parents shake their heads.

"Good. The Bakers I knew there are snobs."

I'm very curious what kind of a creature *she* considers a snob.

"What my mother means to say is, 'Welcome to the family,'" Claire says with a gracious smile. "Please come in. Everyone."

That was just the right thing to say because Mom and Dad beam with happiness—which in turn makes me feel extremely guilty. Neither of them have any family except for me and Layla, but they've always wanted a big one, and now they think they've got it, but it's all fake.

Claire herds everyone through her lavish apartment and into the dining area, where she forces us to put our gifts on top of a giant pile.

"Sit." She extends a hand toward a table that takes up most of the room.

On said table is fine China, sterling silverware, linen napkins, caviar, and a roasted goose—as well as countless fancy dishes I don't know the names of.

A bunch of handwritten place cards command us to sit in specific places, and before anyone can reach for the food, the doorbell rings.

It's Layla. And when she walks in, she's holding a deck of cards in her hands—something she does when she's nervous, or calm, or in a bad mood, or in a good mood, or—

"Do you play bridge?" Sawyer's grandmother asks Layla upon spotting the cards.

"Sure." My sister's smile is radiant. "Do you prefer rubber or duplicate?"

The grandmother's eyes widen. "Snickerdoodle, are you sure you didn't marry the wrong sister?" She pats an empty chair next to her. "Here. Come sit next to me... what was your name again?"

Looking a little intimidated, Layla nevertheless does

what she's told, and they whisper animatedly about something that I can't hear, which makes me feel uneasy.

I give my sister a narrow-eyed look that hopefully says, "Don't you *dare* cheat at cards with my husband's grandmother, no matter how rich she seems."

Layla rolls her eyes, which hopefully means, "Obviously, I won't… today."

"Let's eat," Claire says imperiously.

Not so fast. The doorbell rings again, and it's a woman from Claire's knitting circle. When I try to go for the food again, another member of the same circle arrives. This pattern repeats a few more times until the new arrival is Sawyer's father.

"Hello, Roger," Sawyer's grandmother says. "Have you met Claire's… plumber?" She gleefully gestures at the Hamburglar.

Roger's eyes zero in on the guy. "Didn't you used to do maintenance on our plumbing system?"

I suppress a nervous chuckle. An argument could be made that he's still doing maintenance on Claire's plumbing system. Tightening loose fittings whenever needed. Ensuring the water flow is just right. Checking if all the valves are in working order, or if any leaks require special attention.

"Please, call me Ronald," the Hamburglar says. "The past is in the past."

Did Ronald just quote a line from *Frozen*'s "Let It Go?" Is it because that song deals with potty training—or so I heard—and since plumbers are—

"I'm still confused… *Ronald*," Roger grits out. "What are you doing here?"

"He's my friend," Claire says sternly. "Now sit down." She gestures at a spot between two of the more attractive members of the knitting circle.

Muttering something under his breath—probably the words "let the storm rage on"—Sawyer's father takes a seat between the two women. Claire's knitting circle friends look her ex over with the same avarice that the rest of us have been eyeing the various delicacies on the table with.

Finally, we get to enjoy the food, which tastes as amazing as it looks.

Everyone quizzes me and Sawyer about how we met and other details, and my earlier guilt intensifies about lying, especially since everyone, even the grandmother, seems to be happy that the family has grown. Also, a part of me wishes all of this were true, both the marriage and the story of our insane attraction at first sight—not that I wasn't attracted to my husband on that day.

Hell, if I'm honest with myself, each day I'm getting dangerously closer to falling for my fake husband, and meeting his ex-girlfriend has shown me just how bad things already are.

"This saffron lobster bisque is amazing," Mom says. "All of this food is out of this world."

"I agree." I shake off the thoughts that don't really belong at this table and give Sawyer's mom a beaming smile. "Your son clearly got his cooking skills from you."

I turn and peck Sawyer on the cheek, which shouldn't get me hot and bothered but totally does.

"Claire's cooking?" The grandmother clutches her pearls. "Dear, please tell me this meal came about in a civilized manner—by being catered."

"It was made by a Michelin-star chef," Claire says, sounding a little guilty. "But hey, I chose her, so an argument can be made that I can take some of the credit."

A weak argument.

"Sawyer learned cooking from me," Roger says proudly. "We Worthingtons have always been more practical than the Pembrokes." He darts an odd look at the Hamburglar—who no doubt is more practical yet, being a plumber and all.

"Sure, if by more practical, you mean poorer," the grandmother says snidely.

"Grandmère," Sawyer says with a frown. "There's nothing wrong with working for a living."

Grandmère? Was calling her Grandoodles out of the question?

"Let's not pretend that working for a living isn't vulgar." She looks around the table. "No offense to those of you who do."

"I'm retired," Dad says.

"So am I," Mom says.

"Finally, some reasonable people join this family," the grandmother says.

As insane as it sounds, my parents look pleased at that praise, which reawakens my guilt. It only gets worse as the conversation turns to our plans for the future, and we lie through our teeth about the two children we might have one day: a boy and a girl that I can weirdly picture in my mind's eye. They would have their father's gray eyes and jet-black hair, as well as his fearlessness when it comes to such horrors as beards. From me, they'd inherit the ability to make small talk and—

"Everyone, listen up," Claire says. "It's time to open the presents."

Ah. Right. I feel giddy about finally learning what Sawyer got me, as well as seeing his face when he opens my gift.

Turns out, Claire has purchased gifts for everyone, and she must've hired a private detective or a powerful psychic. She gives my sister a Christmas-themed deck of cards, my mom a soap-carving kit, and my dad a huge sheet of bubble wrap that he so likes to pop.

Even the two dogs each get a gift—something that looks like a hollow butt plug. Claire even stuffs the things with peanut butter, and the two fluffballs go nuts for them.

In contrast, I get a book called *What to Expect When You're Expecting*, a baby blanket, and tiny socks.

Yeah. Not subtle, Claire. Not at all.

Eventually, we get to the gifts that Claire didn't prepare, and that's what I'm most curious about.

What did Sawyer get me?

As I open the wrapping, I feel like a kid—specifically, like I did at my first Christmas with the Bakers. While my birth mother was alive, I never got any presents, so the Bakers' first gift was extra special… and, as it turns out, this one is too.

It's a book of forever stamps, each featuring John Lennon in a different color, starting from orange and ending with blue. It's something I've always wanted but haven't been able to get.

A gorgeous stamp book and the best gift I've ever gotten.

"That's a misprint as well," Sawyer murmurs. "See how the die cuts are missing?"

And that does it.

I can't fool myself any longer.

I'm officially catching feelings for my fake husband. And I want him to fuck my brains out tonight.

22

sawyer

a.k.a. the guy who wants to unwrap something besides presents

"THANK YOU," Sawyer says, looking at me with wide eyes. "Now open mine. Please."

I do so, and a wide grin spreads across my face because my gift is *also* a stamp. It features two cats, a Maine Coon and a Burmese, and it's also a misprint.

"Wow," Mom says when she sees the coincidence. "Talk about a match made in heaven."

"More like a match made by a faulty printer at some USPS facility," Dad chimes in.

The rest of the party participants "ooh and ahh" at the serendipity of our gifts, especially once our parents explain to them about us both being philatelists.

"Now we can have the dessert," Mom announces imperiously.

I go to the table unenthusiastically. What I really want is to go home and take Sawyer to bed, which I realize is insane, but here we are.

My libidinous torment only worsens once at the

table, thanks to the way Sawyer's lips wrap around an éclair.

No. Must think of something else. In theory, there are many distractions at this table, like Mom's boyfriend, because that's what this plumber guy must be—why else would she be acting so happy around him?

"I'm going to wash some dishes," my dad announces to no one in particular.

He, too, must have noticed Mom's unusual behavior.

When there are no replies, he stomps away.

Sawyer elbows me. "You should go talk to him."

"I should?" I whisper back. "Why?"

"He's clearly struggling," she says in a low voice. "No doubt jealous of the Hamburglar."

I'm about to ask who she means, but then I see the resemblance. "I don't think it's necessary," I whisper. "Dad likes his solitude."

Just like me.

Hmm.

"Fine," I say. "I'll go."

She gives me a thumbs up, and I head over to the kitchen. And maybe I *am* needed here, because the way Dad is scrubbing a plate at the sink is borderline homicidal.

"You okay?" I ask, approaching him.

"I got phone numbers from both of those women your mother pawned me off to," he says without turning. "I'll be fine."

I walk over and rinse a dish in silence, then say, "I thought you were happy being divorced."

"I was. I am. I mean, I'm better off than my friend Frank."

"Is that the one who died of a heart attack?"

"Right."

Wow. I take another plate. "I always thought you liked your solitude."

Dad's shoulders sag. "Why did you think that?"

"I have no idea." Maybe because I thought that's what I liked, and that I inherited this from my parents.

"Take my advice: treat your wife well," Dad says. "Amicable or not, divorce sucks, and don't let anyone tell you any different."

He was literally the person who told me different, or at least surely acted like it.

"Will you call either of those women?" I ask.

He shrugs. "Maybe. The blonde one is cute. But—"

"Am I?" asks the blonde, who just happens to walk in at that exact moment.

I snort. "I'll leave you to your debate."

Returning to my wife, I only listen to the ongoing conversations with half an ear. What I really want to do is take her home and treat her well... in bed.

"Is your dad okay?" Sawyer asks.

I nod.

"What time do people usually leave these things?" Sawyer asks, echoing my own thoughts.

Before I can answer, my dad comes back along with

the blonde, both of them looking suspiciously disheveled.

"Well, Claire, thank you for this amazing party," he says. "Sadly, it's time for me to go."

"Me too," says the blonde. "Thank you very, very, very much."

On that disturbing note, they both leave, not even bothering to pretend they're going separately. As often happens, the first departure from the party opens the floodgates for the others, and soon the rest of the knitting circle is gone.

"All right, Mom," I say when there's a lull in the departures. "This was lovely."

"Very much so," Sawyer says earnestly. "It was nice to meet you face to face." She turns to her family. "It was great seeing you guys. I'll call tomorrow. Be safe."

Everyone hugs and kisses us goodbye, even my grandmother—which is a rare treat for me and unheard of for people who aren't members of the family.

Once we're in the cab, Sawyer says, "I really enjoyed myself. Is that bad?"

I place my hand over hers. "Why would that be bad?"

"Because our marriage is fake?"

I sigh. "That doesn't mean we can't enjoy something that's enjoyable."

She darts a furtive glance at the driver. "We keep talking about not repeating... certain enjoyable activities on the same grounds. It's easy to get confused."

"So let's not avoid anything enjoyable," I say huskily. "Maybe it's time we changed the family motto to 'Carpe diem.'"

She moistens her lips. "Our family motto has to include at least a mention of subligaculum."

"Sure." I squeeze her hand. "How about 'Carpe subligaculum!'"

Because seizing her panties—or shredding them into pieces—is something that I'm dying to do.

She nods. "I like that motto."

Did she just agree for me to actually seize her panties? Or should I clarify in English?

"I'm worried my sister will cheat your grandmother at cards," she says before I can pose the question.

I shake my head. "The reverse is much more likely. Grandmother is *very* serious about bridge."

"You sure?"

"Yeah. She's not easy to trick either. A social security scammer once called her, and she claims she hired some shady guy on the dark web to locate him and give him a beating."

Sawyer pales. "She wouldn't do that to my sister, would she?"

"Of course not. Your sister is family, so in that case, Grandmother would give her a stern talking to—which, granted, could be as unpleasant as a beating. But like I said, it's your sister who is more likely to find herself in my grandmother's debt."

Sawyer grins and then imitates my grandmother's voice while paraphrasing the famous quote from *The Godfather* about someday calling upon Layla to do a service for her.

Once we're home, I feed Hermit and hurry to the study to put away my new treasure, the stamp Sawyer got for me.

"Does this mean you like it?" she asks, having followed me in.

"Like it?" I give one last adoring look to the new acquisition before closing the stamp book. "I love it. I'll frame it as soon as I get the chance."

Sawyer beams at me. "I love yours too." She opens her album, frees up some space, and then sticks my gift prominently on the first page.

"The very front?" I whistle. "Seems like a place of honor."

"It is, and it will make Elvis very happy." She gestures at the stamp of the King that she's kept in the same spot.

I arch an eyebrow. "Didn't Elvis dislike John Lennon?"

She closes the album. "Is that true? But John Lennon very famously said, 'Before Elvis, there was nothing.'"

Huh. That's an interesting idea. That quote echoes something that's been on my mind, except instead of Elvis, I've been feeling like before Sawyer, there was nothing. As in, I thought I was cozy in my solitude, but I was just biding my time until—

"You okay?" she asks.

"Yeah." I pull her to me. "Very much okay."

I claim her lips and do my best to show her what I'm thinking using a kiss. And then using my dick.

She comes four times, yet I'm not sure if the message gets across.

I guess there are limits to non-verbal communication.

Fine. As I hold her in my arms in the drowsy aftermath, I decide to sort out exactly how I feel and then speak to her about it—but probably after HR's decision. If we're fired, things will be somewhat simpler: I'll just ask her on a date after we are divorced. If we're *not* fired, things will continue to be a little complicated, but we'll sort something out.

"This was the best Christmas ever," she murmurs sleepily and shimmies her butt deeper into my crotch.

"Today was Christmas Eve," I whisper into her ear. "Actual Christmas is tomorrow, and now I'll make it my mission for *that* to be the best Christmas you've ever had."

"The bar is high," she says over a yawn. "I've lost track of today's orgasms."

I kiss the back of her neck. "Challenge accepted."

IN THE MORNING, I MAKE SAWYER THE MOST scrumptious breakfast in my repertoire, and her moans are my reward.

Then I take her to all the touristy spots that look

best on Christmas, like the tree at Rockefeller Center and the FAO Schwarz toy store. When we get hungry, we go on a hot chocolate tour, and afterward, we head over to Central Park, where we ice skate at Wollman Rink until dusk and gawk at the festive lights and decorations.

"You win," she says. "This is the best Christmas ever."

I smile knowingly. "It's not over yet."

"Oh?"

Instead of explaining, I take her hand, help her into the cab, and tell the driver to take us to SoHo, where we eat a romantic dinner at the Michelin-star-rated Le Coucou.

"That has to be it," Sawyer says as I pay our bill. "I don't want to be ruined for the rest of Christmases to come."

"Actually, we do have more to do," I say, mock apologetically. "So please try to live in the moment and worry about future Christmases later."

Not that there's anything to worry about. I plan to top this next year, and the year after that.

She demands to know the next stop in the itinerary, but I keep her in suspense until we reach our destination: the Nutcracker Ballet.

Judging by her grin, she very much enjoys it.

After the ballet, I ask our cab driver to take the scenic route home, and he passes by places with holiday lights, of which Sawyer likes the Washington Square Park the most.

At home, she watches with an amused smile as I give Hermit the gourmet cat treats and catnip toys that I saved for this occasion. Once the cat is occupied, I lead Sawyer to the bedroom and propose a new Christmas tradition: a hot bath with mutual massages.

"That sounds like a great idea," Sawyer says, her eyes gleaming. "It'll help us sleep."

We get into the bath, and no one is surprised when the massages quickly escalate to passionate, desperate sex during which I remember my challenge and make sure Sawyer comes three times before we get into the actual bed. Once in bed, I lose count of how many orgasms she has before I reach mine.

All I know is that the hot bath isn't the reason why we sleep well that night.

An alarm wakes me up at the usual time, and Sawyer groans.

"I wish I were with the company long enough to be allowed to take days off," she says sleepily.

I sit up. "You *could* call in sick."

"No." She sighs. "I want to be there in case HR has an answer for us."

I don't tell her how skeptical I am about HR even being there.

Oh, well. We get ready and head into work, and it turns out a lot of people decided to come to work today, including some from HR.

What gives?

Maybe because it's a Thursday?

All I know is, more people means more small talk and more chances for someone to involve me in a stupid meeting, so I dive back into work while I can.

By the time Sawyer asks me about lunch, I'm finishing something very important: a way to associate code with the person who pulls it out of the repository. So I ask Sawyer to give me five more minutes. Since I wrote the code to use as bait long ago, I submit it now, and in the box where you explain what you did, I make it sound enticing for someone who works for Circumflex.

As we eat our lunch, I enjoy the sense of accomplishment from a job completed. Once I'm back at my desk, I jump into the more difficult remaining task: getting us an edge over Circumflex despite their earlier theft.

Sometime later, a message from Sawyer pops up.

Ready to go home?

Shit. It's late, and everyone around me has gone home already. I tell her that I'm ready and that the coast is clear—Eugene and Susan are having a meeting in a room nearby, meaning he won't be in the elevator with Sawyer.

When we get home, the evening feels very much like how I've always pictured a random Thursday night for a happily married couple: a nice candlelit dinner and a competitive game of Tetris, followed by slow and gentle sex that feels suspiciously like another word, one that starts with an "l" and ends with "making."

Friday follows a similar script to Thursday: I work and have an amazing evening with my wife. Over the weekend, we stay in and relax, so it's a lot like the two prior evenings in the most wonderful way.

On Monday, an hour after I get to work, Damian comes to my desk and gestures at his meeting room—now free of aluminum foil.

When I enter, he puts a brand-new gizmo on the table and clicks it on.

"What's that?" I ask.

"A device that blocks cell service," he says. "Also firewalls anything unessential on the company Wi-Fi."

"Nifty," I say. "But isn't blocking cell service illegal?"

He shrugs. "I only use it here. How would the FCC catch me?"

"True. So… what's this about?"

"I heard from our person at Circumflex," he says.

I arch an eyebrow.

"They stole new code from us. Again."

"Already?" I exclaim. "That's great."

With Christmas last week and New Year's the day after tomorrow, I didn't expect the spy to—

"Great?" Damian looks at me like he's worried about my sanity.

"Ah, right. I forgot to tell you… That code they stole is bait. If you show it to me, I'll be able to figure out who the spy is."

His eyes widen. "How could you forget something so monumental?"

I frown. "Maybe I was too preoccupied with whether or not I'm still employed here?"

He swats my words away like a meddlesome fly. "So if I get you the code, you'll know who it is?"

I nod.

He opens his laptop, and his fingers fly over the keyboard for a few minutes.

"Here." He turns the laptop my way. "Tell me who it is."

I check a comment on the very top of the file. There's a number there that most people might mistake for a timestamp—and it is that, in part. The date part is an actual date, but the time isn't time. Instead, it's the user ID of the spy.

"Tell me," Damian says. "Who is it?"

"I have to go get my laptop," I tell him. "I now have their user ID, but I need to match it to a name."

"Go get it," he says.

Driven by curiosity, I sprint to my desk and come back with the laptop.

"Let me know as soon as you know," Damian says when I sit down.

Ignoring him, I bring up the necessary screen.

When I link the user ID to the name of the spy, I stare at the screen in confusion.

What the hell?

This doesn't make sense.

I close the laptop and demand Damian show me the ID again, without explaining why. My stomach is churning, and I want to punch something, hard.

"How about I fucking email it to you?" Damian growls.

"Good idea," I snap. "Do that now."

He takes forever with his email, so I run the lookup again using my memory—and get the same result.

Finally, the stupid email arrives, so I copy and paste the ID in order to repeat the lookup one final time.

My chest feels like a billion bricks just fell on it.

The result is still the same: it is my own name that is staring back at me, and I know that I'm not the spy, so it can only be the one person with the exact same name as mine.

Her first name she's had all her life, but her last name she took on very recently.

My wife.

Sawyer Worthington.

23
sawyer

a.k.a. Austin Powers: The Spy Who Shagged Me

I TRY to think through the turmoil in my mind.

No. No, I don't care what the stupid email says.

She can't be the spy.

I know her too well to even suspect such a thing.

Besides, at the time the code was stolen, she didn't even have access to it. At least I doubt it. It was at the very beginning of her tenure here at Octothorpe.

On autopilot, I take a look at the source control history.

Fuck.

She *did* have access, and she did pull the code in question at her workspace—but then again, so did countless other people.

No. I refuse to believe this. She can't be the—

"Hey," Damian says, startling me.

Frantically, I close all the windows that could incriminate Sawyer.

When I look up from my laptop, Damian is arching an eyebrow.

"Were you looking at porn at a time like this?" he asks caustically.

I slam my laptop shut. "Porn? Seriously?"

"You closed *something* in a hurry. Whatever. I don't really give a shit. Who do *you* think the spy is?"

I grit my teeth. "I don't know. There's a bug with the code that was supposed to tell me. I'll have to review it and try again. Sorry."

I could be telling the truth. Unlikely but possible. But even if she were the spy, which I can't bring myself to believe, I wouldn't throw Sawyer under the bus like that. Not after—

"Too bad," Damian says, but he doesn't sound as pissed as I'd expect. "Apparently, when it rains, it pours. The contractor—what was his name?—just emailed that he has zeroed in on a suspect."

"Who?" I demand.

Damian shrugs. "He said he'd tell me in our upcoming meeting. It's in a few minutes. I had hoped you'd give me a name so I could double-check his findings, but I guess we'll have to go on his skills alone."

"I want to join this meeting," I state.

Damian cocks his head. "Didn't you want to be out of all meetings?"

"When it comes to this spy, I'm pretty invested," I say, and it's not a lie anymore.

"All right. I'll send you the invite. Be ready in a few minutes."

I nod, open my laptop back up, and launch the messenger app.

Weird. It's not connected to the network.

Ah.

Right.

Damian's stupid gizmo must deem this thing an unessential part of the Wi-Fi.

I pull out my phone.

No signal.

Stupid fucking device. I slam it on the desk, then shut my laptop with a bang.

"Hey," Damian says with a frown. "I know you hate meetings and all that, but you invited yourself to this one. No need to punish inanimate objects over it."

Fuck. I need to keep myself together, or else I might give something away.

"What room will this meeting be in?" I ask.

"Dreamatorium," he says with an eyeroll. He finds the naming conventions around here ridiculous.

Dreamatorium? That's on Sawyer's floor.

"I'll meet you there." I leap to my feet. "I've got some business to take care of first."

Before he can reply, I'm already sprinting away, and only in the elevator do I realize that I forgot my phone and laptop back in Damian's office.

Whatever. I'm about to see Sawyer face to face, which is better than any phone or messenger app.

Not that I have any idea what I'll say to her when I see her.

The elevator opens, and I leap onto her floor, then rush toward her desk.

Fucking fuck. Even from a distance, I spot that her cute pixie head is *not* sticking out of her cubicle as it should. Still, I get all the way there and glance under her desk—in case she happens to be picking something up from the floor at the moment.

Nope. She's not here.

So where is she? Could she have stepped away to the restroom? Or the breakroom? If it's the latter, I can check—and I do, but she's not there.

When I return, the new guy sitting at the nearby cubicle is looking at me funny.

"Hey," I say curtly.

"Hi," he says. "Happy upcoming New Year."

"Right. Felicitations," I say in as friendly a tone as I can muster. Then, still doing my best to sound friendly, I ask, "What's your name?"

His eyes narrow. "It's Jasper. Jasper Knight. We've spoken at least a dozen times, Sawyer."

"Right. Jasper. I'll remember it from now on."

"We'll see." Jasper glances at Sawyer's empty desk. "Is all this your way to warm me up before asking where your wife is?"

"You're clearly smart, Jasper." Smarter than I previously thought, that's for sure. "Do you know where she is?"

"Ah, there you are," Damian says just as Jasper opens his mouth to reply.

"Give me a second," I say to Damian. "I was just talking to Jasper here."

The look Damian gives Jasper is identical to the one he would give an empty chair. "No. Whatever it is, it will have to wait. Everyone is already gathered." Damian juts an accusing finger at the Dreamatorium.

"I'll be back," I tell Jasper, who is reverently staring at my boss.

When we get into the meeting room, Eugene, Henrietta, and her husband are already here, as well as Susan.

Fuck. My heart squeezes painfully. The presence of Susan implies the spy is on her team. Which—

"Happy holidays, everyone," Henrietta booms.

I clench my teeth. "Let's just get to the business at hand."

Damian chuckles. "Maybe I should bring him to every meeting to speed things up?"

Henrietta shifts in her seat. "She told you already? Is that why you're upset?"

I glare at her. "Who told me, and what?"

"Your wife," Henrietta says. "I figured when I had her—"

"Hold the fuck up," Damian interjects. "What does Sawyer's wife have to do with anything?"

Eugene clears his throat. "I think that's my cue."

"Cue for what?" I clench and unclench my fists.

"Umm." Eugene tugs on his beard. "After a thorough

investigation, Sawyer—your wife, that is—turned out to be the person that I—"

"Stop." I accompany the word with a smack of the table that makes everyone wince. "What evidence do you have against her?"

Something in my voice makes Eugene realize that fast speaking is his best course of action, so he rattles out, "It's a lot of circumstantial evidence that all adds up to a bigger picture. Like the fact that she has been avoiding me and acted super guilty when—"

"That was because of that shit on your face," I growl. "She has pogonophobia. I hope you have better reasons for your accusations than that." Violent fantasies flit in front of my mind's eye, most of them involving spilled milk, crushed cookies, and a beardectomy.

Eugene pushes his chair away from the table. "There's also the fact that she's been looking at the code you submit, religiously. Code that has nothing to do with her job." He glances at Susan, who nods at this.

"Could she not be admiring her husband's work?" Damian asks.

Eugene nods. "Like I said, all of it is circumstantial evidence. Like the fact that the code theft coincided with her arrival at the company and thus her getting access to said code." He stops and looks at me worriedly.

"What else?" I demand.

"I didn't expect you to be here for this," Eugene says to me. "It makes the next part... awkward."

Not as awkward as it will feel once I grab him by the beard and pull until—

"Just spit it out," Damian orders.

"She's highly attractive, even for this odd workspace." Eugene gestures at me. "And he's in charge of the project the spy is interested in, right?"

Damian rolls his eyes but nods.

"Also… he's a known misanthrope," Eugene continues. "Not liked by most people, at least if you ignore professional respect."

Damian narrows his eyes, and Henrietta nods, then looks sheepish as she notices me glaring at her.

"As to Sawyer herself, everyone says her people skills are far above average, which makes one wonder how two people so different would end up together."

The words land like the punches that I was just picturing delivering to Eugene's jolly belly.

"And don't get me started on this hasty marriage," Eugene continues. "It sure looks like the honeypot strategy that spies so very often employ. They get romantically entangled with the target to get them to lower their guard and—"

He continues speaking, but I'm barely listening at this point.

An ugly seed of doubt has dug its tendrils into my brain. As flimsy as every individual piece of this so-called evidence is, when listed together like this, it's *not* nothing. And Eugene doesn't know some things that only I know—like the fact that Sawyer's user ID was attached to the code that ended up at Circumflex. Or how good of a liar Sawyer is when she wants to be. I noticed it when we were telling our story to our families. At that time, it didn't ring any alarm bells, but now…

No.

Plenty of people are good at lying.

As to all the other shit, there has to be some other explanation. "I'm going to talk to Sawyer," I say out loud. I peer through the glass wall toward her cubicle, and my frown deepens. "She's still not at her desk."

"Oh, crap," Henrietta says. "I guess you haven't talked with her yet."

With a jolt, I recall how at the very beginning of the meeting, Henrietta said something about Sawyer having told me something already—something that might be the reason why I'm upset.

"What did you do?" I ask, my tone dangerously level.

"We fired her," Henrietta admits. "That's why she's not at her desk. Security escorted her out twenty minutes ago."

I leap to my feet. "What?"

"Please, calm down," Henrietta says. "We haven't told her it was due to her spying. I told her it was about that kiss so that—"

I do a double take. "The kiss? Are you saying that I'm fired also?"

Damian vehemently shakes his head. "It had better not mean that."

"Well, no," Henrietta says. "We told her that, as the

new employee, she was on a probationary period, and therefore her behavior was supposed to be completely above reproach as far as—"

"That's bullshit," I exclaim.

Henrietta shrugs. "She's a spy. It's not like she's going to lawyer up."

"And if she does," Henrietta's husband chimes in, "I suspect that the financial hit of that lawsuit will be less than the continued theft of our intellectual property."

The room is spinning around me.

"Is this why you sat on deciding their fate for so long?" I hear Damian demand as if from a distance.

"Correct," Henrietta says.

"I should've been consulted," Damian says through his teeth. "I would have told you to—"

"You hate it when we bother you," Henrietta interrupts defensively. "And this is the holiday season on top of that, so you'd be extra mad. Not to mention, I spoke to Susan, who is the female Sawyer's manager—or was. I honestly didn't think you'd mind."

"Are you sure this isn't about getting blindsided with their marriage maneuver?" Damian demands. "It sure made you look like—"

"Enough." I turn my back on all of them and head to the exit.

"Wait!" Henrietta shrieks. "You can't—"

"I can do whatever the fuck I want," I throw over my shoulder.

"Not if you value your job," Henrietta booms.

"Take your job and shove it."

To punctuate my point, I slam the door behind me and run for the elevator without looking back.

"Hey," Jasper pants at my side.

What the fuck? He's running alongside me.

"I didn't get the chance to tell you earlier," he continues breathlessly. "Security came and forced Sawyer to leave."

"Yes." I jam my finger into the elevator button. "I know that now."

He slinks away, muttering something like "Ah, good," or "Good luck," but I'm already stepping into the elevator.

The trip downstairs takes a decade, and I pace the small space like a caged honey badger. Once the elevator doors finally open on the ground floor, I hurry outside—but she's not by the building, as I'd hoped.

On a hunch, I swerve into the coffee shop where we met for the first time, and as soon as I step inside, I hear sobs that make my heart crack.

There she is. Crying into a matcha latte.

When she spots me, she leaps to her feet, wiping at the wetness on her face. "There you are! I wrote to you on the messenger app, and then texted and called."

She did? Oh, right, Damian's stupid gizmo prevented me from seeing all that, and then I forgot my phone and laptop in his cursed office.

"Anyway, I'm so sorry," she gasps. "I can't believe they fired us over that kiss after all that. You're probably—"

"I wasn't fired," I say. "And you weren't fired… for kissing."

Her eyes widen, and a look of faint hope appears in them. "We weren't fired?"

I sigh and scrub my palm over my face. "I'm fucking this up. You *were* fired. It just wasn't for the reason they gave you."

She drops back into her chair. "So… *you* weren't fired, but I was?"

I nod.

She hiccups. "And not over the kiss?"

I nod again.

"Then why?"

"Corporate espionage." I feel like a traitor as I watch her face for some sign of *something*, but all I see there is a complete and utter shock that you'd expect from an innocent who is hearing about this clusterfuck for the first time.

"Is that a bad joke?" She clutches her matcha like a lifeline.

"No. I never got a chance to discuss this with you, but someone stole some code and gave it to our competitor. I've been working on a way to find out who that someone is."

"And you think I'm this person?" The look of betrayal on her face is as genuine as the shock was earlier.

"No. My code did implicate you, but I didn't tell them about that."

She gapes at me. "Your code implicated *me*?"

"And I'm sure there's some explanation for that," I say. "Maybe you—"

"I had nothing to do with any espionage." Her voice rises. "There's zero reason your code should've implicated me. You know me better than that. I can't believe you would let them fire me over—"

"I didn't," I say, but I can tell she doesn't fully believe me. So I hurry ahead with my explanation. "You know that guy Eugene? The one with the beard? Well, he's a private investigator, and he concluded that you're the spy—independently from my code."

She gasps. "And you believed him?"

"I…" I hesitate for a second. "No, but—"

"And you let them fire me?"

"It wasn't my decision—"

But she's no longer listening. Grabbing her bag, she runs out of the café. Cursing, I run after her, but it's too late.

She leaps straight into a waiting cab, and before I can reach for the door, they're already speeding away.

Fuck.

Since I can't run after the cab, I do the next best thing—run to get my phone so I can call her.

24
sawyer

a.k.a. the girl who's not ready to give up the fight

I CRY all the way to Layla's house, and whenever I see a call from Sawyer, I let it go to voicemail and ignore the texts that follow.

"It's okay," the cab driver says when we get to my destination. "You don't have to pay today."

How miserable must I look that a hardened NYC cab driver would make such an offer? My crying intensifying, I not only pay the man, but I leave a big tip as well.

"What the hell happened?" Layla demands when she opens her door. "You haven't cried like this since the time I accidentally deleted your Super Mario Galaxy save file."

"Sure," I say over a sob. "Let's say you deleted that 'accidentally.'"

Her phone rings.

"Weird," she says, looking down at it. "I don't know this number."

"Show me," I say.

She does.

"It's him," I exclaim. "Don't take it!"

"Ah." She declines the call. "I'm guessing this—whatever this is—is husband related."

"Yeah."

"How did he get my number?"

Her phone rings again, and it's Mom.

"I'm a little busy," Layla says and puts Mom on speaker.

"I just wanted to check if Sawyer's husband got ahold of you. He was asking if she was at my place, and I said she wasn't and to check with you, so he asked for your number and—"

"I'm here, Mom," I say in as normal a voice as I can. "I'll call him in a few."

There's no way I'm telling Mom about what happened anytime soon, not until I get my turbulent emotions well under control.

"Ah. Perfect. Okay, I'll let you enjoy sister times."

Layla hangs up and demands that I dish, so I haltingly tell her about getting fired and the conversation with Sawyer in the café that followed.

Somehow, this works like a session with a therapist. I feel a tiny bit better from just having talked about it all.

"Umm." Layla pulls out a deck of cards from a box and gives them a shuffle. "I'd like to clarify a few things."

I wipe my nose. "What things?"

"Sawyer said he didn't believe them when they told him about you being a spy."

I purse my lips. "He hesitated for a second before he said that, but yes, he did."

She fiddles with her cards again. "But… he said that he *did not* believe them."

"Yes." The word comes out whiny, so I clear my throat. "But I don't believe him that he didn't believe them."

She snorts. "I don't believe that you don't believe that he didn't believe them."

I roll my eyes. "He let them fire me."

She cocks her head. "Did he know it was going to happen? Did he have the power to stop them? Or to reverse it once it happened?"

Shit. "He told me it wasn't his decision, and I have no idea if he knew it was going down. I think HR was the deciding party, maybe my manager as well. As to reversing things, I have no clue, but I doubt it."

She frowns. "Look, sis, I'm always on your side… but I have to ask: why are we angry at your husband, exactly?"

I ponder that question and realize that it all boils down to a simple fact: "They only fired me."

"So? Who else should they fire?"

I sniff. "No. You don't get it. The reason they gave is that I kissed Sawyer at the company party. Not the spying."

She stops shuffling mid-way. "They fired you for kissing your husband?"

"They think we weren't married yet at the time of the kiss. Sawyer and I discussed lying about getting married prior to the party, but we never went through with that. Anyway, HR said I was on probation at the time of the kiss, so I'm fired and he's not."

"Oh. So you want him fired too?"

"No." I leap to my feet and pace nervously.

"So what then?" she asks.

I circle around her. "It's possible I didn't think all this through, especially the spy thing, back at the café."

"And now?" Layla demands.

"Now I feel even worse," I say. "I've lost my job *and* my husband."

"That's a bit of a stretch. If you'd lost him, he wouldn't be calling you. And me."

Shit. She doesn't get it. She thinks our marriage is real, and I'm too embarrassed to dissuade her from that. Instead, I pace around her place until she puts a hand on my shoulder and turns me to face her.

"This isn't like you," she says sternly.

"What isn't?"

"To just accept fate without a fight."

I blink at her. "Fighting with him just created more problems. I didn't need to. I shouldn't have done it."

"Not with him, you nincompoop. I mean this thing with your company. If they fired you because you're a spy, and you're not a spy, that leaves a lot of questions, including your husband's role in all this, as well as who the spy actually is."

I stare at her. "Right. Some person *is* the spy, and they let me take the fall."

"Exactly."

I turn toward the door. "I've got to go."

"That's the spirit," she says. "But one correction, *we're* going to go."

"Sure." If I ever needed her moral support, now is that time. "Can you please get ready quickly?"

"I can." She puts her deck of cards down.

"I'll get us a ride in the meantime."

She shakes her head. "We can take my car."

"All right." She won that nice car playing poker, but the guy never gave her the deed, so she can't sell it and use the money. Nor can she take that guy to court—not when gambling is illegal and she most likely cheated to win. Hell, she's lucky he didn't report the car stolen.

"Give me a minute." She hurries to change and is ready ten minutes later, which sets two new records: speed in changing outfits and accuracy in estimating time—ten to one is an amazing ratio for her.

"Where to?" she asks when we get into her car.

"Octothorpe," I say and enter the address into the GPS. "I'm going to get some fucking answers."

25
sawyer

a.k.a. the guy with a puzzle to solve

THE FIRST THING I do after I give up on calling Sawyer is look for her at our place.

Nope.

She's not here.

Purely on autopilot, I feed Hermit as I think about what to do next.

The answer is pretty obvious when it occurs to me. I need to clear Sawyer's name and then get her her job back.

Yes. That's it. And to clear her name, I need to figure out who the spy actually is—because I don't think it's her. I hate that I hesitated back at the café when she asked me point blank. My only excuse is that crap Eugene said about me being a misanthrope. It made me feel like I might not deserve a woman like Sawyer.

No.

Fuck that.

And fuck Eugene.

Even if he's right, even if I don't deserve her, I intend to fight for her and make her mine—and I dare anyone to try and stop me.

"The spy will rue the day he picked Sawyer as the scapegoat," I tell Hermit grimly. "Because that must be what's going on. How else would her user ID end up where it did?"

The cat twitches his tail at me and attacks his food with the ferocity I'll show this spy—once I know who they are.

Well, time to find out.

I get a cab and tell the driver to punch it, and as we drive, I form a plan of action.

As soon as I reach Octothorpe, I get to my desk and do something that's not connected to the spy. Not exactly. It's more of a precaution—or a persuasion tactic—for later. Specifically, I plug a flash drive into my laptop, copy some files, pocket the flash, and delete the originals.

Now it's time to test my first theory, one in which I've cast Jasper Knight as the spy. After all, he is also a new employee at Octothorpe, and his desk is near Sawyer's. It's entirely possible that he stole her log-in credentials for the source control system and then framed her.

As I dig deeper into this theory, I find that there are indeed irregularities when it comes to Jasper's usage of the source control system—and they are similar to the irregularities that I see when it comes to Sawyer's usage of the same.

Both she and Jasper seem to be logging in from too many different machines. Typically, this would include their laptops and workstations, but that's not the case here.

Hmm. There's one specific machine that they both used.

As I follow this clue, I put the puzzle together, piece by treacherous piece.

26
sawyer

a.k.a. the girl who's spying on the spy

WE WAIT AND WAIT. I see many people leave work, but none are from HR.

"Should we go?" Layla asks. "I bet you could just locate your husband and—"

"Wait." I point a trembling finger at the entrance.

The bearded guy—Eugene—exits the building and walks across the street, toward the park.

"That's the consultant," I explain shakily. "He'll have the answers."

Layla's eyes widen. "The one with the beard?"

"That's right."

"Don't beards give you… the heebie-jeebies?"

Understatement of the century, but I do need those answers and I'm going to get them, even if I have to talk to Satan himself—which this comes very close to.

"I *have* started some therapy," I say, not sure if I'm convincing Layla or myself. "I think I should be able to do this." But it would help if I had a couple of Xanax floating in my system.

"Are you sure about this?" Layla asks. "I mean, if you'd like, I could—"

I sit straighter. "No. Thank you, but I have to do this myself."

"All right," she says. "But if you change your mind, I'm here."

It's tempting but… "He wouldn't know who you are and wouldn't tell you anything anyway."

"Right," she says. "Then good luck."

Yeah. I'll need a lot of luck because there's an obscene amount of beard involved.

I step out of the car.

Wow. I'm really doing it. I'm going to approach a guy with a beard and—

In the corner of my eye, I see someone else exit the building.

Oh, thank heavens. It's Susan.

I would much, much rather speak with her instead of Eugene.

I'm about to run to do just that when I see Susan wave at Eugene—and Eugene waves back.

Weird.

I didn't realize these two knew each other.

Hmm. Something about the way he looks at her is disturbing.

It reminds me of how a serial killer might stalk his prey.

Some instinct possesses me to return to the car and

watch what's about to happen stealthily—and I'm right to do so because I see Susan beeline right for Eugene, which isn't victim behavior at all.

"Who is that?" Layla asks.

"My manager," I say, not taking my eyes off her.

At this point, Susan has reached her destination and Eugene bends down to allow his evil beard to maul Susan's face—or at least that's my initial impression. In the next moment, I realize that they're actually kissing, or whatever the word is when one of the participants has a facial growth like that. Hair licking? In any case, the beard just makes it difficult to see their lips, but either way, this is by far the grossest thing I've ever witnessed, and I wonder if Eugene has somehow brainwashed Susan, or blackmailed her into doing this.

"Huh," Layla says when Eugene grabs Susan's ass, and she strokes his crotch over his pants—seemingly voluntarily. "I think the consultant is fucking your boss."

I swallow bile back into my throat. "I think you're right."

"And I bet it's against the rules." Layla smiles impishly. "Could you use this as some sort of leverage?"

"Maybe, but I have another question for you," I say.

"Yeah?"

"That guy... is he hideous-looking? Or are my perceptions colored by his beard?"

She pulls a deck of cards out of who-knows-which orifice. "I'm not sure if I'd go as far as to say he is hideous, but he's certainly punching way above his weight."

Exactly. "It's suspicious."

Layla's eyes widen. "You think she's the spy, and she used her honeypot—as in, her pussy—to persuade him to frame someone else?"

"It's the best theory I've got." I breathe past the sudden bout of nausea.

"Well, given that she's out here, why don't we go snoop around in her office?" Layla says with shocking casualness. "Maybe she left some evidence around."

I gape at my sister. "Are you nuts?"

"Why not? It's not like they can fire you *more*."

"I could get arrested for trespassing. Besides, how would I even get into the building? I was fired, and my building pass was taken away."

She strokes her chin with the deck. "Doesn't your husband have the exact same last name as you?"

I nod.

"Then can't you tell the security guard that you forgot your building ID? You can just show them your actual ID, which matches the name of someone who still works there."

Huh. "All my IDs still have my maiden name," I say. "And that's just the tip of the iceberg regarding what's wrong with this plan. For instance, what if one of the guards who escorted me out is there?"

She rolls her eyes. "We can always turn around if there's the wrong guard. Otherwise, just tell them you've just changed your name—which is true. Show them something to prove it. Is there an online copy of your marriage license?"

"I must be nuts also," I say. "I think I'm going to try this madness."

Layla makes a fan out of the cards and fans herself. "My plans are that good." She unzips her jacket and unbuttons a few buttons at the top of her shirt, to the point where you can see a hint of her bra and the swell of her breasts. "Now you do the same." She gestures at my chest. "If the security person is a guy, this could help."

With a sigh, I do as she asks, and when we get into the lobby, the guard happens to be unfamiliar to me—a stroke of luck. Said luck continues because the slutification pays off. The security guy looks like he might salivate as his lecherous gaze ping-pongs between our cleavages. So, needless to say, Layla's plan works with flying colors. Hell, the guy even lets her up with me "to use the restroom."

As we ride the elevator, I feel like I might burst from the pent-up nervous energy. Doomsday scenarios play out in front of my mind's eye, most of them ending with me being interrogated by a mustachioed detective.

The elevator arrives at my floor, and we face the first major hurdle: the woman at the front desk.

"Talk to me about something," Layla whispers. "Behave like you belong."

The woman looks at us.

"Why not?" Layla chirps loudly. "When a woman looks like a young Leonardo DiCaprio, you kiss her first, then wonder about your sexuality after."

Seriously? This is Layla's idea of idle corporate chitchat?

To my relief, the front desk lady doesn't spare me another glance. She's staring at Layla's lips instead.

"Let's go this way." I gesture at the hallway that leads to the pantry. When we're out of anyone's earshot, I explain that this route will make it so we can reach Susan's office without anyone on the floor noticing me. "Because most of them will remember my walk of shame from before, without a doubt."

Layla fiddles with her cards. "You're misusing the term 'walk of shame,' but I catch your drift."

We reach Susan's office and carefully step inside. I lower the shades to give us some privacy, and we start looking through everything—though I'm not sure what I'm looking for.

Then I hit paydirt. "There's a locked drawer here."

Layla rushes over and grins. "I bet you there's something interesting inside."

"Yeah... but it's locked."

My sister chuckles, pockets her deck of cards, and pulls out honest-to-goodness lockpicks.

I narrow my eyes at the adroit way she takes care of the lock. "So... being a card cheat isn't illegal enough. You're a cat burglar as well?"

Layla pulls out a thick folder. "Do you want this or not?"

I snatch the folder and open it.

Shit. Even on the very first page, there's something incriminating, namely my source control log-in info, plus that of Jasper and many others on Susan's team.

Damn.

I reset mine after she gave it to me, so how did she learn it? Is it because I suck at locking my workstation? But then, how did she get the info for the others? Did they not reset their initial password? Or does she have some sort of hacking tools? I guess she must, being a spy and all.

The next page is a photocopy of some sort of financial statements. I'm no expert on this stuff, but I think they indicate she was doing Octothorpe harm for a while now, even if she only started to steal code recently.

"What the hell is going on?" Susan demands as she enters the office.

Fuck.

I slam the folder shut and notice Layla dive under the desk.

"You were fired," Susan states. "You can't be here."

I wave the folder in the air. "Are you in any position to act indignant?"

Spotting the folder, Susan seems to deflate—and age a decade.

"I really wish you hadn't found that," she says, her hand diving into her handbag. "I liked you. Originally, I was going to have Jasper take the fall, but then you married Worthington and it made much more sense for the patsy to be you." She pulls out something oddly shaped from her purse, followed by a small gun—which she proceeds to point at me.

I freeze in disbelief. Icy dread creeps down my spine, the kind I've never felt before, not even when encountering particularly bushy beards.

"Is that a gun?" I manage to choke out, mostly to warn Layla and have her stay hidden.

In my peripheral vision, I see Layla swiping across her phone screen, likely dialing 911, but I don't let that lower my guard.

There's no way the cops will get here in time if Susan decides to pull the trigger.

"I really wish it hadn't come to this," Susan says.

My heart hammers at my ribcage. "Are you really going to just shoot me? Here? In the office?"

She attaches what turns out to be a silencer onto the gun. "You're disgruntled about getting fired, so you're about to attack me." I can tell she's not as confident as she sounds, but I'm not sure it makes her any less dangerous.

Cold sweat is pouring down my spine as I try for a modicum of calm and common sense. "Susan, listen... You said you liked me. I like you as well. I look up to you. Please. You don't want to do this."

Susan sighs. "I didn't want to do any of it." She takes aim.

"Wait!" My voice is shaking. "So far, what you've

done is minor. If you go down for murder, that's life in prison." My heart is racing with a speed that might kill me without the gun, and I'm shocked I'm able to talk.

She lowers the gun minutely. "If I don't do what I have to do, I'll spend my life in prison anyway. I'm sorry. He didn't leave me much choice."

I must keep her talking. I must not give in to this overriding panic. "Who is this 'he?'"

Maybe I could jump her?

No.

Too far.

She'll put a bullet in my brain before I get there.

"Lex Ravenwood," she spits out. "He does all sorts of dirty work for Circumflex."

Must be her handler. Except… "How does someone positioned to make billions do something she doesn't want to do?"

In my peripheral vision, I spot Layla moving and will her to stop. If I have to die, I don't want her to die with me. Instead, she can stay hidden and tell the cops the truth about what happened here.

Then again, after shooting me, Susan might want to put that folder back into the safe, and then she'll discover my sister.

Maybe I should jump her, after all. Maybe—

"I'm not a billionaire," Susan says bitterly.

To her side, at the door that isn't screened by the shades, I catch a glimpse of movement, and my heart jumps anew.

It's Sawyer.

He's staring at Susan and the gun in her hand.

What is he doing here?

Has he figured out she's the spy?

He must have, and if looks could kill, his would slay her on the spot.

Sadly, looks don't kill. Guns do.

He gently opens the door.

I want to scream and beg for him to run away. There's no reason for him to get shot alongside me—because that is all he's going to accomplish with whatever he is doing.

"Susan Johnson would be the billionaire," Susan says in the meanwhile. "Unfortunately, she's not me. She isn't even real. She's just a fiction Lex created—and he was ready to burn that identity to get his hands on your husband's code, until he decided to make me have someone take the fall for it. My real name is Jennifer Forrest. I was already going to jail for life when I got an opportunity that seemed too good to be true. I took it anyway, and now I know I've made a deal with the devil."

Sawyer is already in the room, but he might as well be miles away because Susan—or whatever her actual name is—takes aim again, and her finger moves on the trigger as she adds caustically, "Seems like the devil is about to claim what little of my soul is left."

Time slows to a crawl as I stand there, paralyzed.

In my periphery, I see Layla standing up.

Sawyer leaps.

Susan squeezes the trigger and closes her eyes like

she's afraid of my blood spattering, or the resulting bang.

No!

The bullet that was meant for me hits Sawyer—who's jumped in front of me.

Layla throws a deck of cards at Susan's temple, followed by the nearby phone.

Sawyer clutches at his side, and I see a blooming red stain spread out from his palm.

Something savage and primal wakes up in me at the sight, undoing my paralysis.

Leaping forward, I smash my fist into Susan's face, once, twice.

My knuckles burn, but it's worth it.

Susan—or whatever her name is—stumbles back, which is when Layla grabs her gun and yanks it out of her hands.

"Freeze," Layla grits out, pointing the weapon at Susan. "Move, and I fucking shoot you. Utter a single word, and I shoot you."

Equal parts terrified and relieved, I spin toward Sawyer, expecting to find him on the floor.

He isn't.

Instead, he's leaning against a wall and pressing on his bleeding wound so hard his knuckles are white. Or maybe they are white from blood loss?

My stomach is cold and hard, like permafrost during the Ice Age. I could have lost him. Could still lose him if he bleeds out, or gets an infection, or if that bullet hit something vital. "Why would you do that?" I demand, rushing over to him. "Why jump into the line of fire?"

He arches an eyebrow. "To save your life?"

"But you got shot!"

The eyebrow goes higher. "I got shot? You sure?"

"This is not funny." My hands shake as I reach for the expanding red stain on his shirt. "You took a bullet for me. You shouldn't have."

"I'd do it again." He grimaces in pain. "Now, please, could you stop all this cantankerous gratitude?"

"Let me see the wound." As gently as I can, I open his shirt and nearly faint from the amount of blood that I see.

"It looks bad," I mutter and grab a loose piece of his shirt to press against the wound. "The blood makes it difficult to see how much damage there is."

"I called 911 earlier," Layla says, still aiming the gun at Susan, who's taken my sister at her word and is blessedly silent in her defeat. "EMTs are hopefully on the way."

"I also called security before I came down here," Sawyer says and winces. "But where the hell are they?"

Four burly security guards rush in at that very moment, and I recognize one of them—he walked me out earlier today.

He looks utterly shocked by the scene in front of him, as do his colleagues.

"Apprehend her." Layla gestures at Susan with the gun.

"She's the spy," I explain tersely.

"And she shot me," Sawyer adds. "Before we took her gun away."

"Holy shit," one of the guards says in awe as two others grab Susan by her arms. Then the guard who spoke takes the gun from Layla, and they exit, leaving one guard behind—fortunately not the one who witnessed my walk of shame, or whatever the proper term for that is.

"The cops are already on the way up," the leftover guard says. "They should have the assailant in custody in a few minutes."

"And the EMTs?" I demand, still pressing the shirt to Sawyer's wound. "My husband is bleeding to death."

And Susan is lucky she's in custody. I want to punch her a few more times, and kick her as well.

The guard contacts someone through his walkie talkie and then confirms that the EMTs have arrived and are on the way.

"Hang in there," I tell Sawyer urgently. "And do not even think about dying."

"I don't think it's as bad as you're making it out to be," he says. "When the bullet hit, there was a sharp stinging, but now I just feel a burning sensation."

Leave it to a man to describe a bullet wound as though it were a UTI.

"You could be badly hurt but not feel it thanks to adrenaline," Layla chimes in. "You could still be on death's door."

"Thanks," I snap at her. "That's very helpful."

"I'm okay, truly," Sawyer protests, but the seed of

doubt has been planted, and I can't help but note the paleness of his skin. Or how much blood there is. The piece of shirt I'm holding against his wound is completely soaked, and my hand is covered in red.

He could be bleeding to death as we speak.

He could die before the EMTs get here—and the last thing I did before he saved my life was not take his calls.

"Sawyer..." My voice shakes as I meet his gaze. "I'm so, so sorry about the way I acted at the café. My emotions were running high after getting fired, and I was caught completely off-guard with the spy story. I quickly realized that you couldn't have stopped them from firing me because if you could have, you would have."

"She 'realized' is code for, 'I made her have an epiphany,'" Layla oh-so-helpfully chimes in again.

"I'm sorry too," Sawyer says and manages a crooked smile. "When you asked me if I believed the evidence against you, I hesitated. Both prior to that moment and a millisecond later, I knew without a shadow of doubt that it wasn't you. I was also a little out of it, and—"

The door opens again, and the EMTs descend on us like a swarm of very helpful locusts. They stop the bleeding and announce that his vitals are good, then do a bunch more things before they put Sawyer on a stretcher and take him to the ambulance downstairs.

Meanwhile, I sprout at least a hundred gray hairs as I picture all the horrible scenarios wherein I become a fake widow.

"I'm going with him," I state when they're about to close the ambulance door in my face.

"Are you his family?" asks one of the EMTs.

"I'm his wife," I say proudly.

"Get in," the EMT guy says.

As I do, I hear Layla explaining that she's his sister-in-law and the EMTs saying they only have room for one.

"We're taking him to NY-P Lower Manhattan," he adds. "So you can meet them there."

"Okay, I'll follow you in my car!" Layla shouts.

"Thanks," I reply as the door closes and we get going.

On the way, the EMTs continue checking Sawyer's vitals, and I hold his hand the whole time, trying not to go insane from worry.

When we reach the hospital, they take Sawyer to a waiting area, which is where three people in civilian clothing find us. Based on their above-average attractiveness, I suspect they work for Octothorpe.

"This is going above and beyond," one of them says to Sawyer. "When I asked you to locate the spy, I didn't mean 'get her to shoot you.'"

"Hello, Damian," Sawyer says. "Are these guys from legal?"

"They are," Damian says. "I figured you've been through enough, so when the cops get here with their pesky questions, you won't have to answer any of them."

"Octothorpe security has graciously provided the

authorities with footage from our cameras," drones one of the lawyers.

"I see," Sawyer says. "How suspiciously thoughtful."

"Think nothing of it," Damian says. "We've also secured a large donation for this hospital, and in return, they are expected to see you swiftly and give you the best care they are capable of."

And that donation seems to work. In an eyeblink, a squad of medical professionals swarms Sawyer from all sides, giving him pain meds, cleaning away all the blood, and rushing him away for a few minutes.

When they bring Sawyer back, they have X-rays that they hand over to a gray-haired, distinguished-looking man, who tells us his name is Dr. Montgomery.

"You are very fortunate," says Dr. Montgomery once he's reviewed the X-rays. "You got off with some grazed skin. No deeper tissue damage. No bullet or bullet fragments left in you. It's the cleanest such case I've seen in years."

"I knew it," Sawyer says triumphantly. "Now with the pain meds, I don't feel like I've been shot at all."

"We'll give you a script for those, along with a broad-spectrum antibiotic," Dr. Montgomery says. "But I doubt you'll need the pain meds. By tomorrow, you can just take Tylenol or Advil—if you need anything at all."

"So... that's it?" My heart is doing jumping jacks and somersaults. "Or does he need stitches or something like that?"

"No stitches necessary," Dr. Montgomery says.

"Could he still get an infection?" one of the lawyers asks.

Dr. Montgomery shakes his head. "Unlikely. Still, we do plan to have him visit me at my private practice every few days to watch for any signs of an infection."

A wave of relief hits me then, followed by a slump as the adrenaline and cortisol drain out of my system.

"When can I go home?" Sawyer asks.

"You can go now if you wish," Dr. Montgomery says with a smile. "Just give me a minute to sign your discharge paperwork."

The medical squad scrambles while Sawyer sits up and says, "Can everyone give me a minute to speak with Damian?"

The lawyers skedaddle, but I stand there until Sawyer looks at me apologetically and says, "Could you also step away? This shouldn't take long."

Feeling a tiny bit put-out, I do as he asks, and on my way out, I bump into Layla.

"So what's up?" she asks. "Are you a widow?"

I roll my eyes. "It was a graze. He's about to go home."

Layla cocks her head. "With you?"

That is an excellent question, and one I don't exactly have the answer to. We had that fight—or whatever it was—and though we've each apologized, I'm still not sure exactly where we stand. Furthermore, if we *are* good now, it doesn't change the fact that we married as a means to keep our jobs, and I've lost mine, which means the need for the marriage charade is over. And if we're not married, we don't need to live together…

"Ah, let me guess," Layla says. "You got married because of that kiss you mentioned, not the other way around."

I gape at her. "How could you possibly deduce that?"

"I'm cleverer than you give me credit for."

Not sure how she thinks this will help her point, but she pulls a deck of cards from her cleavage region and gives them a fancy cut.

"Did you tell Mom and Dad?" I demand.

She halts another fancy cut mid-way. "Why would you even ask that? I'm not a tattletale."

"That's true. Except—"

"You want it to be real," Layla states confidently.

I nod.

I do.

I never fully realized it before today, but I've fallen for my fake husband, and I've fallen hard. Seeing him shot was a true wake-up call because now, I can't picture my life without him.

I want us to be together, for real.

"You should tell him," Layla says.

"Yeah?" How is it that I have any anxiety left over to be afraid of such a confession? I should be tapped out after losing the job of my dreams, almost being forced to speak to a guy with a beard, having a gun pointed at me, and seeing Sawyer get shot.

"He took a bullet for you," Layla says. "And even if he hadn't, just the way he looks at you makes things crystal clear."

I take a deep breath. "Okay. I will tell him."

The critical question is *when*.

27
sawyer

a.k.a. the guy who's been shot by Cupid's arrow
(and by Susan with a gun)

"WHAT'S UP?" Damian asks as soon as we're alone.

I clench and unclench my fists—which doesn't hurt at all, thanks to whatever meds the good doctor gave me.

"Obviously, my wife isn't a spy," I announce.

Damian nods. "I found the idea farfetched when we got ambushed with it, so it doesn't surprise me that things turned out the way they did."

"Oh, please. You don't know her."

"True, but I know you," Damian says. "Unlike that idiot Eugene, I never saw you as someone who'd fall for a honey trap."

A compliment from Damian? What's next: the guys from legal offering me a joint? Hermit volunteering to take a bath?

"You will reinstate her prior role," I say. "Effective immediately."

"That would be a little tricky," he says. "She—

"Let me clarify," I say evenly. "If she's not reinstated, I will hire the top law firm in the city, and we'll hit Octothorpe with a wrongful termination suit that will make the history books."

"Like I was saying, reinstating her in her prior role is—"

"No, you still don't get it. The lawsuit would just be the beginning. If she's not reinstated, I will quit, and I will take the code that would've given Octothorpe an edge over Circumflex *to* Circumflex." I show him the flash drive I made earlier. "This is the only copy."

"Impressive," Damian says. "Maybe your wife isn't the only one who should get a promotion."

"What?" I stare at him in confusion.

"Like I've been trying to tell you—reinstating her *in her prior role* is tricky because she's gotten a promotion with her reinstatement, which I took care of on the way here. The current team lead will take Susan's job, and Sawyer will be the new team lead."

"Oh."

"Yeah." His smile is smug.

He reaches for the flash drive, but I pocket it before he can touch it.

"Once I've verified what you've said is true, you can have it," I say. "Oh, and I still need to finish the code." I give him my own smug smile.

"Well played," he says. "Now, if you don't mind, I've got two more fires to put out."

With that, he leaves.

A nurse comes up and tells me I'm discharged.

I push to my feet and head for the door, which is where I bump into Sawyer and her sister.

Sawyer is holding a phone, and her eyes are wide.

I wait until she hangs up and let my eyebrow ask the obvious question.

"That was Henrietta," Sawyer says. "They gave me my job back—but with a promotion."

I smile. "Does that mean you'll take it? The promotion?"

She nods so enthusiastically it could double as headbanging at a heavy metal concert. "I'll have to dive into all the code if I want to lead this team, but yeah. Of course. I'm skipping about a decade in my career plan."

Layla yawns. "I think I'm going to let you lovebirds talk corporateese." She puts her hand on Sawyer's shoulder. "But before I go, I've been meaning to say... I'm sorry I didn't react as quickly as I should've when that bitch pulled that gun on you. I was so overwhelmed that even dialing 911 was a challenge."

"Are you crazy?" Sawyer says. "My biggest fear was that you'd make that move—and get yourself killed."

"And it all worked out," I add. "I'm free to go now."

"All right," Layla says sheepishly. "Thanks. Talk later, okay?"

"Of course," Sawyer says.

As soon as her sister is gone, she turns to me. "How are you? Dizzy? Does it hurt?"

"No. Totally fine."

She eyes the hospital gown that I was allowed to keep in place of my bloody shirt. "You sure?"

"Yeah. Let's go home."

We do, and she fusses over me the whole way back.

Once inside the apartment, she insists on helping me change, but I refuse. Changing with the dressing is a pain, but I manage it.

When I meet up with Sawyer in the kitchen, I see that she's fed Hermit.

"Thanks," I say. "How about we eat as well?" I open the fridge. "I can make some—"

"No." She closes the fridge. "If anyone is going to cook, it will be me."

Is it my imagination, or does Hermit look terrified all of a sudden?

I catch Sawyer's gaze. "Can you please stop treating me like I'm made of cotton candy? I was just going to make us some sandwiches—not dig a ditch."

"I don't want you to overexert yourself," she says.

Hmm. "The doctor didn't say I wasn't supposed to overexert myself." And I'm glad because some activities I desperately want to do would fall under that umbrella.

"How about we order some takeout?" she suggests. "As a compromise?"

I nod, and the cat looks relieved.

As we eat, I can't help but relive the moment I've suppressed until now—the blinding panic I felt when I saw Sawyer being held at gunpoint. The moment when I thought I might lose her. The moment I—

"That was delicious." She pushes her plate away. "What do you want to do now?"

I give her a look that makes her flush and she asks if the doctor said *that* was okay to do.

I stand up. "He didn't say it wasn't okay, which means he recommended it."

Hell, even if he forbade it, I'd take the risk. The near-death experience has made my usual need for Sawyer impossibly more intense.

I need to have her. Now.

"Okay," she says softly. "But you have to take it easy."

"Sure," I growl, advancing on her.

No idea how that's supposed to work, but I'll agree to pretty much anything just to have her in my arms.

Turns out, I'm a fan of "taking it easy" because it translates into a slow, mindful lovemaking, during which we interlace our fingers and stare into each other's eyes as we reach our respective climaxes together.

"Does anything hurt?" she asks as we lie there afterward, facing each other.

"No. The opposite."

She grins. "The opposite of hurt is healed."

"And that is exactly how I feel."

Healed in multiple senses of the word. Healed in ways I didn't even think I needed to be.

She tenderly strokes my cheek. "I think that's the pain meds talking."

"No. I'm overdue for another pill, but I don't need it." There's a slight burning where the wound is, but it's overshadowed by the positive feelings and emotions that I'm overflowing with.

"That's good." She scoots closer. "I was actually waiting for when you're not under the influence to tell you something."

I inhale a big breath, pulling in her intoxicating lavender scent. "I've been wanting to tell you something also."

"Oh?" she asks breathlessly.

"I thought I enjoyed solitude, but that was because I hadn't met you yet. With you, I feel better than if I were alone. I feel complete. Whole. Like a solved puzzle." I frame her face with my palm. "Locky, I love you. When I saw that gun pointed at you, it was like the universe was about to collapse onto itself. Your company has become more precious to me than anything, even the rarest stamp misprint. I can't imagine my life without you in it, and I—"

"I love you too, Key." Her face glows. "I think I fell for you the moment we met—which is why it's been so easy to tell our families that story about our 'love at first sight.' It never felt like a complete lie."

"Neither does this marriage," I say. "Which is why I'd love to stay married to you. See if we can make it real."

"I'd love that," she says, and we seal the deal with a kiss.

A kiss that inevitably leads to more.

sawyer

Two Years Later

AS WE STEP into the famous Monte Carlo Casino, the opulence and the grandeur hit us like a jar of caviar to the face.

A bearded porter asks if he can help us out. I take a deep breath and tell him to scram—which shows just how much progress I've made in therapy.

Sawyer whistles sexily. "These ceilings are so high that a herd of giraffes could stand upright in here."

"Dear," Claire says, "the collective noun for giraffes is a tower."

I smile. My mother-in-law is here with her boyfriend, whom I still mentally refer to as the Hamburglar. Roger, Sawyer's father, isn't giving those two dirty looks anymore, probably because he's here with his girlfriend, the woman from Claire's knitting circle whom he met during our first Christmas together. Incidentally, said woman's name turned out to also be Claire, or as I secretly think of her, Claire 2.4.1.

"I feel right at home here," says Sawyer's grandmother.

Yeah. The ritzy place does look like her mothership.

"Where is the gift shop?" Layla looks around frantically.

I roll my eyes. "To buy a deck of cards?"

"To buy a whole collection of decks of cards." She glances at Claire. "A shoe of decks?"

Claire shrugs. Her knowledge of collective nouns was clearly exhausted by giraffes.

"I'd like to know what the big surprise is," Dad says. "Why did you two bring us all here?"

"Not that we're ungrateful," Mom adds.

Claire glances pointedly at my belly. "There's a lot of alcohol here. Are you planning on drinking any?"

Subtle. "He's the one with the surprise." I give my husband a mock narrow stare. "Now that we're here, will you spill it?"

Because I'm holding off on sharing my own surprise until he's fessed up to his—and let's hope no weird ass miracle makes it so that his announcement will mirror mine.

Having the same name is bad enough.

"Right then." Before I can blink, Sawyer's knee hits the marble floor, and he's looking up at me, eyes gleaming. "Sawyer," he says solemnly. "We've been together for—"

"Wait." I rub my temples. "We're already married. You can't propose."

He pulls out a ring box. "In that case, today is National Rubber Ducky Day. To honor it, I got you this ring." He opens the box, and everyone is blinded by the gorgeous diamond inside it, which is attached to the most delicate band of platinum I've ever seen. "Also," Sawyer continues. "Purely coincidentally, on this day, I want us to renew our vows."

"Oh." I look down at him, the speech center in my brain malfunctioning.

He gives me a cocky grin. "Is that your version of 'Yes, Key, I will renew our vows with you?'"

"Right," I say breathlessly. "Please. Let's get married. I mean, renew our vows."

He slides the ring onto my finger, and everyone claps, though nobody besides Layla completely understands what is happening on the account of us never telling them that this marriage started off as fake.

When Sawyer gets up, I clear my throat. "I guess I also have an announcement to make."

Everyone looks at me with rapt attention, especially Claire.

"Here." I pull out a puzzle box that I've purchased for this very occasion. "It's inside."

Looking confused, Sawyer solves the puzzle in three seconds flat, and then takes out a fancy envelope to which I've affixed my duplicate copy of a stamp depicting Lucille Ball—because *I Love Lucy* makes me think of family.

His eyebrow reaching almost mid-forehead, Sawyer opens the envelope and takes out the black-and-white image within.

"Is this what I think it is?" he asks, sounding awed.

"If you think it's a Rorschach blotch, then no. If you think it's an ultrasound of a lentil-sized six-week-old baby, then yes."

Layla caterwauls and everyone else otherwise loses their shit, especially Claire.

Sawyer looks a little shellshocked as he mutters, "How?"

I heroically refrain from the obvious joke about how babies are made—something he's very good at. Instead, I say, "Remember how you thought I was late from work the day before we left for the trip? I was getting this. Sorry about that. I wanted to be sure before getting our hopes up. And, if I'm honest, I wanted to have a surprise of my own."

"And what a wonderful surprise it is." He envelops me into a hug. "I can't believe it." He sweeps me up into a passionate kiss, his hand falling protectively to my belly.

"I *can* believe it," Claire mutters grumpily. "It's about time."

Eventually, Sawyer releases me from the kiss—but not before his heated gaze tells me there will be a very private celebration in our suite.

"Have you thought about names yet?" my mom asks.

"And is it too soon to know if it's a boy or a girl?" asks my dad.

"No way to know that yet," I say. "But I do have a name picked out that will work for every eventuality." I catch a warning look from Layla, who had called dibs on the names of our parents a very long time ago. Well, she can rest easy. I pause for drama and then announce, "The little Worthington shall be called... Sawyer."

sneak peeks

Thank you for participating in the Sawyers' journey!

Want more romance at Octothorpe? Read *The Love Deal*! When Honey gets caught red-handed making fake coupons for her elderly neighbors, she has two choices: jail, or working under Gunther Ferguson, her high school nemesis.

Ready for another steamy, laugh-out-loud, feel-good romance? In *Fit for Love*, Ashton and Kendall have an incredible night together…until a name mix-up turns their firework romance into a dumpster fire. Years later, will their best friends' fateful destination wedding reignite the sparks between them? Read now to find out!

To make sure you never miss a release, sign up for the newsletter at <u>mishabell.com</u>.

Turn the page to read previews from *The Love Deal* and *Fit for Love*!

excerpt from the love deal

By Misha Bell

Honey Hyman (do NOT call her "hon") is all leather, piercings, and tattoos. And yes, she may be just a tad deal-obsessed, but who isn't? It's not like her using coupons is stealing from anyone... unless, of course, those coupons are the fakes she created to help her elderly neighbors afford groceries from the Munch & Crunch, the uber-expensive supermarket that's replaced their local grocery store.

It really isn't fair for her to go to jail. Or to be blackmailed into working for the Munch & Crunch CEO whom she's supposedly defrauded—a CEO who turns out to be none other than Gunther Ferguson, her high school crush who once ruined both her school record and her life.

Let the war begin.

———

The police? What the hell?

Heart thumping, I check the peephole.

Yep. They're dressed like cops.

Did a neighbor call them because of the caterwauling? It did sound like bloody murder. But how did they get here so fast? Unless…

Fuck. It can't be about the coupons again, can it?

"Open the door, or we'll be forced to open it," a hard-faced cop says.

Well, shit. I can't afford to repair this door.

There's no choice.

I open the door.

The cop looks from me to Pearl. "Honey Hyman?"

"That's me." And yes, I know my name sounds like a virginal membrane that people with diabetes should avoid.

"You're under arrest," he informs me. "For fraud."

My stomach drops. I turn to Pearl, who is as pale as the ghost of a toilet. My voice is strained as I say, "Let Blue know, okay?"

Blue is our clutch mate who used to work for the government, so if anyone can help with this, it would be her.

The rest is like a nightmare. I'm led out of the building, put in a police car, brought unceremoniously into the station, and shepherded into a room—all the while fielding a surge of adrenaline so strong I barely register any of it.

Did someone read me my Miranda Rights? If not, do I get a refund?

They didn't take my butterfly knife, which is weird because I always thought going to jail was like flying on a plane—weapons aren't allowed.

Maybe I'm not going to jail? Dare I hope?

I think back on the last two times I was in trouble. Both were actually interrelated situations.

First, there was Tiffany, a cheerleader who bullied me for ogling her uber-hot boyfriend, Gunther—something I *was* guilty of. Eventually, I stood up to her with a knife—only as a threat, though, since the last thing I wanted was to draw any blood. Unfortunately, the dumdum didn't notice said knife and got up in my face anyway, accidentally slicing her arm open. To this day, I don't know how bad the cut was, as I couldn't look at the wound on account of the blood. Since Tiffany didn't end up with a scar, I imagine the cut wasn't so bad—not that it helped me escape the resulting suspension and mark on my permanent record. On the bright side, that incident is what started my "don't mess with me" reputation, which I don't mind at all, as it has kept the other Tiffanies of the world away.

The second incident took place a year later, still in high school. It involved Gunther again—who was no longer with Tiffany at the time. Not that I kept track. Much. That time, not only did I get suspended and *really* tarnish my permanent record, but I also barely dodged the juvenile justice system.

It all started when I was little. For whatever reason, I became obsessed with all things saving money, including deals and coupons. After taking an art class my junior year, I realized that tweaking percentages on coupons with a white pen was just as profitable as counterfeiting money—so I did it, first for myself and then for the other kids at my school. As it turned out, one of the stores that lost money because of my creative initiative was owned by Gunther's family, so when Gunther learned of my activities, he tattled to the principal. Shit hit the fan, and I'm paying for it to this day.

My phone rings.

Huh. Another thing they didn't take.

I check it.

It's Blue. Good. Pearl must've told her to get in touch.

"Hi," I say, switching to a form of Pig Latin Blue developed when we were kids. "Let's talk quick. They might come back and take my phone."

"The quick version is, whatever they have against you is physical, not digital, so there's not much I can do here," Blue says.

Blue hasn't had any trouble with the law, but she doesn't seem to have much respect for certain legalities after working for—as she calls it—"No Such Agency." Case in point: she's just admitted to hacking into the police department's computers as casually as I'd admit to watching cat videos on TikTok.

"Can your former colleagues help?" I ask.

"Sorry, no," she says. "I know some feds, but that doesn't help your case. If you want, I can text you the name of an excellent lawyer."

"Sure." Except I have no idea how I'd pay said lawyer. Thanks to my high school mishaps, no college wanted me, and I never achieved my dream of becoming a wealthy business owner. Currently, I work part-time sweeping floors at a tattoo parlor and cutting hair at a barbershop.

"I can lend you some money," Blue says, clearly reading my mind.

"No." I hate charity. "I'll take the public attorney."

"It's coupons again, isn't it?" she whispers.

"I'm not sure I should talk about it," I whisper back. "Even in code."

I hear her type a few keystrokes. Then she whispers, "You don't need to say anything. I just checked, and the answer is yes."

Fuck. I want to smack myself. After years of walking the straight and narrow, I got tempted to play Robin Hood, and this is the result. My neighborhood family-owned grocery store was recently replaced by the uber-expensive Munch & Crunch supermarket, and my elderly neighbors told me that they're struggling to afford food. So I fudged a few coupons for them. Why is that even a crime?

"Someone is coming your way," Blue says, startling me out of my reverie. "Talk later."

Before I can wonder how she knows that, she hangs up and the door opens.

I gape at the man who walks in. The epitome of tall, dark, and handsome, he has neatly cut, smoothed-back brown hair that makes me think of corporate boardrooms and OCD. His strong chin and muscular jaw are clean-shaven to the point of shine, and his eyes, a vivid emerald-green two shades brighter than mine, are narrowed with disapproval, his full lips pursed tight.

Who is he, and why does he look familiar?

In that perfectly tailored suit, he's unlikely to be a cop. Perhaps a lawyer that I can't afford? It's possible, but there's something annoyingly honest and noble in his features that I associate more with Boy Scouts than with ambulance chasers.

"Honey Hyman," he says with distaste—and shock rolls through me as I recognize his deliciously deep baritone, one he's had since his teenage years.

"Gunther Ferguson?" I blurt incredulously.

Is it possible that I conjured him up by thinking of him on the way here, kind of like invoking a demon? Or maybe I fell asleep in the police car and I'm dreaming?

If not, then this man is what happened to the boy I hate, the one who got me into trouble in high school, thus proving that karma is a fucking myth. If there were any justice in the world, he would've grown warped and deformed with time, like an evil lord of the Sith, but the opposite has happened.

Like an Anne Rice vampire, the evil transformation has made him hotter.

"Is playing dumb your latest game?" Gunther pulls out a stack of coupons and tosses them on the table. "Are you going to pretend you didn't know that it's my store you've been stealing from?"

Stunned, I glance down.

Yep. Those expertly faked coupons are for that small-business-crushing Munch & Crunch. And indeed, they are my handywork—but that store is part of a multinational chain of supermarkets, so how can it be his? Unless...

"You own that Munch & Crunch, like a franchise?" I ask stupidly.

He scoffs. "I own the whole company. Like you didn't know that."

I blink. "How would I know that?"

He gestures at the coupons. "The same way you know how to make those look indistinguishable from the real thing."

Hold on. Is he just a clever cop? "I'm not about to incriminate myself. Assuming those are actually fake, I'm sure whoever created them did it to help out their elderly neighbors who used to shop at the place that your Munch & Crunch ruthlessly drove out of business. Those folks can't afford your regular prices. In any case, how could that mystery person know that you had anything to do with the store? I know the likes of you think you're the center of the universe, but that's just not true."

He sighs. "First, you did this same thing to my dad. Now me. If this isn't targeted, I have to assume you make so many fraudulent coupons that this has inexorably happened again."

I push the coupons away. "Not admitting anything —but what about bad luck?"

His full lips curl in a sneer. "I don't believe in luck."

"Oh, luck exists." Bad luck is the only thing that can explain how tempting his mouth looks—despite what it's saying.

"You can prevaricate as much as you want, but the case against you is airtight. In fact, I've been led to believe you'll face jail this time. Unless…"

Wait. Is this blackmail? "Unless what?"

A dozen naughty scenarios of what he might demand of me play out in my mind—some involving handcuffs (because police station), others candle wax (no idea why), and a bunch more featuring a bed covered in BOGO coupons.

His green eyes gleam triumphantly. "Unless you work for me. Then I'll drop the charges."

Go to <u>www.mishabell.com</u> to order your copy of *The Love Deal* today!

excerpt from fit for love

By Anna Zaires & Misha Bell

I slept with my trainer. And as it turns out, I'm not the only one.

Apparently, he sleeps with all his clients.

So I block him—the last thing I need is another a-hole in my life. Especially one as irresistibly charming and handsome as Ashton Vancroft.

The catch? Three years later, our best friends, Emma and Marcus, get engaged, and we are both forced to play nice at their destination wedding in Florida.

Is he really the self-centered playboy I've made him out to be? Or is there something more to this fitness-obsessed now-billionaire that I missed the first time around?

Well, after getting stranded on a secret island together and being forced to hunker down in the same cabin, I guess I have no choice but to find out…

———

As I fly from the treadmill, time seems to slow, giving me a cruel opportunity to picture myself breaking a limb. Or my neck. Or my tailbone. Either way, I will be so full of negative juju Tierre will fire me for sure.

Assuming I survive.

To my huge surprise, I don't hit the ground.

Instead, I land upright, smashing into something hard yet pliant and enveloping at the same time.

Something that smells deliciously masculine.

Realizing my eyes are squeezed shut, I open them and… holy fuck.

My savior is built like a Greek statue but with more muscles. His sun-kissed hair is a couple of inches too long, a surfer's look. Only instead of the ocean, he smells like lime zest, clean skin, and toe-curling sex.

Speaking of sex, his blue-gray eyes are hooded, and I can feel something big and hard against my belly. Something that is definitely not a flashlight.

"Thank you," I manage to say, albeit a bit breathlessly. I'm really hoping Mr. McScrumptious can't feel my drumming heartbeat or my pebbled nipples.

"You're welcome," he murmurs in a deep, soft voice

that reminds me of melted things—like caramel, hearts, and panties.

With effort, I pull myself together—not an easy task since he's still holding me. Since he didn't get the hint from my thank-you, I say, "Seriously, you can let go of me now."

I guess I could also push him away, but I'm not sure I can bring myself to do it—not with all the jolts of sensual energy zapping through my body, leaving gooseflesh in their wake.

Sadly, he listens to me and lets me go.

Grr. Why did I insist on that? I could've enjoyed his embrace for a few more minutes before it would've seemed too weird… right?

He even steps away—and the idiot that I am, I immediately miss his proximity.

As he stands there, his gorgeously carved face goes through a series of expressions, settling on something dark, which, for some reason, only makes me want to jump back into his arms—or into his bed.

Crap. *Focus, Kendall. You've sworn off men, remember?*

I swallow and pull myself together, again. "Aren't you going to say something?"

Between the silence and his dark expression, I'm starting to feel all kinds of uncomfortable, and not all of it down south.

"Yes," he growls. "Don't you ever, ever, do something like that again. Is that understood?"

My hackles—which I thought I'd lasered off a long time ago—rise. "Ex-fucking-cuse me?"

A muscle in his jaw ticks. "How could you have been so careless? You could've hit your head."

What the fuck? Who the hell does he think he is?

"If I had, I'd still be smarter than you," I retort caustically.

He blows out a breath. "Is it that hard to attach the safety key?"

So that's what the thingy is called? "I didn't realize I had to. I usually run on the street."

His eyes narrow dangerously. "The street?"

Is he picturing me running through Manhattan traffic? What kind of an idiot does he take me for?

"I run in the park," I clarify. "'On the street' is just a turn of phrase."

"Which park?" he demands. "Some are worse than the street."

"East River. Not that it's any of your business."

Seriously, what is up with this guy?

He cocks his head. "I'm your fitness trainer, so anything to do with you running is my business."

"Wait. You're Ash?"

For some reason, I expected someone more boring-looking. Not to mention dressed in the gym's uniform instead of short shorts that expose his powerful legs and a tank top that shows enough lickable skin to make one salivate.

He grimaces. "You can call me Ash if you insist, but I prefer to go by—"

"Don't worry, I won't be calling you anything. This whole thing was a mistake. I'm just going to leave."

He crosses his arms over his impressive chest. "Do you want a trainer who'd let you break your arms? Your neck?"

I roll my eyes. "What I want is a rush of endorphins to cheer me up. This—whatever you're doing—is accomplishing the opposite."

"You came for endorphins?" he asks, and the gleam in his eyes tells me he's picturing a completely different endorphin-generating scenario from the one I meant.

And there I go again. My panties are officially damp.

"This conversation is over." I turn to leave, as much to get his perfect face out of my sight as to make a statement.

"Wait," he says—and fuck, his voice alone is doing things to my insides. He steps around me to block my way. "If you don't want a session with me, let me at least show you a few machines that can help you get those endorphins."

What he seems to leave unsaid is that these machines are the second-best way to get endorphins when he's involved. The number one way is, of course, to fuck his brains out. Or is it my brains?

Also, why is "brains" plural in that expression?

I give him my best glare. "You really think I can't use a machine without your supervision?"

He smirks, and damn him, it's a sexy smirk. "Use safely? I think we just saw the answer to that."

I resist the urge to growl. "You're insufferable. What happened was a freak accident, nothing more."

"If you say so." He pointedly glances at the cursed treadmill.

"Let me show you how little I need your so-called help." I stomp over to the nearest machine—an upright bench with two paddle-like things at waist level. I have no idea what it does, but there are instructions on it, and I learned how to read when I was five.

"That one?" He arches his eyebrow in an infuriatingly cocky way. "You sure you don't want to make your point somewhere else?"

"Stop following me. Or shut up."

"This should be interesting." He folds his arms across his chest again and watches me, eyes gleaming with amusement.

I read the small font.

Sit upright, with back against the pad.

Hmm. As I plop onto the seat, the paddle thingies align with my legs, which I should have expected but somehow didn't. This gives me an unpleasant suspicion, like maybe I've seen this exercise before, on a less fancy machine and—

"Hip abduction?" he murmurs. "Interesting."

I turn from the instructions to glare at him, but it's a mistake, insofar as I get ensnared by his ridiculously handsome looks again. "Abduction is not hip, no matter how cool the aliens."

He snorts. "Hip as in those that don't lie in that song by Shakira." He gestures at his own narrow hips, but that just draws my attention to the nearby bulge in his shorts. "As to abduction, it means your limbs will move *away* from your midsection. Both words are homonyms, but I bet you knew that."

I snort. "I don't know what a homonym is, but it sounds vaguely homophobic."

It also sounds like Ash might've gone to college and/or read a book, which makes him impossibly more attractive.

Crap. Even his exasperated sigh is sexy.

"Go on then," he says after said sigh. "Let's see if you're as smart with this machine as you are with your mouth."

Is that his way of asking me for a blowjob?

No. It's a challenge, so I read the rest of the instructions… and my heart sinks. My earlier suspicion was correct. This is that machine where you push apart the paddles with your knees to end up with your legs spread, like you're begging someone to fuck you—or summoning a gynecologist.

Usually, in an empty gym or if surrounded by women, I wouldn't have a problem spreading my legs, no matter how obscenely wide. But to do so with Ash staring, and while I'm so wet…

"Nope." I leap to my feet. "There will be no abductions today."

He smiles—and it's like a glorious sunrise after a hurricane. "I can show you a better way to work those same muscles, using movements that are more natural."

"Oh, yeah? Let me see this alleged way."

He leads me to a machine with cables sticking out of it and grabs two thingies that look suspiciously like a collar a sub would wear in BDSM—with a metal ring attached and everything.

Is this workout about to turn kinky? And... do I want it to?

"You put these around your ankles," he says, demonstrating on himself.

He then clips the ring on the collar—or shackle—to the cable on the bottom of the machine, which still looks kind of kinky now that my mind has gone there. With four of these shackles, two on wrists and two on ankles, one could be restrained in a spread-eagle position and then—

"Next, you do this." He extends his bound leg to the side, lifting the weight attached to the cable.

Fuck me. All his muscles—but especially those in his powerful legs—flex in the process of this demonstration, doing damage to my sanity and panties.

"And then with the other leg." He clips his other ankle in and stands with his back to me, giving me a view of his perfectly sculpted back and ass.

"Now." He frees himself from the shackles and hands them to me. "Your turn."

———

Go to **www.mishabell.com** to order your copy of *Fit for Love* today!

www.ingramcontent.com/pod-product-compliance
Lightning Source LLC
Chambersburg PA
CBHW011319310726
48973CB00011B/2983